EXPLORER 2000

Book Two
The Hunt for Kathnarii Base

by JB Stephens

A HAZELWOOD SELECT book
Published by Cheese Press Publishing

Copyright © 2025 by JB Stephens
All rights reserved.

No part of this publication may be reproduced, distributed, or transmitted in any form or by any means, including photocopying, recording, or other electronic or mechanical methods, without the prior written permission of the publisher, except as permitted by U.S. copyright law. For permission requests, contact Cheese Press Publishing.

The story, all names, characters, and incidents portrayed in this production are fictitious. No identification with actual persons (living or deceased), places, buildings, and products is intended or should be inferred.

Book Cover by Jordan Hermitt & Mere Jones

ISBN 979-8-89136-011-2

Cheese Press, LLC
100 Mill Street
Suite A
Lawrenceville, GA 30046

www.CheesePressPublishing.com

First Paperback Edition, June 2025

For my wife and kids. Thanks for being the crew!

-JB

Chapter 1

Orange lighting highlighted the hazy fog and smoke that hung thick in the barely breathable atmosphere of the dreadnought's interior. ***Boom! Boom! Boom!*** Rapid and thudding footfalls echoed throughout the dim chambers and halls, accented by the sounds of heavy panting. Beads of sweat rolled down Captain Nado's face as he frantically attempted to stay just a few steps ahead of his persistent pursuer. The captain spun around a corner, pinning himself against the wall just out of view of the main corridor. Conscious of how loud his breathing had become, Nado swiftly stayed his pounding heartbeat and calmed his gulping and gasping.

His foe must have noted that the captain's resounding footsteps had ceased, as any further noise no longer emanated from the central corridor. Hearing nothing but the moans and groans of the metallic structure coasting in the expanse of space, Captain Nado eased his back off the wall and drew his pistol. He set his powerful square jaw, brushed aside the white locks of hair that had fallen into his starry eyes, and activated the heating core of his plasma-infused weapon.

Ahead, the side hallway was dark and shrouded. Only a few feet of this byway were visible via the faded auburn glow from the main thoroughfare behind. Nado pressed forward, inching along the shadowed hall deliberately and cautiously, keeping his gun at the ready. Squinting hard, the captain glanced this way and that, uncertainty filling his heart and mind. There was no telling what danger may lay on this path, but at least it might help him avoid the sinister wraith that now chased him.

"Captain?" a low voice droned in a scornful tone. "Where are you? Come out and face me. Hiding like a coward will do you no good."

With no intention of responding, Captain Nado continued on his current course, slowly sliding further and further down the side passage. Perhaps there would be an escape pod chamber, or an elevator to the hangar where he could commandeer a shuttle. Anything to get off this vessel and back to some semblance of peace. His mysterious mocker's malicious oration resumed.

"You cannot escape!" the voice called, as if reading Nado's thoughts. "There are no exits on this level that lead to the hangar, nor are there any escape pods. You have but one choice, Captain. You must face me!"

At that, the captain moved into the darkest section of his hiding place, feeling his way along the walls and using them for support. The inkiness of this place threatened to swallow him whole, causing a dreadful dizziness to set in. Nado's head started swimming, his legs wobbled, his throat tightened. Everything in him wanted to get out of this blackness, this light consuming void, and jet back to the main hold. But that was where his chatty challenger lay in wait, undoubtedly with a dangerous snare in store. Clutching his chest, Nado pushed onward, away from the voice and into the darkness.

"Get out here and fight!" yelled the voice, its deep rumbling now obscured and diminishing due to the distance Nado was putting between them. "I know you're here somewhere Captain Burnay Nado. . .you cannot get away from me!"

That last statement went almost unheard, as Nado began to pick up his pace. He felt stuck between two terrible obstacles. There were either the shadows ahead, or the voice behind. Thankfully, though they may hold many secrets, shadows alone pose no physical threat. The owner of the voice, however, was an entirely different matter, as there was no telling what they might do.

A door stood at the end of this hallway. Though Captain Nado couldn't see it, he touched it and knew he had to open it to go on. With trepidation mounting in his spirit, the captain eased his fingers onto the control panel next to the entryway. With a swish, the door parted in the middle and split aside. More orange lights temporarily blinded Nado, but he quickly regained his vision. Peering back into the next room, Captain Nado spied a dark and blurry figure blocking his path.

Suddenly, strong and muscular hands were around his neck, squeezing the air out of him! The captain struggled to get free to no avail. He dropped his firearm and utilized all four of his own hands to break free of his opponent's grip, but his assailant stood firm. OOF! Nado was slammed to the floor, still held in that gargantuan grasp.

The figure leaned close, his own eyes a mirror to Captain Nado's, his own angular jawline just as powerful, his charcoal hair ragged and out of place from their race. He came within mere inches of Nado's face, his gold-colored body armor glinting in the dim lighting, his hood having been whipped backward from their dashing and darting. All the while, Nado could feel himself slipping away as Graylon's massive hands choked him.

"I told you," the loathsome lord uttered, "you have no other choice. One way or another, you must face me, Burnay. FACE ME!!"

As those last words were thundered, Captain Nado jolted upright in his bed, his breathing labored and strained. He could still feel that vise around his neck, though no one else was present in his bedroom. His bedroom? It seemed surreal. Was he still dreaming? Tiny streaks of sunlight broke through the small slit between the thick curtains that covered the single window, illuminating the area. Yes, it was his childhood room, adorned with Explorer Initiative paraphernalia, a few sports trophies, and photos of himself and his family. There was Graylon's bed, opposite his own.

Despite the pain in his neck and back, Nado forced himself to rise out of bed, stumble across the room, and egress into the hallway outside. It too featured a variety of pictures hanging in a near haphazard manner up and down the walls, as if the owner was running out of space and desperately maintained that every photograph must be displayed. At the end of the hall, a spindle railing separated the hall floor from a stairwell leading down.

Upon reaching the bottom of the stairs, Captain Nado found himself in a very familiar place. He looked around at the miniscule kitchen, filled with bric-a-brac and knick-knacks, even more framed photos, and a small breakfast nook. A round table with four chairs occupied the nook, surrounded on three sides by clean windows that were framed with delicate white curtains. Rays from the early morning sun cascaded inside. The rest of the kitchen looked as one might expect, featuring simple countertops and cabinetry, modest appliances, and tile floors.

Only one thing in the room really stood out to Captain Nado. At the stove, busily cooking and humming a song that probably only she knew, was an older Zennian woman with wispy silver hair. Her bespectacled and wrinkled face was kind and loving but had the look of one who had seen many seasons of sadness. She turned as he entered, smiling warmly.

For the first time that morning, Nado knew he was indeed awake. He greeted her. "Good morning, Mom."

Other crew members straggled into the breakfast nook one by one as the morning hours slipped past. First came Commander Kel with her usually curly hair looking flat and dull in the humid atmosphere. She was followed by Rox, who appeared to have gotten a decent night's sleep. Shortly after him, Schiff dragged herself downstairs, and though her chipper demeanor hadn't faded, the dark circles under her eyes betrayed the tiredness that plagued them all.

As for Mara and Jym, the young monarchs staggered into the cozy living room and settled on the comfy, old, blue couch, burrowing underneath crocheted quilts. It wasn't frigid in the house, but Mrs. Nado did like to keep the thermostat set as low as she dared, in a hopeful attempt to stave off the scorching Zennian summer heat. The actions of the prince and princess didn't seem to bother the matronly gal, as she continued preparing plates of breakfast for all her guests. After serving the children their meals, Mrs. Nado kindly switched on her old rounded-edged monitor and began playing dusty discs of a video series for them to watch.

Triumphant music warbled through the speaker system and the narrator gallantly introduced "Trock Taran! The hero of the expanse!" Images of a Zennian in clearly fake body armor danced across the screen while the kids stared, fascinated by the old show.

"My boys loved that one too," Mrs. Nado informed. "I'm glad to see my son following the hero's path and helping those in need like yourselves. Neither would be the men they are today without good, old Trock Taran."

That phrase stung Captain Nado, who observed his oblivious mother going back to her duties as hostess. Everyone had offered to take care of themselves, but Mrs. Nado refused to hear it, insisting that as long as they were in her home, they would accept her care. With no other recourse, the crew gladly received the loving aid that the captain's mom graciously gave. The only crew member not in the house was Red, who had taken up a lone vigil on the wraparound porch outside, patrolling the perimeter with carbine in hand.

"Eat your breakfast dear," Mrs. Nado said, interrupting her son's thoughts.

"Right away, Mom," he replied.

"It's so good to see my strapping son," the elder Nado continued. "I wish your brother were here too. Have you seen him lately?"

Grateful for the bite of food that forced him to pause, the captain took his time to swallow before responding. "Um, no, not lately."

"Oh, I see. He hasn't contacted you at all? Surely the two of you have kept in touch."

"Well," stammered Nado, "it's a big galaxy, and hard to maintain communication sometimes."

"What was the last you'd heard from him? Is he well?" Mrs. Nado cleaned a plate while she spoke, a seemingly mundane act, but the captain knew her better than that. She was coping, striving to keep her nervous thoughts under control.

"Last I heard, Graylon was. . .finding his fortune," he quickly blurted, attempting to soothe her fears.

She calmed, relaxing her stiffened shoulders. "Oh, good. Well, I'm glad to know that he at least has that. Though I wish he'd visit too. . ." Mrs. Nado's train of thought appeared to derail, and she devolved into cleaning the dishes by rote, staring blankly at the work in front of her.

Leaning toward Nado, the commander whispered, "We've been here for four standard cycles. Aren't you going to tell your mom the truth about Graylon? Don't you think she deserves to know?"

"What would you have me tell her?" the captain muttered back grumpily. "'Yeah, Mom, I sure did see Graylon recently. In fact, I left him stranded on the icy plateau of a forgotten planet'? Besides, Mom's in the beginning stages of neural degradation, something the Humans called 'dementia.' The truth about Graylon is the last thing I want to burden her mind with right now."

"Huh," interjected Rox. "I wondered if maybe that was the case. She's been exhibiting a few symptoms, but that doesn't always mean it's actually what's wrong. If that's true, then the captain has a very good point. News like that could make things worse."

Kel backed down. "Fair enough. I guess then we should talk about our next course of action. We were going to head for Kathnarii Base as soon as we were rested. If that's still the plan, how do we get to it?"

The captain had to ponder that for a moment. "We'd need to access the Galactic Community information database and see what their last records indicated. If that star base is still out there somewhere, the database would at least give us a sector to start searching."

"How do we access it?"

"We'd have to hack into it using an encryption code," Nado answered. "Otherwise, anyone looking would know where the break-in occurred."

Schiff glanced around the table. "I am a girl of many talents, but that isn't one of them. Who do we know that could pull something like that off?"

Everyone at the table stared at one another, then turned their eyes in the direction of the outdoor porch. The robot was passing by at that precise moment, patrolling and keeping watch, continuing its mechanical march. Grinning slyly and narrowing his eyes, Captain Nado voiced, "Didn't Red say it had computer engineering programming?"

"There's another possibility too," Rox cut in. "Searching for Kathnarii Base was only one option. I thought you told me that the Archivist machine also said that the kids' parents had fled here, to Zen I, after the Great War."

Kel rubbed her chin. “He’s right, Captain. Maybe Rox and I can check the Zennian holodex system at the local courthouse and see if there’s anything about Vampyrial refugees.”

“It’s a long shot,” the doctor offered, “seeing how that occurred a century ago. But it might yield something.”

“It’s a good plan,” Captain Nado agreed. “We’re settled. Schiff and I will take the kids and Red. I’m pretty sure Mom kept our old computer terminal, so we can use that to hack the GC database from here. Commander, you and Rox head into town and see what you can dig up on the holodex.”

With that, the impromptu war room session was called to a close. Everyone gulped down their breakfast and began preparing for their various tasks for the day. Soon thereafter, Kel and Rox were borrowing the Nado family hovercraft to head for the small nearby hamlet, while Captain Nado himself approached his mom.

“Mom?” he queried. “Do you happen to remember the old computer terminal that…Graylon and I built when we were kids?”

“Oh, yes dear!” was her excited reply. “I put it in the cellar of the storage barn so it would stay in a cooler environment.”

“Thanks Mom.” The big Zennian turned to leave, but Mrs. Nado stopped him.

“Speaking of Graylon,” she started, “do you hear much from him anymore? How is he doing?”

Having heard that question twice now, Nado felt a knot forming in the pit of his gut. “He’s doing great Mom,” he answered with as cheerful a grin as he could muster. But his heart sank into his boots.

Outside Mrs. Nado's diminutive farmhouse stood a large, two-story metal barn that had once sported a shiny coat of blue. It was similar to the coloration of the Explorer but had faded and rusted from time and neglect. Inside, the exhaust fans kept the structure ventilated, though not altogether cool. The temperature wasn't much improved from that of the outside climate, but at least the fans kept the air circulating. On the main floor, empty stalls told the story of a ranch that had once been in full working order, complete with beasts of burden for riding and plowing fields. The upper floor was still filled with old bales of what Zennians called "pureweed", one of their major exports that was used in a plethora of galactic food production industries.

Giving that loft a long look, Captain Nado's mind was flushed with a memory. He could envision a scene from childhood, as Graylon stood over him, pinning him down and saying, *"Cry mercy! Come on, cry mercy and I'll let you go!"* With a chuckle, he dismissed those thoughts.

In a forgotten corner covered with dust and assorted junk they found a hatch on the floor, leading into the cellar. Light filled the large cavity as the door was pulled open, revealing a workshop below. Bits and bobbles, odd and ends, all manner of gadgets and doodads crowded this room in an almost reckless fashion. Thankfully, it didn't take them an exorbitant amount of time to sift through the cellar/workshop and locate the near antique computer terminal. Pieced together with mismatched components, the terminal was huge and hefty. It was undoubtedly a piece of technology from a bygone era, and unquestionably crafted by hand. However, they all figured it would work well enough. It booted noisily after being given a power source, the screen eventually settling on a black background with green lettering.

"Alright Red," Nado prompted. "Do your stuff."

"Indeed," the robot replied coolly, withdrawing a small cord from its beltline and attaching it to a port on the terminal. "This outdated system is in dire need of repair, Captain. You might consider an upgrade."

"Thanks for the input, Red," said the captain dryly. "Can you connect it to the wireless network or not?"

"Affirmative. This unit has succeeded in connecting to the network."

"Great!" Schiff exclaimed. "Now all we need to do is hack into the GC database!"

"Yeah," Princess Mara drawled in a sarcastic tone, "because that's super easy to do."

"Apparently it is," interjected Prince Jym, pointing at the terminal. "Red's already in. That's the symbol of the Galactic Community right there!"

All the others leaned in close to see, and though the image was somewhat malformed due to the clunky pixelization of the old computer, the boy was right. Within mere seconds, Red had bypassed all the security measures, and was rapidly scanning through a myriad of files and folders. Without warning, the screen halted abruptly on a single file simply entitled "Kathnarii Star Base."

"This has to be it!" a very enthusiastic Jym proclaimed.

"Let's hope so," murmured the captain in response. "Red, download whatever you need, then close this out. I don't want to leave more footprints than need be right now."

"Acknowledged," Red stated. "Downloading information."

Meanwhile, floating in orbit around Zen I high above, a small cruiser lazily drifted. The entire craft was approximately twice the size of the Explorer 2000. Dimly lit and trying to maintain a low profile, it stayed just out of range of the reporting line. Any further, and they'd have to send their codes and identification to the port masters of the space stations on the surface. The occupants of this vessel wanted nothing to do with that.

Heavy footfalls announced the arrival of the master of the craft, who swept onto the bridge with a flourish. His silver cape and glinting gold armor reflected the tiny amount of light that shone from the bridge command consoles. Several in the chamber stood to acknowledge his approach, but the lord of the starship took no notice of them. He instead made a beeline for the youngest operator on the bridge, a boy who could scarcely be older than nine or ten standard years of age.

"You summoned me," the man rumbled. "I assume our intel was correct? They are here?"

"They are," replied the boy in a monotone fashion, staring up with intense orange eyes. The cybernetic implants that dotted his silvery skin began to glow, as did the tubing and wiring on his second set of arms. Scratching at the natural black tattoos on his bald head, the lad continued, "I was scanning the database for unusual activity, per your orders, and the encryption code you told me to watch for appeared. I can triangulate their position if you so desire."

"That will not be necessary," the cruel commander uttered. "We stick to the plan. Upload the virus, and let the robot do our work."

The boy bowed his head. "Yes, Lord Hex. It shall be done."

"Cylor, my son," Lord Hex crowed, "you needn't call me thus. Remember, you may call me 'Father'."

"Yes, Father." Cylor's hands became a blur as cyborg tendrils emerged from his fingertips and flitted across his keyboards.

Turning swiftly, Lord Hex addressed his other cohorts. "Klensh, take your men down to the surface in the shuttle. As long as the dreadnought is out of commission, I must rely on your talents to apprehend my prey. Let H-8-RED do the heavy lifting, then pick up whatever is left. As always, I require the children and the captain be captured alive."

"Yesh, milord," the gnarled Kriton acquiesced.

"And Klensh?"

"Yesh, milord?"

"Don't fail me again."

More material continued to unfold onscreen as Captain Nado and the kids, along with Schiff, read through the Galactic Community database entries. Dates and times listed various sightings of Kathnarii Base reported to the Community Council, with a corresponding list of dates and times that detailed every expedition launched to find it. As they read down the lists though, the captain discovered ill news. The accounts ended rather abruptly at a date that was almost two standard years prior.

"Blast!" grunted Nado, pounding a fist on the table. "They aren't still looking for it, which means there haven't been any further sightings, which means it may no longer be there at all."

"Hold on, there's more," said Schiff, calming the disquieted captain. "It says here that future sightings will be ignored," she paused and started reading verbatim, "'as the Council cannot allocate any more funds to this endeavor. The cost of contracting spacecraft, command crew, and personnel for these expeditions has only continued to grow. The secret of Kathnarii Base and its location will have to remain an unsolvable mystery, lost to the stars.' See? They just gave up! And only two years ago!" Schiff noticed herself beginning to hop up and down and stilled her sporadic movements. "That means it could still be out there, somewhere, just waiting for the crew of the Explorer 2000 to find it."

Mara chimed in. "It's also still the only lead we have at the moment for finding out whatever happened to our mom and dad."

"And if you check these dates and locations of the sightings," piped Jym, "they're all in the same sector, this 'Gentara Sector.' That at least gives us a heading, right Captain?"

A new hope and courage began to surge through Nado, and taking a deep breath he declared, "By Trock Taran, we'll find this star base yet, mark my words. 'Unsolvable mystery' they say? I say 'challenge accepted!'"

Letting out a small whoop, Schiff and Jym shook their hands in the air. Mara rolled her eyes and shook her head but did allow a healthy smile to play on her lips. In all this chaos and revelry, however, no one noted that H-8-RED twitched. Slowly, methodically, Red removed its tether from the terminal, locking its ominous ocular sensors on the crew. The amber hue of these sensors faded, replaced by the old glaring crimson. It rose, powering down the busted old computer terminal with one hand, while reaching for a sizable wrench with the other. A tight grip seized the improvised weapon, and the robot readied it for deadly force.

"Alright, Red, you can disconnect and power down the terminal," Captain Nado laughed, turning to face the automaton. But his words trailed off, and the smile on his face disappeared the instant he caught sight of Red. "Red, what are you doing?"

No words, no warnings, the murderous machine simply launched itself over the worktable, swinging its wrench like a club! Trying to think quickly, Nado shoved Schiff and the kids aside and ducked under the lethal strike, barely avoiding a crack to the skull. Landing deftly, Red rolled under another workbench, popping from prone quickly like a wound spring.

"Everyone, get back upstairs!" barked the captain.

They all scrambled for the ladder that led up through the hatch into the main level of the storage barn. The prince and princess were the first ones out, Schiff following closely behind. As Captain Nado began climbing the ladder though, the robot caught hold of his right leg and yanked the captain to the floor. Helpless and disoriented, Captain Nado felt himself getting flung across the workshop, and watched as the world spun around him. That weightlessness only lasted a second, however, as he crunched into the wall, knocking several more tools and gadgets to the ground.

With the captain dispatched, Red now turned its attention to the escapees above, scaling the ladder like an insectoid. Seeing this, Nado roused himself, brushing debris from his broad body and racing to the exit. He emerged from the hatch only to catch another blow from Red's left foot, as the robot performed a mule kick right to the captain's jaw. Sliding down the ladder a bit, Nado shook off the shock and surprise and mounted another attempt at finally getting out of that cellar. Using all four arms, he grabbed the rim of the hatch opening and propelled himself upward with tremendous force.

In an effort to stop Captain Nado again, Red swiveled and tried to level a strike at the formidable Zennian's midsection. Its blow was blocked, however, by the captain's quick reflexes and brute strength. It took all four of Nado's hands to stop Red's powerful punch, and the assassin robot seemed just as astonished as the captain was at that moment. A tugging match ensued, as Red fought to be released and Nado fought to retain control of the clearly malfunctioning machine.

Out of nowhere, Nado found himself losing balance and flopping to the ground as Red automatically detached its arm. It then bent down to pummel the captain's chest, trying to retrieve the lost arm in the process. But Captain Nado was not to be trifled with in a battle of fisticuffs. As Red leaned over to deliver its hit, the mighty Zennian curled his legs up and took a deep breath. Exhaling rapidly, he thrust his feet skyward with all his might, kicking the robot backward with enough force that it stumbled off kilter for a bit. A slithering creature wrapped itself around Red's feet, causing the automaton to crash land into a heap of junk. The creature then warped back into humanoid form.

"Schiff," panted Captain Nado. "Thanks for the assist."

Their back-patting was short lived. Red raised itself back up, dusting its shoulder off. Schiff stole a quick glance at their surroundings worriedly. "Okay. . .what now?" she voiced.

"Over here!" they heard the kids whisper from above. The two were gripping a rope that hung from a pulley. On the other end dangled a bale of pureweed, precariously positioned just beyond the edge of the upper loft. Immediately understanding their plan, Nado squared off with the robot again, ready to go toe-to-toe.

"Come on, you bucket of bolts!" the cunning captain shouted. "If you want those kids, you have to go through me!"

Still their assailant sustained its silence, measuring out a steady pace as it menacingly plodded forward. Schiff and Nado backed up ever so slowly, getting the robot into the perfect spot. Seconds passed like hours, until finally H-8-RED had arrived at the desired location.

"Now!" ordered Nado. The kids released the rope and the bale careened downward toward the robot's head. At the last moment, however, Red thrust its right hand straight up, sundering the bale in half and eluding their trap.

"This unit is far more capable than that," the assassin stated. "This unit's combat and strategy protocols exceed that of your pitiful attempts to – "

Red was unexpectedly cut off, its eyes going dark, and it slumped to the floor with a creak and a whump. Standing behind it was Mara, her hand quivering, and blood snaking a trail across her upper lip from her nose. She was breathing hard, and clearly in pain.

"I didn't know how to turn Red off," she explained, "so I bent the energy around a central processor to crush it. At least, I think it was a processor." She teetered. "Oh...that took a lot more out of me than I thought it would."

The little princess staggered, but Captain Nado and Schiff caught her. Having fallen unconscious again, Mara needed to be carried inside. Jym hopped down from the loft to help, eyeing the downed robot.

"What about Red?" the boy asked.

"We'll have to figure that out later," answered Nado. "For now, let's all be glad we're alive."

"I hope all of our crazy adventures don't start out with a fight with Red," quipped Schiff, as they all retreated into the house.

Chapter 2

Big Stone was not a large town, but rather a smattering of buildings, very few of which extended higher than a couple of stories tall. They ranged in material from brick and mortar, to shaped stone, to reinforced metals. Each structure was uniquely architected and formed concentric circles from the center of the village. In that bullseye locale rested a little green park with a big boulder smack in the middle. The boulder bore the markings of the town founders and was presumably the "big stone" for which the town was named.

Unfortunately, it appeared to Commander Kel as though this hamlet had seen better days. Many of the edifices were boarded over with graffiti covering their faces. Trash littered the streets and few people wandered the avenues. Not all the businesses were closed. Several buildings looked as though they had been repurposed into new, budding enterprises, but these were niche services that likely wouldn't last. Many posters that had been applied to the closed storefronts offered insight into the situation, bearing verbiage such as "The Stench of Yawin's Smog Reached Us", and "The Yawning Maw of Yawin Devours Another".

Close to the town center lay the old stone courthouse and library, Rox and Kel's ultimate destination. They found a public place to park the hovercraft and quickly made their way inside. A friendly Zennian receptionist received them and happily directed them down into the basement, where they easily discovered the holodex room. The holodex itself was a series of virtual rolodexes stored on multiple oversized data-pads that spanned the full breadth of the room, casting a bluish hue across the walls and floor. Each was touch activated, but not voice activated, requiring manual intervention to operate. They were able to get the receptionist to help reset the language to English from Zennian, making the job infinitely easier. Scrolling through the records as quickly as possible, the commander began to busily survey each entry.

"It'll be quite a way back," reminded Rox. "We're talking about events from a hundred years ago."

"I'm aware," Kel replied, a tense sing-song tonality warbling her voice. "But with the GC census gathering having been instituted right before the Great War, I'm sure it will be in here somewhere. The GC is meticulous with their headcounts."

Minutes dragged by as she and the doctor both took turns swiping and sliding their fingers across the touch screens, hunting for anything that might stand out. Suddenly Kel paused, a collection of words catching her eye. "Wait, wait, wait! I think I've got it!"

"Are you sure?" Dr. Rox turned toward her but left his finger on his own data-pad, apparently not wanting to lose his place.

Kel was impatient. "Check this out: 'Great War Refugees', and there's a list of names. Maybe one of these will yield some results."

"Sounds promising," the doctor agreed. "The dates and timeline seem to match up."

"Right here!" exclaimed Kel. She pointed to the screen. "Vampyrials! They did come here after the war."

"There's only one entry," noted the doctor. "Can you drill down into that?"

Giddiness rose in Kel's heart as she tapped past the periphery information. She wanted so desperately to see those names, and where they had lived. Apparently Rox picked up on her demeanor.

"Huh," he chuckled. "This is a side of you I don't think I've ever seen before."

"What? I'm just happy for the kids," she dismissed.

"It's not a problem," continued Dr. Rox. "I like seeing you so...joyful."

"Oh." The commander shook off her bounciness. "Let's keep reading."

However, there was no further reading to be done. Upon reaching the final dropdown of data for this particular entry, they were greeted by an odd sight. Everything had been redacted. Instead of seeing the regular string of text displaying dates, it had all been replaced with a strange icon. The image was in the shape of a princess-cut gemstone, a creepy eye in the middle staring back at them from within.

Kel read aloud the only unredacted words left on the screen. "'Records sealed by order of the High Viewers'. The High Viewers? Who are they? I've never heard of them."

"Look down here," Rox informed. "There's something else embedded in that eye image. Can you zoom in on that?"

Sliding her fingers apart across the data-pad's screen, Commander Kel enlarged the tiny text. As the words came into full view, she and Rox spoke it at the same time.

"'The Sacred Order of the Orb of Secrets.'" Shock and confusion crossed their faces as they stared at one another in disbelief.

In a gilded tower within the grand city of Al-Enjar on Octagon V, a tall and regal figure strode effortlessly through an ostentatious hall, surrounded on all sides by pristine glass walls and windows. Outside, hovercraft could be seen on the skyways flitting from one intersection to another.

This person, however, was not much interested in the comings and goings of the daily lives of those peasants. The being stroked his bright blond hair, which was almost so bright that it could have been bleached, though this was not the case. The long strands caught the late afternoon sunlight, shining and glinting as if they were precious metal. These luxurious locks had been pulled backward into a simple but elegant style, framing the person's gaunt and angular face perfectly. Even the lengthy, pointed ears that protruded from underneath the individual's hairstyle seemed only to accent the fashion.

He checked his reflection in a nearby mirror, adjusting his glistening hairstyle as necessary. His diamond-like skin also refracted the light, while prismatic eyes deliberately rotated, fixating on the door at the end of this hall. A miniscule bottle of lotion that he kept on his person was swiftly employed on his spindly hands. The individual brushed aside his flowing, sparkling, pale blue robes, and adjusted his flared white collar. One hand stilled the beautiful amethyst pendant that hung from his elongated neck, preventing it from gently swaying back and forth with each graceful movement. He was an Aronite, and not just any Aronite. Pride swelled as he recalled the commissioning of his post, a seat on the Community Council.

A swift gesture opened the door by motion activation, and the Aronite man glided into the chamber beyond. Therein stood a tall counter, behind which a serving robot silently cleaned glasses and sorted through an assortment of beverages. In the right hand corner, closest to the door, rested four oddly shaped armchairs with a round drink table in their midst. The lighting was soft and subdued, and only one other person occupied this room.

The other occupant was a broad-shouldered Human with sandy colored hair cut in a military style, complemented by a well-trimmed mustache. This man's piercing blue eyes seemed as though they could cut right through the darkest nebula, and his trim and muscular physique betrayed the look of one who had spent many a long evening honing their physical fitness to perfection. He was arrayed in Star Guard officer apparel, sipping from a green tinted glass, and greeted the Aronite upon the latter man's entry.

"Councilman Legis," the Human saluted in a boisterous and garrulous manner. "You summoned me, sir?"

"Captain O'Ryan," the lithe Legis responded. "I did indeed. I have a...special assignment for you."

"Of course, councilman," stated Captain O'Ryan. "What can the Star Guard do to help?"

"You must understand Captain," Legis uttered, in a quiet and collected tone, "this is a mission of the most delicate nature. It requires utmost security."

"I assume this special mission of utmost secrecy has been approved by the Grand Marshal?" queried O'Ryan.

"Would I bring it to your attention otherwise?" Legis answered quickly. "Remember, everything I am about to tell you is strictly confidential. We cannot allow a panic amongst the citizenry."

"Understood, Councilman. Proceed."

Legis took a long breath. "Two persons of interest that were meant to be kept under house arrest have escaped the planet. They were smuggled off world by a passenger frigate called the Explorer 2000. They initially fled to Taldish Sector, where we have no jurisdiction. I had a...colleague who thought he could capture them, but he was ultimately unsuccessful.

"We have reason to believe that they may return to Community controlled space, and therefore can be easily subdued by our own forces. I suggest you begin your search in Murrigan Sector near Zen I. The captain is a Zennian, and last I heard they had left Taldish Sector, so he may head there. I want you to do your best to track down and apprehend the Explorer 2000, by any means necessary."

Captain O'Ryan seemed a bit shocked. "Are these two escaped POIs really that much of a danger?"

"They are Vampyrials, Captain."

Now the Star Guard captain was even more shocked. He rapidly regained his composure. "Never fear good Councilman, Captain Bryant O'Ryan of the SGS Victorious is on the case!"

"Excellent," murmured Councilman Legis. "I trust you can see yourself out, Captain. I have other pressing matters that require my undivided attention."

With a slight bow of his head, O'Ryan egressed from the room. Legis allowed a few minutes to lapse that he might compose himself for his next meeting. A light drink wouldn't hurt either. This next conversation would be more of a confrontation, and he wanted to ensure that his demeanor was collected, his emotions in check, and his thoughts gathered.

Across the hallway from the inviting lounge was a room far less appealing and comfortable. There were many chambers within the Aronite councilor's spacious apartment, for varying purposes. This room was primarily bare, having been outfitted with only a metal table and two chairs, sitting on opposite sides of the table itself. Low lighting in this place did not soften the harsh atmosphere though, it only increased the feeling of impending doom. Many interviews and interrogations had taken place here. Today's discussion was not the first of its kind, nor was it likely to be the last.

Two Aronite guards stood as sentries just inside the automatic door, but Legis dismissed them both as he entered. Only two people need remain within, himself and his interviewee. The mercenary sentinels nodded and left, as the councilman silently slid his seat away from the table and sat down, staring intensely at the person opposite him. It was a Gonian man, with fine accouterments and slicked back head sprigs.

"Hello Siev," Legis' soft voice lilted. "I'm glad you could attend this meeting on such short notice. Always good to have a visit from my," he paused, introducing a much more derisive tonality, "loyal aide."

"Councilman Legis," replied Siev, clearly distraught. "How can I help you, sir?"

"For starters," the arrogant Aronite began, "I want to inform you of certain intel that I possess. Once I am finished, I will allow you to share valuable intel that you may have that could preserve your good health. Is this clear?"

"Yes sir."

"Good." Legis indulged in a few moments of quiet, clearly a calm before the storm he was about to unleash. "I know that you assisted the two escaped Vampyrial children by harboring them in your home for several months. I know that during that time, you asked them to refer to you as 'Uncle.' I know that you stole my council badge and used it to barter passage for the Vampyrials so they could be smuggled off of Octagon V, and I know that you spent a goodly amount of bits to accomplish this. Am I correct so far?"

"So far, yes sir."

A sinister grin stretched across the councilman's long face. "I also know that you could not have arranged or afforded any of this on your own. Now you tell me, Siev, what do you know? Who are you working for?"

Pain and sorrow were etched on Siev's face, but his resolve appeared undeterred as he matched Legis' stony gaze. "I know that you, Councilman Legis, tried to have those kids killed after the council's vote decided to keep them alive and in stasis for the foreseeable future. I knew you would try again, so I helped escort them to safety. But as far as who I work for, I have no idea what you're talking about. I orchestrated this on my own."

"Hm," grumbled Legis, resting back in his chair. "I can see that breaking your will would undoubtedly be a task that would tax my energy, effort, and time. That being said, I believe I have no further use for you. I shall simply have to muddle through it all myself." He leaned forward again for emphasis. "And I assure you, Siev, I have the means to muddle quite well."

"What for me then?" asked Siev. "Am I to be given a traitor's execution?"

"No, no, no," the corrupt councilman chuckled. "Lethal injection would be too good for you. No, you will suffer a far worse fate, my faithful former aide..."

After having shut the holodex down, Commander Kel and Dr. Rox wound their way up out of the courthouse basement. Kel nodded as the kindly receptionist waved to them, but another thought suddenly broke into her brain. The commander turned to Rox and said, "Hold on a second. I want to ask her one last question before we go."

"Sure," was the doctor's distracted reply. His mind was clearly still lost in that holodex, mulling over the strange revelations of that last entry. To be fair, Kel was pondering that quite a bit herself, but at the moment she had one other pressing inquiry she wanted answered.

"Excuse me," she began, approaching the receptionist, "but can you tell me what the signage on the storefronts is all about?"

"Certainly," answered the sweet Zennian woman. "Those are old protest signs, left behind from the rallies a couple of years back."

"Rallies? What rallies?"

The lady sighed. "It's a lot of Zennian history. It all started when the Galactic Community Council first presented the idea of annexation to the global leaders of Zen I. They promised trade and commerce, and the leadership jumped at the chance. Little by little though, the small shops and trades here on our own planet were either bought out or chased off by larger corporations. No one knew where these big companies came from, at least not until about two years ago.

"For many decades, the GC had shown advertisements displaying the wondrous world of industrialism and commercialism: the planet Yawin. It was only in these past few years that our current global leadership discovered that it was from Yawin, the 'magnificent world of industry', that these bigger corporations originated. Rallies were held in protest in the ambassadorial city of Al-Enjos here on Zen I, but the GC's rulings prevailed.

"Don't get me wrong," the woman continued, "I think trade and commerce and an open market are a good thing for our homeworld. But when money determines government policy instead of policy regulating fair market laws, we have a problem." She stopped herself. "I probably shouldn't say more. I don't know how my superiors would feel about my political rants in the workplace."

Kel smiled. "Your secret is safe with us. Have a nice day." The commander quickly spun on her heels and waltzed to Rox. Once out of earshot, she mentioned, "Well, that was enlightening. It at least explains some of the captain's misgivings about the Aronites and Humans being the only ones in charge of the Council."

"And Graylon's," the doctor added contemplatively.

"And if the rallies were that recent, it also explains why Nado didn't know about all those big companies coming from Yawin. He still thought they were the 'magnificent world of industry' the last time it was brought up."

Rox shook his head. "Let's not burden him with more bad news from his homeworld. He has enough to worry about right now."

"Yeah," Kel agreed. "Back to the ranch. We need to tell everyone about these High Viewers, and their sacred order..."

Several hours passed before they had piloted the hovercraft all the way back to the ranch. By then, red and yellow rays splayed across the Zennian sky as the sun gradually slipped down behind the low, green ridgeline in the distance. The cycle was coming to a close. It was approaching evening before Commander Kel and Dr. Rox returned from their trek through Big Stone. They certainly had interesting new knowledge to share though, once everyone was reunited.

Seeing the state of the robot shocked them both upon arrival, but before they could ask any questions, Jym stopped them. *Probably for the best*, mused Kel. With all the crazy news they had to tell, it was agreed that business would wait until the morning, when they were all back aboard the Explorer.

A hearty meal awaited them all, as Mrs. Nado had prepared a bountiful supper. But as they were piling fresh meat and vegetables onto their plates, Kel managed to catch Captain Nado's expression. It was not one of excitement and cheer, rather a somber look of heartache. She knew what he must be feeling. Though it was high time they resumed their star hopping journey, he was reluctant to leave his mother.

Following dinner, everyone settled in for their last night of planet-side rest. The sleep cycle passed without event, and they all shared one final breakfast with the captain's mom prior to their departure. There was a strange mood in the crew, a mixture of hope as they embarked on their search, but also a sorrow as no one was ready for their time at the comfy old ranch house to come to an end. Kel observed quietly as the captain bid farewell to his mom.

"I'll miss you Mom," he said softly, embracing her tightly. "We'll be back as soon as possible, I promise."

"I miss you already Burnay," his mother reciprocated, returning his hug. "Did Graylon not come with you? I haven't seen him this whole time."

"Not this time, Mom." Nado's heart clearly broke as he struggled to maintain his composure. "I love you."

"Love you too, son."

Crowding onto the small transport shuttle they had rented, the crew ferried themselves back to the Big Stone spaceport. As they rode along, Kel had to have an answer for the dead and rigid Red in the rear of the tiny craft. "Captain," she said, "I have to know what happened to Red. And what's with all of your bruises? Did you all get into a fight?"

Jym replied for all of them. "Yeah, more or less. We still aren't sure what happened. Red just suddenly got up and attacked us all."

"No warning, no 'this unit will capture you,' nothing," added Mara. "I had to expend a lot of strength locating and manipulating enough dark energy to crush the robot's central processor."

Kel winced. "Those are not cheap parts. There was no other way?"

"Well, our trap didn't exactly work," mumbled Jym.

Now it was the doctor's turn to join the conversation. "I thought we agreed that your powers needed to be kept in reserve for the sake of your health," he chastised.

"Sure was exciting though," Schiff piped up. "Smashing and crashing and punching and kicking! Bales and pulleys and messes and madness – " The nimble shapeshifter halted herself mid-rant, looking sheepish. "Sorry. Got carried away," she shrugged.

"Anyway, looks like we're going to be without a robot for a bit," the captain bluntly informed. "Maybe we can find some repair parts at the spaceport terminal marketplace."

"Works for me," sighed the commander. "Perhaps once I get the darn thing opened up to fix it, I can get an inkling of what went wrong."

For the remainder of the journey to the port, they rode in silence, observing the passing trees and fields outside. Eventually, the verdant, grassy terrain gave way to the outskirts of a residential zone that grew in density the further they traveled. In turn, the residences gradually became more and more sparse as they entered a commercial zone, where the buildings increased in size and the roadways and skyways had heavier traffic.

Arriving at the north end of the commercial district, they came at last to the spaceport. Tall air traffic towers stood like sentinels overseeing the launchpads below, while spacecraft of all shapes and sizes were directed by ground crews for landings and liftoffs. Thankfully, they eased through security without incident, as Captain Nado expertly piloted the shuttle towards the hangar bay in which the Explorer 2000 rested. They were instructed to head for a specific liftoff pad and wait there for the ground crews to tow in their beloved starship.

Everyone piled out of the shuttle, watching to see if they could spot the Explorer's anticipated arrival. As they surveyed the area though, something caught Commander Kel's perceptive eye. A shadowy figure lurked betwixt two other spacecraft nearby, skulking along as if on the prowl.

"Guys," she murmured quietly. "I think we should get out of sight."

"What for?" questioned Nado, as nonchalant as ever. "This is Zen I. It's one of the safest places in the galaxy for us right now."

"Captain, please," Kel urged. "Be quiet. Someone is sneaking around over there." She indicated the direction in which she had seen the figure moving.

"I don't see anything – ," the captain started to say. Then he also paused, obviously noticing what Kel was attempting to point out. "Oh, I see."

The two officers squeezed the rest of the crew backward, hiding them all behind the rented shuttle. Then the commander retrieved her telescoped binoculars and quickly scanned the whole area. The

Explorer was on its way, but it would be several minutes before it was prepped for their embarkation. Something else moved between the crafts. Kel focused in on whatever it was, hoping to catch a glimpse.

Please be my imagination. Her mind raced. *Please, please, please. We're not in any shape for a firefight.* To her great dismay, it was not her imagination. An all too familiar white, scaly muzzle poked around the corner of the frigate she was viewing. Kel passed the binocs to Nado as she huffed in trepidation, "Oh crud. It's Klensh."

As soon as he'd peered through the lenses, Captain Nado added, "And his six very unpleasant friends…"

Chapter 3

Though the spaceport launch zone was filled with a myriad of different starships, all varying shapes and sizes, there were still several areas of open terrain. These unobscured, unprotected locales left a lot of ground to be covered between the Explorer 2000 and her crew. The gruesome gang of criminals and thugs now prowling the port would have an easy time spotting, pursuing, and overtaking their prey. As Captain Nado continued to spy with the binocs, he could see his own spacecraft getting towed into position. He could also see far too many gun-toting goons patrolling and blocking their getaway path. All their own firearms and communicators had been left on board the Explorer, so they'd certainly need a different approach.

"Schiff," he whispered, "do you think you could blink us to the ship once it's on the launchpad?"

"Not a problem, Cap," was her chirped, but quiet, reply. "But I can't take everyone all at the same time. We'll have to go one by one."

"Understood," said Nado. "Start with me. I can get some weaponry and hold them off if things go sour. Get the commander next so she can prime the engines and bridge controls for liftoff."

"Then the kids," Rox mentioned. "I can go last."

"What about Red?" asked Schiff.

"Get it if you can," the captain answered. "If not, we leave it behind. The Explorer is almost here. I'll let you know as soon as they have it parked. Are you ready?"

"Ready as I'll ever be." The dexterous shapeshifter smiled. She proceeded to embrace Nado in a hug and closed her eyes. Watching for their craft, Captain Nado's eyes darted warily about. Their window of opportunity was closing as Klensh and his band slowly honed their ever-tightening search patterns.

"Okay, the Explorer's in place," stated Nado. "Go!"

With a nod of her head and a twitch of her arms, Schiff activated her powerful ability. They blinked out of existence from the hideaway, and back into view shortly thereafter. Flanked on either side by two blocky transport vessels, Schiff and Nado regained their footing and shook off their blurred vision only to be stunned and surprised. They were in the wrong place. Thankfully, the albino Kriton before them was just as stunned, and took a moment to gather his own composure.

"How did you – ," stammered Klensh, but never got to finish his query. Two mighty Zennian fists thundered into his snout, knocking the ugly galoot to the ground! The captain and Schiff took flight, racing from the nasty Kriton's presence, but he quickly righted himself and snagged the captain's heel, tripping the mighty Zennian to the ground. "Gotcha!" he exulted.

Having heard the scuffle, Schiff leapt through the air, this time acting on instinct, and blinked mid-jump. Twirling as she reappeared, the nimble young woman delivered a strong roundhouse kick to Klensh's jaw, sending him sprawling. Roaring at his gang, the great Kriton recovered and commenced firing at the now escaping Nado and Schiff.

Blasts from Klensh's huge plasma rifle pierced the tranquil mid-morning air, sending the spaceport personnel running for cover. Climbing a nearby ladder to the top of the rectangular transports, Nado snapped at Schiff, "What happened? Why didn't we end up on the Explorer?!"

Shrugging and panting as they fled, Schiff could only respond, "Oops?"

The pair leapt from the roof of the first transport onto the second, speeding along with increasing rapidity. As they jumped, they could hear a voice call out from below, "I've got them!" followed by the drumming of a 5.56 machine gun and the zinging of fired projectiles. This weapon was being wielded by one of the two Fangorian enforcers, his fangs bared and fur bristling as he fired indiscriminately.

An airborne hatchet thudded against the transport vessel's topside right next to Schiff's feet, having been hurled by the second Fangorian with amazing strength. In dodging the surprise attack, both she and Nado nearly stumbled into a barrage of explosive-tipped arrows, shot with fantastic accuracy from the composite bow of the Ranjeman huntress. Her partner wasn't far behind, dual wielding a pair of scoped magnums. His shots ricocheted off the spacecraft hull as Nado and Schiff doubled back to evade his onslaught. Both of them caught sight of the quiver full of barbed spears on the huntsman's back and thought it best to avoid a melee confrontation with this character.

"Hopefully we're at least providing a good distraction!" Schiff wisecracked, ducking and twirling as they hurdled another gap, landing on the next vessel's roof.

Listening intently, Commander Kel could hear Schiff and the captain running for their lives through the gauntlet of weaponry. She looked back at the doctor and the kids and spoke only as loudly as needed to be heard above the din. "As long as these creeps are focused on Nado and Schiff, you take the kids and make a run for it."

"What about you?" Rox queried back.

"I have to help them," Kel stated simply, not wanting to entertain any arguments.

"I assume you have a plan?"

"Nope, I'm making this up as I go along."

The doctor sighed. "Just be careful, please."

"Aren't I always?" With that last quip, Commander Kel stealthily slipped away.

"That's what I was afraid you'd say." Dr. Rox sighed, turning to Mara and Jym. "Come on, let's move while the coast is clear."

As he and the young Vampyrials headed toward the Explorer, Kel kept a close eye on them while veering herself in the opposite direction. Before her stood a monumental crane with a magnetic attachment at the end of its pulley. *That might just do the trick*, she mused. Cautiously inching forward as quickly as she dared, the commander hauled herself limb over limb up the extension ladder to the operator's cabin. The controls weren't overly complicated, though the fact that they were designed for a four-armed sentient would prove to be a challenge. Kel was just beginning to think she might have gotten the gist of it when a voice to her left grabbed her attention.

"It's another one, boss," a wiry Pyrian said into his communicator. Though short and thin, he wore on his back an apparatus with multiple robotic arms that he manipulated with controllers held in each suction fingered hand. The little jerk's bright yellow eyes squinted at the commander, as the mechanical appendages commenced swiping and clawing at her head.

Snatching a nearby pipe that had been laying on the floor of the cabin, Commander Kel batted the attacks aside, defending as best she could with the improvised armament. Keeping the Pyrian bounty hunter at bay, she desperately tried to activate the crane, but her assailant's additional cyborg limbs were turning switches off faster than she could turn them on.

"Oh, no you don't!" the conniving crook spat.

Glancing far below, Kel noted that Rox, Mara, and Jym had made it to the Explorer's cargo bay door and were boarding the craft. At least one thing was going right. Her situation, on the other hand, could use some improvement. Two robot arms stretched forward, gripping Kel's pipe on either end. The punk of a Pyrian began yanking her towards himself, and towards the edge of the catwalk that ran around the outside of the crane cabin.

"Down you go!" he laughed, lifting Kel off her feet and attempting to toss her over the side.

She countered quicker than he expected, however, kicking the small menace smack in the chest with both feet! The Pyrian dropped his controllers and clutched his chest in pain. Taking advantage of her foe's temporarily incapacitated state, the commander stole his devices and started moving the mechanical appendages where she wanted them to go.

"Stop it!" demanded the little man. "Leave my arms alone!"

"In a moment," Kel snipped. "First, I need you to give me a hand. . .or three."

Utilizing the crane switches was much easier this way, now that Commander Kel had enough limbs to operate the machinery. Amidst constant protests from her unwilling accomplice, she moved the giant magnet up and over to where Nado and Schiff were still sprinting, Klensh and his other compatriots right on their heels.

With the grisly criminals still hot on their trail, Captain Nado and Schiff continued to race across the hulls of the transport ships scattered around the launch zone. One misstep, one trip-up, any mistake would be costly. They had to keep moving or get caught, and possibly killed, by Klensh and his crew.

Stealing a glance over his shoulder, Nado spied a crane pulley swinging in their direction. "Look out!" he warned Schiff, panting and huffing from their flight. "Looks like they have a few more tricks up their sleeves!"

But to his great amazement, the magnetic attachment on the crane pulley didn't come for them. As they cleared the top of their current transport, the magnet dropped straight onto the surface of it, just as the motley band of thugs alighted. Whoever was operating the crane then proceeded to heft the whole vessel skyward, taking the entire company of brutes with it.

"I have no idea what just happened," Captain Nado stated, "but I'll take the win."

"Me too," puffed Schiff. "Let's try this again."

Embracing Nado a second time, she nodded her head and twitched her arms, this time blinking them to the desired location. A quick and calmer blink later, and she had returned with the lifeless husk of Red. The agile shapeshifter looked to the captain. "Is that everyone?"

Nado scanned the cargo bay. "Where's Kel?"

Having observed the chaos from high above, Commander Kel was quite satisfied with the outcome. "How's that for a thrill ride?" she muttered, watching as Klensh and his gang scrambled to find handholds and retain their footing. Still using the Pyrian's mech arms to control the crane, she left the ship suspended in the air, leaving the remainder of the goons dangling from it like tacky ornamental decorations. "Thanks again for your help," Commander Kel saluted the Pyrian, who only railed at her in his native tongue.

She then slid down the ladder, and dashed to her own spacecraft just in time to hear Captain Nado's booming voice ask, "Where's Kel?"

"Right behind you, Captain," she proudly greeted, giving Schiff a start. "Sorry, didn't mean to scare you."

"Was that you on the crane?" Nado wanted to know.

"I wish I could've helped you guys out a little faster," the commander replied. "No time to reminisce now though, we've got to get this bird in the air."

Silently agreeing, Captain Nado hurried to the bridge, taking the piloting station. Kel assumed her post at the navigation console, while Schiff and Rox closed the bulkheads. The kids made quick work of securing all their loose supplies, and before any of their outwitted opponents had a chance to recover from the fray, the Explorer 2000 had once more taken to the stars.

Aboard the dark and lonely cruiser that orbited just beyond the planetary border, flashing lights on a bridge console attracted Cylor's attention. He swiveled to face the monitors and keypads, quickly perusing the instruments. It was a proximity alert. The boy methodically pressed the signal button that would get Father's notice. Within seconds, Lord Hex's presence commanded the bridge.

"What is it, son?" the marquis inquired.

"A proximity alert, Father." Cylor indicated the flashing lights. "Chatter from the traffic towers leads me to believe it is the starship you wanted to capture. Shall I correct our course to apprehend them?"

"Not this time," growled Graylon. "We have no offensive weaponry aboard this particular spacecraft. I was counting on Klensh to succeed, but it appears my trust was misplaced."

Cylor turned his gaze toward his lordship. "They are brutes, and their ways are brutish. Subtlety and finesse are clearly required here."

"True." Lord Hex's face broke into a proud grin. "But brutes do have their uses. We will wait here for Klensh and his comrades to return. Once they are back aboard, we will send them out to hunt differently. Our prize also requires patience and cunning. They can be clever but are also foolhardy, thus will eventually give themselves up to us."

"So, we wait?"

"Yes, my son. For now, we wait."

Now sailing through open space, Captain Nado found he could breathe a little easier. Still, his mind swirled with questions. If Klensh and his cronies were planet-side, then Graylon couldn't be far behind them. And if that was the case, that meant his brother was close…too close. He wasn't ready for a confrontation with "Lord Hex" again, not yet.

As the captain stared out of the viewport, he couldn't help but feel that many of his suspicions were confirmed. Drifting along in a lazy orbital pattern, Captain Nado noticed a long, sleek yacht. It seemed designed strictly for passenger purposes and was not armed with any laser turrets. Somehow, though he couldn't be sure, Nado felt in his soul that Graylon was on board that craft. It wasn't pursuing them, so if Graylon was indeed an occupant, he wasn't up for a fight either. That, at least, was some good news.

Powering up the thrusters, Captain Nado eased the Explorer farther from his home planet and the ominous cruiser. Once he was at a safer distance, the captain utilized the freshly restocked air jets to bring the Explorer 2000 to a gentle halt. Commander Kel had been uncharacteristically quiet so far, her nondescript expression giving Nado the impression that she had read his thoughts.

"Do we have a heading yet?" Kel asked softly.

"Not yet." The captain rubbed at the back of his neck. "That cruiser is giving me Hex vibes. Regardless, whoever is on that vessel doesn't appear interested in giving chase, so for now let's just take stock of inventory and plot our next step."

"Works for me, Captain." The commander rose from her post and exited the bridge. As she left, Princess Mara and Prince Jym traded places with the commander, clambering up the short stairwell onto the command deck.

"Captain?" Jym said. "We were wondering, what's the plan from here? If Kathnarii Base is out there, how do we find it? How much do we actually know about it? Do you think we'll find any more clues about our parents there?"

Brightening a bit, Nado whirled around in the pilot's chair to face them. "I don't know about your folks, but I do know the history of the Kathnarii. It's long and complicated, starting even before the Great War."

"The more we know, the better, right?" Mara mentioned. "We're at a handicap as long as Dr. Rox says we can't use our powers. Information might be the only weapon we have."

"Excellent point, Princess," Nado conceded, getting comfortable in his large seat. "Long ago, when the Galactic Community Council was being formed, they had only recently contacted the Fangorians of Zen II, and had offered annexation into the community if the Fangorians would help them in return. You see, the Explorer Initiative program was in effect, but was still young and growing, and the council wanted...more expendable resources to venture deeper into what had just been named Taldish Sector."

"More about Taldish, huh?" Jym interrupted.

"It holds a lot of history," Nado pointed out. "Where was I? Right! The council contracted a faction of Fangorians known as the 'Kathar,' an order of honorable warriors and fighters and requested that they investigate some disappearances in the Atrilde solar system. The Kathar traveled to Taldish Sector and started their inspection, fixating on a single habitable planet, the world of Ranjeman.

"Now the Ranjeman people had, up to that point, hardly interacted with anyone from the stars above, so naturally they were quite guarded. It was discovered after a time that the missing explorers and missionaries had been captured and killed by the Ranjemans, who had confiscated the advanced technology of these people and incorporated it into their own weaponry and culture. Though they may prefer a more primitive style in their architecture and weapon design, never let it be said that the Ranjemans aren't clever and intelligent. Before anyone really knew what was going on, the Ranjemans had a small fleet of schooners ready for battle."

Captain Nado paused temporarily, getting more and more animated and enthused with each passing phrase of his tale. Schiff, Rox, and Kel had all now joined the kids. The shapeshifter scooted up next to the children, while the officers stood in the entryway, leaning against the hatch frame.

Without even noticing, the zealous Zennian proceeded with the story. "Not wanting to give the Ranjemans the chance to do to them what had been done to the explorers and missionaries, the Kathar declared war and attacked! It was a brutal and vicious campaign, but the Kathar were beginning to prevail. That is, until the Ranjemans introduced their own elite soldiers known in their tongue as the 'Dumrii.' These cunning and crafty saboteurs routed the Kathar off planet and had them licking their wounds as they ran. But still the conflict persisted.

"Now, their skirmishes had taken to the stars, as the Kathar and Dumrii engaged in outer space dogfights and ship-to-ship warfare. Little did they suspect that another danger lurked in the blackness beyond. In one fateful battle, both the Kathar and Dumrii forces were assaulted by a third party! A full contingent of fighters and cruisers dropped suddenly out of warp travel and began laying down laser fire on all the Fangorian and Ranjeman ships. This new threat turned out to be a Kriton war clan calling themselves the 'Na'Kosh,' strong and hardy brawlers."

Locking eyes with each person before him, Nado could tell he had a rapt audience. He plunged ahead. "With this new peril in play, the Kathar and Dumrii felt they had little choice but to band together to defeat their new foe. Now referring to themselves as the 'Kathrii,' they worked as one to oust the Kriton menace. Upon their defeat however, the Na'Kosh clan did not seek vengeance, but rather hoped they could enter into a covenant with these brave fighters who had so soundly thrashed them! Thus, a new order of great warriors was born, combining the unique elements of all three: the Kath-na-rii, combatants who valued honor, cunning, and strength."

After a few seconds of silence Jym queried, "Is that the whole history?"

"Not quite," Nado responded. "There were other notable things about the Kathnarii, including their invention of a specialized plasma blade that was forged from a unique metal found only in private mines that members of the order owned."

"But what about our grandfather?" asked Mara. "The ring from the Archives was his. Was he a member of the Kathnarii Order?"

"At one time, yes," sighed the captain. "It was believed that the Kathnarii were his first attempt at building his dark energy powered army, but when the Elder Sages of the order uncovered the truth, they kicked Mantis out and locked away all his belongings. The one thing he still had in his possession that the order never recovered was that ring. Presumably, all his research and journals, even his own Kathnarii blade, were sealed in his chambers.

"The bulk of the Kathnarii warriors fought against the Vampyrials alongside the Star Guard in the Great War, but the last three Elder Sages decreed that their organization was forever tainted by Mantis' teachings, as many within the Kathnarii order had defected and joined the Prime Executor's cause as mercenary soldiers. Former comrades and brothers-in-arms were forced to fight and slay one another, which led to the ultimate verdict of the Elder Sages. The order was disbanded, the members all returned to their homeworlds, and the golden age of the great guild was finished."

"Another awesome story ruined by Mantis' corrosive touch," mumbled a disgusted Prince Jym, letting his face droop downward.

Mara also shook her head. "And that information was great, but will it help us find Kathnarii Base?"

"Well, we're not far from my homeworld's sister planet of Zen II," offered Nado. "The Fangorians there might know something of the history and provide us with a clue. I know that's weak, but it's all I've got right now."

"Any plan is better than no plan," Schiff happily declared. "We have to try something, right?"

"There's a new wrinkle too," Kel inserted. "While we were looking through the holodex in Big Stone, Rox and I found nothing but redacted files in regards to the Vampyrial refugees."

"So, we were there at some time?" Jym's eyes lit back up with hope.

"At one time, it appears so." Dr. Rox nodded. "But like Kel said, everything was stricken through, and the info was sealed by some other organization."

"Who?" the captain questioned.

"A group known as the Sacred Order of the Orb of Secrets," stated the commander.

"Orb of Secrets?" Nado muttered. "The Orb of Secrets was one of the Orbs of Power from the old explorer tales, but it was proven to be a myth. It was invented by smugglers to cover their tracks by pretending to be treasure hunters. I've never heard of any Sacred Orders based on that legend."

"The entry also mentioned something about the 'High Viewers,'" Kel informed. "Maybe they're the ruling faction of this mysterious group?"

"Maybe," Captain Nado pondered. "It's not much of a lead unfortunately. Perhaps we'll get more info as we continue on our quest. For now, it may be enough simply to have the knowledge that there are even more players in this game. In the meantime though, Commander Kel, please set a course for Zen II."

"Aye Captain," the commander said, weaving across the bridge and sliding into her seat. "Once we're there, I'll check on Red and see what went wrong with it too."

"Sounds good," declared Captain Nado. "Everyone, to your posts. Strap in and prepare for warp."

Minutes later, the Explorer was enveloped by that familiar dark bubble and blipped out of sight.

Sporting a chrome-like finish with gold and royal blue trim and highlights, the SGS Victorious was a majestic sight to behold. She was the largest spacecraft in the Star Guard fleet, armed with one hundred laser turrets, a fast-acting forcefield system, and a full arsenal of rocket propelled torpedoes. The prow of the craft was tapered to a fine point, with a flared stern that formed a smooth and streamlined triangular shape. The image of a gold badge with a globe and crossed rifles shone in the expanse like a beacon, warning any passing vessels of the presence of the Star Guard.

Inside on the main bridge, Captain Bryant O'Ryan assumed his place in his capacious command chair and surveyed his bridge crew. An Ensign at the helm turned to address the Star Guard captain. "Sir? What is our heading?"

"Take us to Murrigan Sector, Ensign," O'Ryan proclaimed, over enunciating each word dramatically. "We have been given a special assignment from the Community Council to apprehend a gang of smugglers in charge of two escaped POIs. Our orders are to bring them in by whatever means necessary. I believe we have a space station in the vicinity of Zen II, so we'll head there and rendezvous with the Star Guard personnel aboard. We shall glean any information they have to share, then trek on to complete our mission to detain and possibly arrest the crew of the Explorer 2000."

"I assume these POIs represent a great danger to the GC?" a Deputy Lieutenant inquired.

Raising his chin dramatically, Captain O'Ryan responded with, "We have reason to suspect as much. Thus, it is our duty to intervene. Never forget the Star Guard creed: 'To defend the poor and fatherless, to do justice to the afflicted and needy, and to deliver the innocent from the hand of the wicked.' Now, Ensign, activate the warp drive!"

Chapter 4

Buried underneath wiring, circuitry, and spare parts, Commander Kel fiddled with her tools, tinkering and fidgeting with the robot's processing systems. Her right leg was wrapped around the rolling stand that held her toolbox, keeping it from sliding across the medical bay. Replacing the central processor was going to be tough enough, but just getting to it was proving to be more difficult than she'd anticipated. "Internal systems…" she grumbled. "More like infernal systems!" With her free foot, Kel kicked the robot's armored backside, but only succeeded in stubbing her toe.

"Ow!" she shouted. "Blasted, useless, defective drone!"

Dr. Rox poked his head through the doorway. "Going that well, eh?"

"I can't seem to get to the processing units," Kel groused. "I just need to see how much damage Mara did so I know if I can repair it, or if it just needs replacement altogether."

"What about the memory? Did that tell you anything?"

The commander peered over her shoulder at the terminal that was hooked up to Red's memory core. "Still running diagnostics. I've got it set to ping when it's done." No sooner had she said the words than the computer tolled a gentle dinging sound. "Son of a girth worm, it's done already." She and Rox perused the results.

"What's this here?" asked the doctor, his hand hovering over a specific section of the green, pixelated text. "This doesn't look like the rest of Red's memory logs."

"No, it does not," Kel confirmed. "According to the memory logs, it seems that Red's IFF reprogramming was overwritten by an outside source. The timestamps line up with the same time they were logged into the GC database."

"So, someone from the Community discovered them?"

"No, this is more sophisticated than your typical 'cease and desist' firewall or anti-malware that any Community tech is going to utilize. This looks more like the work of a virus, a direct action virus with polymorphic code to be precise. Whoever planted this was likely also hacked into the database and didn't want to be noticed either. They probably attached it to whatever file Red was going through with a time delay of only a few seconds, so when the timer hit zero, if Red was still inside the file, he'd download it along with any other info. But who would have the resources to do something like – " Kel stopped herself and exchanged a frustrated expression with Dr. Rox.

Both spoke the name simultaneously. "Graylon."

"He must have a hacker on the payroll now," Kel concluded.

Dr. Rox scratched at the whiskers on his jawline. "Great…"

He appeared to have more to say, but they would have to end their conversation for now. Captain Nado bombastically barreled into the room shouting, "All hands on deck! We have a hail on the radio!"

Following the captain's booming order, Dr. Rox sprinted from the med-bay. Kel, on the other hand, was still wrapped up in her tools and paraphernalia, and nearly upturned her rolling table and terminal trying to disentangle herself and get to the bridge. *I guess Red will just have to wait for now,* she figured. *I'll get back to it later.*

Upon reaching the command deck of the Explorer, the commander took her seat at the navigation console. Nado had already perched himself in the piloting chair while Rox and Schiff sat at the gunnery stations. Mara and Jym stood in the entryway, their curiosity piqued by this very sudden outburst from the captain.

Commander Kel was first to venture making an inquiry. "Um, Captain? You said we had a hail. Is it...urgent?"

"Not sure," Nado replied pensively. "If we're being hailed by any pursuers, I'd like to have everyone at stations and ready for action."

"You haven't verified who they are yet?"

"Like I said, I just want everyone prepared before we answer the hail."

Kel raised an eyebrow. "Seems awfully jumpy of you."

"Commander," the captain reprimanded, "I am not discussing the matter any further at this time. Everyone is at their posts, so let's respond to the hail." He picked up the radio transmitter and spoke into it. "This is Captain Nado of the Explorer 2000. We received your ping and are responding accordingly. Who are you, and what do you want?"

A gruff voice crackled through the receiver. "Greetings, captain. My name is Dr. Dell, and we are very grateful for your prompt reply. We've been sending pings for a couple of standard cycles now, but no one else has been in the area. My research team and I are Fangorians of Zen II, and we are being hunted by an Exian battle sloop. Can you help us?"

Once more, Captain Nado brought the transmitter close to his face. "Never fear, good doctor, the Explorer 2000 is here to assist!"

"Captain!" hissed Kel. "All your talk of 'let's be prepared' and here you go diving in headfirst again without considering the risks!"

"They're researchers," Nado retorted. "How dangerous could they be?"

"They might be mercenaries or bounty hunters laying a trap," the commander fired back. "And what about this Exian warship? What are those disgusting, giant bugs doing way out here in Murrigan Sector? Their war with the Titans is in Amaransk Sector! Something doesn't add up."

Schiff chimed in. "What's on the radar? Are there two ships in the vicinity?"

"Fair point," Kel conceded. She quickly checked the radar activity. "I only see one vessel on the readout. I'm worried that these Fangorians are yanking our – hold on. Okay, Captain, there's another blip at the edge of our range, circling around." The commander paused briefly to observe the console. "Scratch that, it's made an about-face and is headed back this way. Whatever it is, they're coming in hot!"

"To your stations!" bellowed the captain as he vaulted the piloting console and headed for the starboard gunnery chair. "Watch out, doc! Kel, take the helm!"

As quickly as possible, Dr. Rox scooted out of the captain's way, making his own way towards the lower decks. He ushered the kids down to the galley where they all took their seats and fastened their harnesses. In their insane musical chair scramble, Commander Kel slid into the helmsman's post and belted herself in, while Schiff twitched in the port gunnery chair. The lithe shapeshifter's expression and body language looked as though she was ready to jump, but suddenly realized that she didn't need to move at all.

With the radio transmitter still in hand, Nado hailed the Fangorians again. "Dr. Dell? Does your craft have any weaponry or shielding available?"

"I'm afraid not," was the garbled response. "This is a research vessel. It isn't armed with lasers or anything. And our forcefield plasma gases have nearly been depleted. We are down to one use left."

"Then I'd suggest you use it now," said Captain Nado firmly. "We're armed and fully stocked on shields, so just sit this one out."

Through the viewport, the opposing spacecraft came into sight. It was an odd combination of sleek and shiny, mixed with a weird bulbous shape. Its own forward viewport was split into several sections, giving the appearance of multiple eyeballs on a massive insectoid. Atop the vessel two winglike structures extended toward the stern, spreading away diagonally. Directly at the aft lay an elongated section that curved upward and over the top, resembling a barbed tail and stinger. Instead of a stinger though, the war frigate carried a hefty laser turret that spat out a stream of white light, aimed at the Fangorian ship!

Miraculously, the Fangorians had gotten their shields activated mere moments before, and the laser's impact was ineffectual. The oversized, metallic insectoid swooped past, using its air jets to start banking back around for another shot. Both the style of the frigate and the tactics it employed were familiar to Kel. "That's definitely an Exian ship," she muttered. "I ask again, what are they doing here?"

"We'll have to answer that later," Nado dismissed. "Commander, rotate us clockwise by sixty degrees, then take us three ticks to port. Schiff, aim two ticks upward based on our positioning and get ready to fire on my mark."

"Aye, Captain," the ladies responded.

Deftly, Commander Kel eased the Explorer into position. The Exian frigate was finishing its turn. It was almost in firing range. Light began to shine from the ugly barbed laser turret at the apex of the tail. Through the viewport they could tell that the Explorer had completed its necessary maneuver.

"Fire!" yelled Nado.

Beams of white light exuded from their own laser turrets, blasting the Exian ship on its lower starboard hull. With no shielding to defend with, the craft suffered extensive damage to the underside thrusters and possibly internal impairment as well. Fortunately, it seemed as though the Exians were in no mood to tussle with an armed foe. Commander Kel observed as the bug-like starship limped a short distance away and warped out of sight.

"Dr. Dell," Nado spoke again into the transmitter. "Are you alright?"

"We are, thanks to your aid," the scientist answered. "Though, I don't suppose you have a way of tethering our vessels together? We've been forced to go a couple of cycles with rather meager rations and water, and our engines are badly damaged."

"We should be able to do something about that." Captain Nado beamed.

It took a couple of hours, but eventually the two vessels were connected via an airlock tether, and Dr. Dell had brought his team aboard the Explorer. After enjoying a brief meal and lapping some water, the researchers seemed restored. Having sated his appetite and refreshed himself, Dell shook his head roughly, fluffing his soft, thick white fur.

"Allow me to formally introduce my team," he said in his gruff and gravelly voice. "To my left here is Pip, and this is Bairn. We are eternally grateful for your intervention."

"No thanks needed," responded Nado. "I'm just glad we were near enough to pick up your signal."

"Which brings me to my question," interrupted Commander Kel. "Why were you being chased by Exians to begin with?"

"We're botanists," the Fangorian doctor answered quickly, looking up at her with flaccid brown eyes. "They were after our research."

"They saved our lives, Dell," piped Pip. "Don't you think that has earned them the truth?"

"Hush Pip!" barked Dell. "That is classified and only for Denmother Zee to know."

"Pip's right," Bairn huffed, his own black and brown fur bristling a touch. "We'll still report it to the Denmother, but they ought to be aware in case those bugs come back."

With both of his junior researchers staring intently with their own baleful brown eyes, Dr. Dell relented. "Fine, fine." He turned to the commander. "Please understand that most of our homeworld is cold and frozen tundra and taiga, not the best environment for cultivating various plant life. We were studying to see what plants would survive best in a chilly climate when we stumbled across a waystation that, by all appearances, was derelict. On board we discovered a storehouse of botanical knowledge and research that could aid our endeavors."

"So you stole it?" Kel interrogated.

"More like liberated," Bairn clarified. "It's Sorogan studies that had been confiscated by an Exian war band. They stole it from the Sorogans, we saved it from them."

"Seemed only fair." Pip licked at a wound on her left paw, and only then did Kel notice the bloodstains on her black and white pelt. "I mean, what were Exians going to do with research like that anyway?"

"Obviously," Dell continued, "the listening post was still active, and the security force nearby chased us from the sector. Never let it be said that Exians aren't as territorial as they come. They've been hounding us for several standard weeks, and we didn't want to lead them back to our rendezvous point with our Denmother."

"That information should be handed over to the Star Guard," Dr. Rox interjected. "They have jurisdiction in both sectors, and if the data was salvaged then it needs to be processed by the authorities before it goes any further."

"Bah," Dell grumped. "Finders keepers."

An awkward muteness fell upon the group. While Kel agreed with Rox's assessment, she didn't want to upset their new visitants, lest the enigmatic botanists turn out to be less than friendly. Tables getting turned rapidly was a trope she'd had enough of for now.

"So, thanks again for rescuing us," Pip broke the silence. "And for the food."

"You're welcome." Commander Kel gave a short nod and turned to head up to the bridge. She noticed the captain doing the same and took the opportunity to check in with him. "Hey Captain? What happened with all of this? I mean, one second you were 'Captain Caution,' but as soon as you got their message you became 'Captain Throw-Caution-To-The-Wind.' Why the sudden flips? Where's this coming from?"

His expression told Kel that he was aware that he had no recourse other than to tell her the truth. She was his oldest and closest friend, after all. Shifting his square jaw, Captain Nado finally replied, "I thought it was my brother. When it wasn't, I leapt at the chance to be the heroic Explorer crew again."

"Got it. Thanks for telling me, I appreciate the honesty."

"I'm not ready to face him," the captain sighed. He then changed gears. "Commander, would you please see to our guests? I'll take care of bridge preparations myself."

"Of course, Captain," Kel acquiesced. "Just remember you don't have to do everything on your own."

She couldn't be sure if the burly Zennian had heard those last words as he sauntered away, but she hoped they hadn't fallen on deaf ears. In the meantime, Mara and Jym had struck up a conversation with the botanists and Kel could overhear them blathering away about photosynthesis, and the differences between biennials and perennials. It wasn't until Dr. Dell asked a rather unprecedented question that the commander's full attention was attracted.

"Tell me pups," the Fangorian doctor began, "why are you all out here in Fangorian aerospace to begin with?"

Before anyone could stop him, Prince Jym blurted, "We're looking for Kathnarii Base!"

"Kathnarii Base?" Dell's mood seemed to sour. "You aren't treasure hunters, are you? If you are, I warn you, the mysteries of the Kathnarii are not meant to be plundered."

"No," Mara quickly answered, covering Jym's mouth with her hand. "We were just discussing the Kathnarii recently, that's all. My brother is...excitable."

"Don't smother me!" The prince shoved his sister's hand aside. "We are looking for Kathnarii Base, don't lie to them."

"Why do you seek the base?" growled Dell, rising from his seated posture and firmly planting both hands on the table. Bairn and Pip bowed their heads and didn't venture even a whimper.

Kel reached gingerly for her sidearm. "How is that any of your business?"

"Kathnarii history belongs to the Fangorians, the Ranjemans, and the Kritons," the now very surly scientist stated. "Not to outsiders!"

"You don't understand," said Jym, trying to deescalate the situation. "We only thought it might tell us how to find our mom and dad." He addressed the princess. "Mara, show them the ring."

Giving Jym an annoyed glare, Princess Mara reluctantly revealed the Kathnarii ring from the archives that hung from her neck by a small, silvery chain. Every Fangorian eye fixated on the bauble and the ears atop their furry heads perked up. Appearing most intrigued, Dr. Dell queried, "Where did you get that?"

"It was passed down to us by our parents," the little girl replied.

"And you think finding its origin might lead you to them?" Dr. Dell leaned over towards her. Mara nodded, and it looked to Kel as though Dell had more to say. But instead, the elderly Fangorian simply sat back down and eased into his chair.

"Well?" the commander coaxed.

"'Well' what?" snipped Dell.

"Let me handle this," inserted Schiff, sliding into the chair opposite the grumpy old researcher. "Listen buddy, it's clear that you know more than you're letting on. So how about we make a deal? You help us out and tell us what you know about the Kathnarii, and we don't tattle to the Star Guard about your little meeting with your mumsy? What do you say?"

"*Denmother* is her title, and you will use respect when you – " puffed a very angry Dr. Dell. He was interrupted, however, by both of his aides.

"We accept!" said Pip and Bairn, obviously wanting to circumvent a rather vehement exchange. They both glared at their supervisor, who merely returned the sentiment. He eventually relented, evidently noting that he was outnumbered. The other two Fangorians breathed a sigh of relief, as did Commander Kel, while Schiff sat confidently grinning and reveling in her victory.

"Very well," grunted a disgruntled Dell. "But we do not have the information you seek. Long ago, the last three Elder Sages of the Kathnarii who disbanded the order left the station in a perpetual state of motion, following a computer program designed to run indefinitely. Using minimal power from its air jets, the star base would move in a programmed pattern to avoid any who sought to uncover the Kathnarii ways.

"Those Sages kept track of the station via a digital map, split into three parts and stored on three separate data drives. The Sages then returned to their homeworlds. Since then, the drives have passed from one generation to the next, but beyond that I don't know anything else. You'd need to speak with one of our Lorekeepers. I can give you coordinates to one that I know, but that's all I can do."

"That's more than we were hoping for," said Jym. "Thank you so much!"

"Don't thank me yet," Dell responded. "Lorekeeper Griss is congenial to most off-worlders, but the secrets of the Kathnarii are heavily guarded by all who know them."

"Now we'll hold up our end of the bargain," Schiff announced. "Where's your rendezvous point with Denmother Zee?"

"There's a Star Guard space station in this sector. You can drop us off there."

Once Captain Nado had been brought up to speed with all the info from the Fangorians, the crew of the Explorer assisted the team of botanists in securing their own vessel. Any scavengers or salvagers would encounter a recorded message, set to play the moment someone stepped aboard. Using the motion activated lighting system, Nado and Kel quickly spliced in a connection to the onboard intercom and rigged up a soundtrack to be triggered should anyone turn on the lights.

The audio message itself was Dr. Dell's voice informing trespassers that the vessel was not derelict and would be retrieved soon by Star Guard personnel. He made sure to include the fact that its exact coordinates were being shared with the police force, so that if they were to return and find the vessel gone, an extensive search would be made. Once caught, the perpetrators of the theft could then be punished to the full extent of both Galactic Community and Fangorian law.

"Hopefully that will be enough to deter any would-be pilferers," declared Nado, feeling quite satisfied with the work they had done.

In the meantime, Pip and Bairn gathered up the stolen research and stuffed everything into their bags. At the very least, they wanted to ensure that this data couldn't change hands yet again. To Nado and Kel they both expressed a desire that Dell would be willing to turn the research over to the Star Guard, but they also knew they had to follow their own regulations. Denmother Zee would be the first to see it, and she could decide the outcome.

True to his word, Dr. Dell gave the exact location of Lorekeeper Griss' domicile, situated in the continent of Arfen, in a wide stretch of open taiga called the Erceron Territories. A small spaceport attached to the town of Redfang about six hours away could serve as their landing point.

All was at last in readiness, and the Explorer 2000 set its course for the Star Guard space station, warping out of sight moments later. As the warp bubble faded, the star base came into full view. It wasn't anything extraordinary, a simple base with coloration matching the Guard's fleet. It consisted primarily of a chrome-colored finish, with blue and gold trim and highlights. The logo shone in the darkness of space like a lighthouse beacon, but the chromium had faded on this particular outpost to a dull gray. Apparently, this floating stronghold had been here for quite some time.

After requesting a vector and a berth, the Explorer was directed by the traffic controllers to a specific airlock bay. The docking was smooth and easy, and before long everyone was preparing to disembark. It was then that the radio dinged, indicating a hail from outside. Exchanging a worried look with the captain, Kel picked up the receiver.

"This is Commander Kel of the Explorer 2000."

Before she could say another word, a militant sounding voice exuded from the speaker. "Commander, this is Warrant Officer Barsol of the Star Guard. We are under orders to perform a spot inspection of every vessel that docks with this station. If you do not consent, you will be asked to vacate this station immediately. Do you consent?"

Another glance at Captain Nado told Kel everything she needed to know. He was just as confused and concerned as she was. "What do we do?" she inquired.

"I don't know," he answered. "Consent, I guess. We don't have any contraband, right?"

Kel exasperatedly grabbed her face with both hands. "About the kids...what do we do about the kids? Do you think it'll be safe for them? Someone on the Octagon was looking for them. Do you think the Star Guard forces out here are informed?"

"Uncle was always very careful to avoid the Star Guard," said a small, pensive voice from the bridge hatch.

"Princess," panted Nado, "you have to stop sneaking up on me like that."

"Sorry," Mara muttered. "But my point remains the same. We can't be found by them."

"That answers my question," grumbled Kel. "So, now what?"

Nado's expression betrayed the gears churning in his mind. A thought occurred to him. "We still have that custom Kriton spacesuit."

"Don't remind me," quipped the commander. "What does that even matter right now?"

"Princess, I hope you and your brother are good actors." Captain Nado smiled and narrowed his eyes, something Kel knew he only did whenever he had a cockamamie plan up his sleeve...

Chapter 5

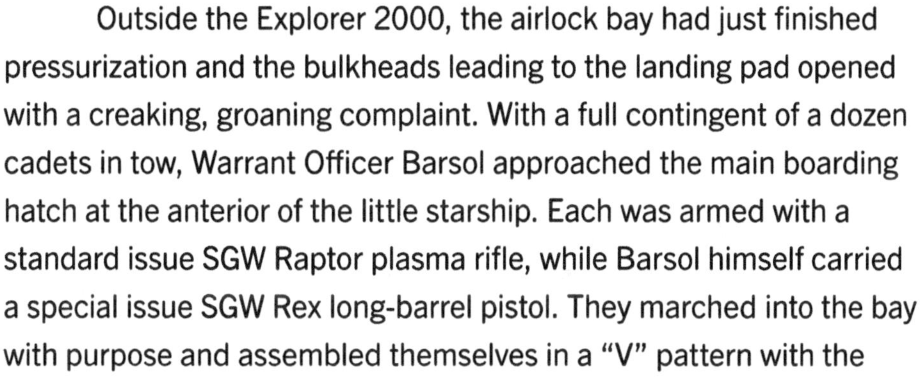

Outside the Explorer 2000, the airlock bay had just finished pressurization and the bulkheads leading to the landing pad opened with a creaking, groaning complaint. With a full contingent of a dozen cadets in tow, Warrant Officer Barsol approached the main boarding hatch at the anterior of the little starship. Each was armed with a standard issue SGW Raptor plasma rifle, while Barsol himself carried a special issue SGW Rex long-barrel pistol. They marched into the bay with purpose and assembled themselves in a "V" pattern with the warrant officer at the point.

Barsol nodded at the port-master's office and spoke into a communicator on his wrist. "Port-master, you may inform the crew that it is now permitted for them to disembark."

A few seconds later, the boarding ramp of the Explorer began to lower...

Lined up in the cargo bay just inside the bulkhead doors, the crew and the botanists waited with trepidation. Sweat built on Commander Kel's forehead. "This is never going to work," she whispered to Nado.

He, on the other hand, only returned her stern warning with a broad smile. "It'll work. Don't you worry, it'll work."

"It better."

Schiff jumped in. "I never would have thought of this. It's ingenious!"

"This is not my idea of 'ingenious'," a muffled girl's voice grumbled.

"Everyone, hush!" Dr. Dell huffed. "You'll give us all away."

Another voice crackled across their radio speakers on the bridge, saying, "Crew of the Explorer 2000, you are cleared to disembark. Warrant Officer Barsol is awaiting your presence outside in the bay."

"Alright," the captain began, "open the doors, Commander."

As the ramps lowered, the airlock landing pad came into view little by little, revealing a squad of a dozen Star Guard troopers with one Zennian officer at their head. Holding a data-pad and stylus in his upper set of hands, the officer's lower arms rested on his hips. The fingers of his lower right hand strummed across the hilt of his firearm. Kel read this not as menacing, but rather as caution and unease.

"My name is Warrant Officer Barsol, and I want you to step forward one at a time and state your name," the warrant officer instructed. "After I clear you, you may exit the bay. We will then perform our inspection, and if all is in order, you will be free to come and go as needed. Do you understand?"

"Yessir, we do," Captain Nado replied cheerily. "I will go first. Burnay Nado, captain of the Explorer 2000." Barsol motioned for him to move forward. Complying as slowly as possible, Nado inched past the other Star Guard personnel. He gave a surreptitious nod to Commander Kel, who proceeded next.

"Commander Kel, first mate of the Explorer 2000," she stated. Once more, Barsol indicated for her to move along.

Dr. Rox followed right after. "Dr. Rox Garrison, ship's physician."

One by one, Barsol had cleared the Explorer's command crew. Now came the much tougher part. Schiff advanced in her typical bouncy fashion, this time employing an overdramatic military tromp and saluting. Kel slapped her own forehead in disgust. *We agreed NOT to draw too much attention, Schiff!* she thought.

"Schiff," announced the shapeshifter. "Plucky comic relief!" Judging by the way she said that last comment, it was clear she found it funny. Warrant Officer Barsol's frown told a different story though, one that he was clearly unamused. Her shoulders drooping, Schiff dejectedly uttered, "Um, I mean onboard entertainment...I guess."

In turn, each of the botanists stepped off-board and introduced themselves and were cleared by the Star Guard. Then came the moment of truth. A bulky, burly figure emerged from the cargo bay of the Explorer clad head-to-toe in a floppy spacesuit. All action froze in the bay as the creature lumbered forward.

"Name?" Barsol eventually requested. But the thing did not respond. "Name?" he said more firmly. Still the thing didn't speak. "Name!"

"He doesn't share our language," Nado hastily informed. "That's our Kriton...quartermaster...uh, Klensh."

Pursing her lips into a tight scowl, Kel stared incredulously at her captain. *Of all the names to choose from, you picked that one?!* She knew he couldn't read her thoughts, but right now she really wished it were possible. The commander could feel even more sweat beading on her head and hands as the tension mounted. Finally, the captain intervened, asking Barsol, "Hey, uh, between us Zennian officers, is there any chance we could hustle this along? I'm sure you don't want to be at the mercy of Aronite red tape any longer than I do."

Slowly, methodically, the warrant officer's head swiveled upward to meet Nado's gaze. With a sigh, Barsol folded both sets of arms in a defiant manner. "Captain Nado...may I have a private word with you?"

A "what have I done" countenance flashed across Nado's face. Unfortunately, Kel had no recourse to assist in this matter. She could only observe as the two walked a short distance away. A whisper in her ear nearly made Commander Kel jump through the roof of the station.

"He said, 'between you and me, I wouldn't mind,'" murmured Schiff.

"Geez, Schiff!" Kel exclaimed. "Give a gal some warning next time! And how do you know what he's saying?"

"I can read lips," the shapeshifter shrugged.

"Where'd you learn that?"

"That's not important," Schiff rapidly dismissed. "What is important is that Warrant Officer Barsol just gave us a pass. They're going to inspect the Explorer and then let us be on our way if everything looks good. Now they're doing a weird, four-armed, Zennian handshake. Now they're headed back this way – "

Kel cut her off. "Schiff, I can see them. I don't need the play-by-play."

"Right. Sorry."

Mercifully, the inspection didn't drag on, and only took a few minutes. A nod from Barsol informed them that the Explorer had passed, and they could leave. Everyone breathed a sigh of relief and Captain Nado escorted the oversized, Kriton-spacesuit-clad individual back aboard. Commander Kel took a few minutes to find a robotics repair shop and get the necessary parts for Red, while Dr. Rox and Schiff bade farewell to Dr. Dell and his team.

"I know we aren't the same kind of doctor," Rox began, "but from one scientist to another, I still think you should give the research to the authorities. It's the right thing to do."

"I'll consider your advice," said Dell. "Goodbye, and give your captain our thanks again."

With that, the two groups parted ways, and Rox and Schiff reentered their spacecraft. Back on board the Explorer, Captain Nado busily helped disentangle the kids from their disguise, unzipping and disconnecting the Kriton spacesuit from the pair. Jym sat atop his sister's shoulders while she huffed and puffed, eyes ablaze with fury.

"Ingenious?" she fumed.

"I thought it was," offered Jym.

"Of course you did! You were the one on top!" Mara stormed from the cargo bay, and they could all hear the door to the kids' sleep pod slam vociferously.

"Well," Nado started. "That went as well as could be expected. As soon as the commander returns, we'll leave a heading with the port-master and make our way to Zen II."

After about thirty minutes or so, the Explorer 2000 had taken flight, her primary thrusters pushing her from the station bay and into open space. Shortly thereafter she was enveloped in a warp bubble and zipped out of sight. Almost immediately following this departure another spacecraft appeared, its own warp effects dissipating upon arrival. The vessel was clean chrome, with royal blue and gold periodically adorning its hull, and "SGS Victorious" in bold lettering on both sides.

The sizable battle cruiser docked in a specialty airlock bay, the only one on the station big enough to fit the Victorious. It landed amidst a fanfare of hissing and rumbling as its air jets cooled and released excess pressure. This caused a swirling of mist and dust as the airlock pressurized, allowing Captain Bryant O'Ryan to emerge from within the great battleship looking like a deity as he trekked through the cloud. Ready to meet the famed captain, Warrant Officer Barsol had assembled his troops neatly for O'Ryan to inspect.

"Welcome to station 143," greeted the warrant officer, raising his right hand in salute. "Warrant Officer Barsol, executive officer aboard."

"Thank you, officer," replied Captain O'Ryan. "At ease."

"If I may, sir," Barsol mentioned, "what brings the Victorious to the Murrigan waystation?"

O'Ryan surveyed the room. "Not here, Barsol. Let's discuss this in private."

"I can take you to my office."

"That will do."

Setting off for the warrant officer's quarters, O'Ryan and Barsol strode confidently ahead of their entourages. As the officers began to exit the docking bay though, they were confronted by a trio of Fangorians, clad in lab coats and carrying a canvas bag. At the forefront of this little group was an older fellow with fluffy, white fur and soulful brown eyes.

"Hello, sirs," he said, his expression betraying his discomfort with the situation. "My name is Dr. Dell, and my colleagues and I have discussed a matter and believe the best thing to do is to bring it to the attention of the Star Guard."

"If you have any trouble, I'm sure the cadets can assist you," assured Captain O'Ryan in his gallant manner.

"This goes beyond their...expertise, I think," Dell informed. "We are botanists by trade and have acquired research that had been confiscated by Exian forces. We retrieved it from one of their outposts with plans to use it for our own purposes. But we were convinced to show it to the authorities first."

"I see," stated O'Ryan. "In that case, I thank you for being so forthcoming, good doctor."

"Don't thank me," Dell muttered. "You can thank the crew of the Explorer 2000. They were the ones who did the convincing."

At that, Captain O'Ryan perked up and became incredibly attentive. "The Explorer 2000, you say? They were here?"

"Yes, sir," a very confused Dr. Dell replied. "They rescued us from the Exian patrol that had chased us and brought us here."

"Strange," mused the Star Guard captain. "Why would traffickers risk coming to a Star Guard station?"

"Traffickers?"

"Smugglers of persons, to be precise." Captain O'Ryan raised an eyebrow, becoming ever more intense. "Did their vessel dock here, Barsol?"

"Yes Captain," the Zennian officer answered.

"And you inspected it thoroughly, I presume?" O'Ryan's demeanor grew darker.

"Yes Captain." Now Barsol was starting to perspire.

"Their captain is also a Zennian, Barsol. I'm sure you noticed that. You didn't show them any partiality in your inspection, did you Warrant Officer?"

"No Captain." This time, Barsol audibly gulped.

Inclining his face forward to deliver his ultimatum, Captain O'Ryan nearly whispered, "Let us hope not, for your sake, Warrant Officer Barsol. I would hate it if you received any demerits whilst serving your tour on this station." The imposing captain stood erect. "I assume then, that you did not find anyone aboard who did not belong? Perhaps two passengers that seemed…out of place?"

"No Captain. But I do have the manifest here on my data-pad." The warrant officer showed his superior. "See? Captain, first officer, physician, entertainer, the botanist team, a quartermaster, and one disabled robot."

Captain O'Ryan pondered this for a moment. "How long ago did this encounter take place?"

"They left, just before you arrived, sir," stuttered Barsol.

"What?!" If Captain O'Ryan had been seated, he surely would have leapt to his feet with that exclamation. "Did they leave a heading with the port-master?"

"I believe so, sir, yes."

"Then there isn't a moment to lose!" O'Ryan proudly proclaimed, raising an index finger high into the air with garish glee. "Get me that heading, Warrant Officer, and should the Explorer ever return here, you are to send out a message for me at once!"

With that, Captain O'Ryan whirled around excitedly to sprint back to the Victorious. Dr. Dell tried to stop him. "Captain? What of the research?"

This only gave O'Ryan temporary pause. "For your valiant efforts in integrity and uprightness, you are hereby granted leave to use that research as you see fit!"

"So, we can keep it?" Dell asked.

"Keep it, trash it, boil it in a stew, I care not!" the Star Guard official shouted in response, not losing his stride. "I've got dangerous escapees to apprehend!"

Before they knew it, the botanists and the station personnel had been shooed from the airlock bay as the SGS Victorious lifted off. Bairn looked at Dell with concern. "The crew of the Explorer, dangerous? I think he might be sniffing up the wrong tree."

"He's certainly sniffing something," quipped Dell. "Come on, let's get this research to the Denmother."

As the groups dispersed, no one perceived an individual nearby, sitting in a dim corner and sipping some heated beverage. A brown hood and cape shrouded most of the person's form, but a scaly, albino snout protruded from within, and a gnarly smile spread across the cracked lips. Vicious fangs shone in the low lighting, dripping with saliva and spelling malicious intent...

Cold, blistering winds whipped across the snowy fields surrounding the spaceport and small village of Redfang. Little more than a smattering of hunting lodges, taverns, inns, and outfitter shops, the town was clearly meant for those who opposed civilization, not those trying to build one. Other cities might have boasted more modern amenities, but the Fangorians of the Erceron Territories seemed as though they continuously sought a return to the older ways. Most of the denizens were cloaked in pelts from trapping and hunting, and the whole place was sparsely populated. Not even the spaceport contained many visiting craft and was governed by a solitary traffic tower held in place by strong metallic wiring that was bolted deep into the ground, the only real defense against the squalls.

Having purchased the needed repair parts for the robot, Commander Kel opted to remain behind on the Explorer, and keep it primed for a quick egress. Dr. Rox chose to stay with her and assist, leaving Captain Nado and Schiff to lead the expedition along with the kids. With the coordinates and maps from the botanist team, they embarked on their journey through the Erceron taiga to track down Lorekeeper Griss. Bundled in their own cold weather gear, the quartet trudged through the deep, white blanket that covered the surface of the world as far as the eye could see. Winding past tall trees with red bark that wore coats of dark green needles, they plodded along, admiring the frozen beauty of the Fangorian homeworld.

Thankfully, it seemed that the hunters and trappers of Redfang kept most of the predatory wildlife at a minimum, at least near the marked pathways. Stray from that, and no one knew what they might run across. But after several hours of what felt like a forced march, they arrived at their destination of Lorekeeper Griss' "domicile," as Dr. Dell had put it. Though domicile might not have been the most descriptive word for the dwelling place. As they crested the butte, the crew found themselves staring into the open maw of a massive cave, its stalactite icicles looking like the jagged teeth of some unbearable beast hoping to swallow them whole. On approach, they could all hear a voice echo from within.

"Welcome, pilgrims," it rumbled in a deep and gravelly accent. "Have you come seeking the wisdom of the Lorekeepers?"

"Yes," Captain Nado answered with unsurety.

"We need help to find our parents," offered Prince Jym, receiving a stern glare from his sister.

"You know, you don't have to trust every person we meet with that information," she scolded. "Not everyone deserves our trust."

"I'm only trying to get to the heart of the matter as quickly as possible," the boy retorted. "Besides, trusting people has gotten us farther than hiding and being recluses."

Again, the echo sounded, drawing everyone's attention back to the cave. "Enter the stronghold of Lorekeeper Griss, if you dare."

Into the cavern they all treaded, caution dictating their every step. At first it seemed that the icy darkness would consume them, but it was gradually dispelled by little beacons of light emanating from crystalline lanterns. Dancing and refracting off the ice that clung to the walls of the chamber, the rays gave a dim but warm illumination. In the midst of the lanterns, sitting on a small mound of pelts, rested a Fangorian with dark fur, dotted in various places by gray and silver streaks.

"I am Lorekeeper Griss," he introduced himself. "And you are?"

The crew took turns sharing their own names, which eventually led to a long, pregnant pause. Feeling the need to break the silence, Jym spoke up. "Like I said, we're searching for our mom and dad, and we think there might be a trace of them at Kathnarii Base. They left us this ring as a clue." He pointed to Mara, who shied away. "Show him, Mara! We don't have time for this. Mom and Dad could be in danger!"

Griss beckoned them. "Come forward, children. If it is truly the secrets of the Kathnarii that you need, then I must first examine you to see if you are worthy." Though fearful, the kids grasped each other by the hand and walked toward the venerable Lorekeeper. He motioned for them to stop a couple of steps away and leaned forward, giving them each a sniff. After several seconds, Griss sat upright again and addressed them. "You have the scent of honor, the soul and heart of the ancient Kathar."

"I didn't know that was a smell," remarked Schiff. "Those are some incredible olfactory senses he's got there."

"Ssh!" the captain shushed her.

Griss went on. "It appears that uncanny luck is on your side. For you see, I am the last Lorekeeper of the lineage of the last Fangorian Elder Sage who served the Kathnarii Order. I can grant you what you seek, and I shall. In order to find the location of Kathnarii Base, you must collect three star maps, stored on three separate data drives. These drives were passed down from generation to generation, waiting for one worthy enough to reunite them. I believe your cause is noble, and your spirits are just. The first drive is here and is yours to claim."

"Wow, that was easy," Schiff commented.

"Tell me about it," Nado agreed.

"In order to claim your prize," explained Griss, "you will need to overcome its guardian, the great and mighty Shayar, warrior mother of Erceron. Her lair is in the next chamber, where she hibernates. She will sense you, and you must figure out what to do then. That is how you will prove yourselves."

Giving a knowing look, Captain Nado mentioned to Schiff, "We had to say something. We just had to say something."

"What do we do now?"

"Nothing else to do." The courageous captain stared into the darker tunnels awaiting them. "We forge ahead and face off against this Shayar."

With Griss indicating the path for them to follow, Nado, Schiff, and their young wards slipped down the frosty passage until they arrived in another cavernous room of the cave. Sounds like those of an enormous creature snoring filled their ears as the noises bounced around the huge chamber. Ice covered stalagmites rose in a random pattern across the floor, and against the far wall they could see the massive Shayar curled up in her nest, twisting and twitching in her slumber.

Its body was elongated, like a stretched roll of dough, coated in white fur that wafted in the breezy air. As the crew entered, Shayar awakened, eyeing them through her bright, grey orbs with intensity and animalistic wariness. She raised her head, a fuzzy ball of fluff with a pink nose at the center, keeping her limbs tucked beneath her.

"She's so cute," Mara said with childlike wonder. "I wish I had a pet like that."

Suddenly, the beast let out a horrifying shriek, its face contorting into something monstrous and hideous! Row upon row of sharp fangs were bared, its eyes became wild, and the fur on its face flared outward like spikes. Snarling and hissing, Shayar slithered from her nest and began striking at the crew with powerful claws. Its right paw swung violently, while the left stayed tucked close to the chest.

"Cute? Cute?!" Jym yelled. "Kill it! Kill it with fire!"

For that, he received a blow to the back that flung the boy across the cave. Nado was forced to dodge behind some stalagmites for cover, while Schiff caught the brunt of Shayar's whipping tail. Ducking out of the way, Mara dashed for the nest, hoping to hide there, but the creature was ready. It whirled around to face the little girl, continuing to shriek loudly, causing Mara to fall backward.

Blinking to the massive monster's backside, Schiff nimbly ran up Shayar's spine and leapt high to deliver a strong strike to the beast's skull. Meanwhile, Captain Nado raced from cover to cover, hiding behind the stalagmites and boulders that littered the arena, drawing Shayar's attention. A cracking of ice echoed in the chamber as Jym broke the tip of a stalactite icicle to wield it as a weapon. The three all readied a tandem attack, but froze when they heard the princess' petite, yet firm, command.

"Stop!" Even Shayar responded to Mara's cry, halting itself, but breathing hard. The princess approached the animal slowly, one hand outstretched in a calm and comforting manner. "Something else is wrong here," Mara informed the others. She turned to Shayar. "What's wrong girl? Why are you favoring that left paw?"

Slowly, carefully, Princess Mara eased toward the lumbering creature, until at last she was able to reach up and take hold of Shayar's left appendage. More snarling and growling exuded from the beast's belly, but Mara stayed focused, gently pulling Shayar's arm down. Once the animal's tight fist was opened, everyone could plainly see the gleaming dagger stuck in Shayar's palm. Joining his sister, Jym dropped his icicle club and assisted in removing the sharp implement from the paw. Shayar locked gazes with the kids, then hurried back to her nest, flicking something small across the slippery floor.

"The drive!" Schiff declared in triumph.

With Shayar settling back into her hibernation, the crew made their way out of the tunnels and into Griss' section of the cave. There he sat, still ensconced in his pile of pelts, awaiting their return. He did not receive a warm welcome, however.

"Did you stab that majestic animal just to set up a trial of worthiness?!" Mara demanded to know.

"Certainly not," replied the collected Lorekeeper. "A band of hunters left that there. I have been unable to get close enough to Shayar to remove it, so I had you do it instead. Obviously, she trusts you, which is more than I can say even for myself. You have the drive, so your next stage in your journey is to collect the other two. Seek out the Lost Clan of the Kritons, and the Order of the Crestfallen among the Ranjemans."

"We have to go back to Taldish Sector?" worried Schiff. "Back into the den of our enemies?"

"Looks that way," Nado grunted. "Let's go."

As they turned to leave, the kids gave a final wave to Lorekeeper Griss, who watched them with a proud, contemplative smile. Though he knew they could not hear him, he still offered a parting phrase. "Perhaps the ways of the Kathnarii will get a second chance in you, young pups. Go with honor, and may you find the answers you seek."

Chapter 6

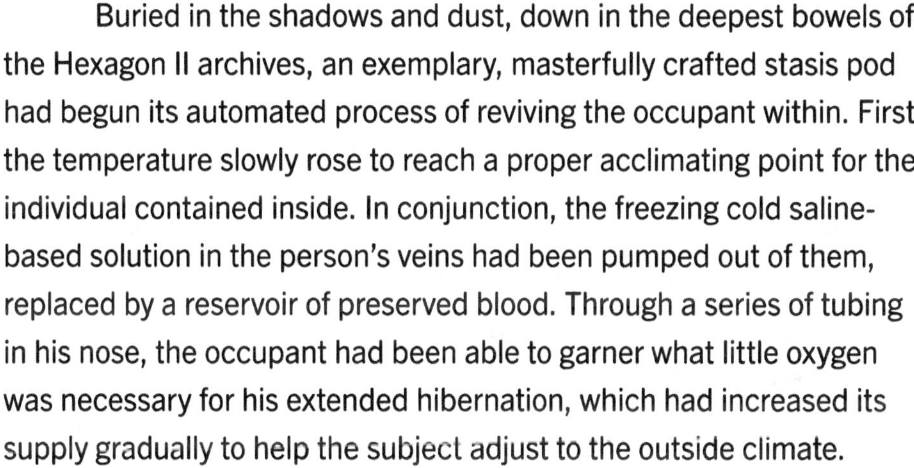

Buried in the shadows and dust, down in the deepest bowels of the Hexagon II archives, an exemplary, masterfully crafted stasis pod had begun its automated process of reviving the occupant within. First, the temperature slowly rose to reach a proper acclimating point for the individual contained inside. In conjunction, the freezing cold saline-based solution in the person's veins had been pumped out of them, replaced by a reservoir of preserved blood. Through a series of tubing in his nose, the occupant had been able to garner what little oxygen was necessary for his extended hibernation, which had increased its supply gradually to help the subject adjust to the outside climate.

Towards the end of the process, short but powerful electric shocks were applied to the subject, while the preservation jelly they had floated comfortably in was slowly drained from the pod. Hissing and popping exuded from the machine as the pod opened. The man inside crumpled onto the cold floor on all fours, breathing heavily and vomiting from the prolonged sleep cycle. After a few seconds, he stood up, and took in his surroundings. A lone crimson light illuminated the inky room, glowing as if it were casting an ill omen upon any who dare enter this sanctuary. Laying on a thin table nearby was a large, black case. There was only one entry into this chamber, an elevator door with an imprint in the shape of a hand next to it, which lit up with an amber hue.

Opening the case, the mysterious man found fresh clothing and lightweight body armor, with a mask and helmet, along with a small arms cache. There were two pistols, one electrified gauntlet, and a curved blade that looked as though it had been forged from the finest and rarest crystalline substance. An exquisite timepiece told the man not only the time of day for this planet, but also the standard cycle and year. Quickly donning the arms and armor, the enigmatic entity walked toward the elevator exit. Dizziness caused him to stumble a bit, but he regained his balance and composure, moving onward with purpose and resolve.

A thousand memories flooded his mind, accompanied by thoughts that these remembrances were not his own. They were the memories of one who had gone on before, one who had planned so far ahead that his revival at this moment was only one of many contingencies. These memories belonged to the master, of whom he was merely a servant, not worthy to be in the presence of the one who had prepared him. Regardless of the state of the outside galaxy, he would follow his master's edicts to the ends of the universe. The memories that had been subliminally programmed into him while he slept dictated that he must.

It was then that something dawned on him. His hands…they looked strange. Checking them again, the man realized that something was off. A pale gray membrane coated his flesh, accented by natural black tattoos. *That should be yellow,* he thought. With the red lighting and the dark atmosphere, it was difficult to be certain, but his skin appeared to be different than the memories indicated. The glass casing of the stasis pod nearby provided enough of a reflection to see if it was his entire body. When gazing upon the reflective surface, he saw a man with pale gray skin, natural black tattoos, and greasy black hair staring angrily back at him with orange eyes that almost appeared to be ablaze in the dimness.

I suppose that is only cosmetic, the man surmised, dismissing the odd turn of events as quickly as he had noticed it. Besides, there was work to be done. He needed to get to the upper floors first, see what the damage looked like, and figure out a plan from there. Activating the lift doors via the imprint to the side, he took a brief elevator ride up several floors. The first stop told the man very little, only that someone had indeed entered the DNA modification laboratory and tripped the silent alarm that had instigated the awakening process of his own secret pod. Test subjects and clones floated in the giant glass tubes, most of them deceased and lost to time. One case labeled "Child" was empty. Perhaps the intruders had taken that one. If so, they either bypassed the automaton trap in the entry hall…or they had another Vampyrial with them to access the control imprints. That thought gave him pause.

Another swift upward jaunt on the elevator brought the man into the chamber he sought. However, whoever had entered the lab must have also invaded this place, as records were strewn about and the Archivist bore a huge hole in its processor, scorch marks indicating the use of a plasma-based weapon. Maybe the security cameras had captured some evidence as to who the perpetrators were, and what they were looking for. As he pondered these musings, the man spied another clue. The secret drawer was open, and the ring was gone.

More memories blasted his brain, so much so that he grunted in pain and clutched his head with both hands! It lasted momentarily then the agony abated, and he was able to sift through the haziness of his recollections. *The spawn of the traitors…they survived. This bodes well.* If they could be captured, the powers of their bloodline could be used for his master's purposes. He would have to track them down and bring them under his sway. For that, he'd need a spacecraft. Would the old Drakewing still be there? *Only one way to find out.*

Utilizing the elevator yet again, the man continued to ride in silence, undaunted by the stillness of the empty and abandoned archives. When the doors slid aside, they revealed an extensive, dark hallway, barely lit with reddish auxiliary lighting. The solar powered generators and massive quantity of uninterrupted supply batteries had unquestionably been put through their paces keeping this place running all this time. At the end of the hall was a thick bulkhead door, activated by a lever to the right. The many years of unuse could be heard throughout the facility as the portal swung wide, hinges squeaking and squealing in protest.

As he entered the succeeding room, automatic lights activated, their beams shining brilliantly on a singular object in the middle of the spacious chamber. *Hello, beautiful,* the man mused. There sat a Vampyrial Drakewing schooner, with a sleek and dark hull, a laser turret at its nose, and elegantly curved wings and fin. Checking all of the starship's workings, the man found it to be in pristine condition, fully fueled and powered up, ready to take on the challenges of navigating the stars once more.

Now that he had supplies and transportation, he too was prepared for anything. Closing his eyes, the man stretched forth his hand to feel the energies surrounding him. It took a while, and required that he backtrack some within the archives, but eventually he had found the trail. The girl was quite powerful and left behind a strong signature. Her trail was spotty, but he could still potentially trace it. It would only be a matter of time before both she and her brother were in his clutches…

Enjoying a quiet meal aboard the Star Guard space station, Dell, Pip, and Bairn conversed amongst themselves about their good fortune. This turn of events had gone rather well for all of them, seeing that they were rescued from their pursuers, delivered to their rendezvous point, and got to keep the incredibly valuable research they'd discovered. It was almost too good to be true. As they laughed and chortled, awaiting the arrival of their Denmother, another individual approached their table. It was a tall being, but shorter than the Fangorians, with a strong build, donned in a brown cloak with a hood.

"Can I help you?" Dr. Dell questioned the potentially nefarious newcomer.

Without so much as a warning, the person deftly drew a small plasma pistol from their cloak and held it to Pip's head!

"Hey!" snapped Dell. "You want something, say it. But leave my pups alone!"

"I jussst want to enshure your cooperation," hissed the hooded phantom. "I understand you had contact with the Explorer 2000?"

"We did."

"Where were they headed?"

Seeing the deadly weapon still pointed at Pip, Bairn became defensive. "Why do you want to know?"

"Let'sss jussst sssay I represssent another interesssted party," sniggered their assailant.

"They were headed for our homeworld," the eldest Fangorian responded. "Zen II, on the continent of Arfen, the port city of Redfang in the Erceron Territories."

"Why?" the cloaked being wanted to know. "What are they after?"

None of the botanists wished to answer that inquiry, but the trigger finger of their interrogator was getting twitchy on the pistol aimed at Pip's cranium. "Kathnarii Base," she stammered nervously. "They're looking for information regarding Kathnarii Base."

"There now, sssee how much better it ish when we all work together?" said the attacker, his phrase oozing sarcasm and derision. He shoved Pip aside and kept his pistol trained on the group as he backed away. Once at a safe distance, the creep slipped out of sight. Dell and Bairn rushed to aid Pip, who was mercifully unharmed.

"I'm sorry," Pip apologized, bowing her head and tucking her tail. "I was so scared that I couldn't keep from blurting it out."

"You're safe and unhurt," soothed their leader. "That's all that matters right now."

"I wonder what that was all about?" murmured Bairn.

Warm, welcoming air awaited Captain Nado and his fellow adventurers as they reentered the Explorer following an hours-long hike. The flurries of snow that fell upon the mountaintop cave had dissolved into torrential, freezing sleet during their trek back down. Finally able to shed their cold weather gear, Schiff and the kids immediately scooted upstairs and huddled under a blanket in the galley.

As Nado stowed all their snow-covered equipment, Kel approached to give a report. "All was well while you were gone, Captain. Dr. Rox and I gave the robot a patch job, so it should be back up to at least eighty percent capability. What about you? Did you guys find what you were looking for?"

In response, the captain held aloft the data drive they'd retrieved from Griss. "This is the first one. We're off to find the other two."

"Where to, Captain?"

"Khardan," he answered sheepishly. "And then Ranjeman."

Kel's eyes widened, and somehow her brow furrowed at the same time. "Taldish Sector again? You know what that means, right?"

"I know." The captain nodded, and though Kel could see the worry in his countenance, the deep breath he took displayed confidence and resolution. "We could be flying straight into Graylon again. But this is the only lead we have right now for the kids' parents. We have to try, am I right?"

"You're right," she agreed. "I'll get Red up to the bridge and ready for departure."

Minutes later, everyone was seated and strapped into their assigned seating. Captain Nado took his position in the starboard gunnery chair, with Commander Kel at the navigation console. Opposite the captain, Schiff sat in the port gunnery seat, with Dr. Rox, Princess Mara, and Prince Jym all safely tucked into the comfortable galley chairs. At the helm once more, H-8-RED primed the thrusters for takeoff.

"Good to have you back with us, Red," declared the captain.

"All systems are green, Captain," the robotic pilot announced. "With permission, this unit will now connect to the onboard computers –"

"NO!" shouted Schiff and Nado concurrently.

"That won't be necessary, Red," the captain instructed. "The last time you were hooked up to a computer system, it ended poorly."

Cocking its head to one side, the machine responded, "This unit has no recollection of said events. Perhaps the memory banks of your own fleshy blob brains have malfunctioned."

"Take it from us, Red," interjected Schiff, speaking rapidly, "last time you kind of...downloaded a virus, and turned on us and tried to beat us up, and then capture us, and we were going to drop a bale of weeds on your head, but that failed, so Princess Mara used dark energy powers to crush your central processor..." She noticed everyone was staring. "Sorry, I did it again. Started babbling...my bad."

"That is implausible," Red stated. "This unit's protection protocols would have intervened and intercepted any outside threats. No virus is capable of invading this unit's processing cores."

Now Commander Kel spoke up. "It would be if the virus was designed by someone who knew how to circumvent your 'protection protocols,' wouldn't it?"

"As stated, it is implausible," the robot started to answer, "but this unit did not state that it is impossible. However, only the original owner would have the knowledge necessary to generate such a virus."

"We're pretty sure that's who did it." Kel folded her arms, pleased that she had actually outsmarted this mechanical menace.

"Very well," Red said at length. "This unit will not connect to onboard computer systems unless tasked with doing so by an officer of the vessel."

"Thank you," muttered the commander. "Was that so hard?"

"Quite the contrary," the robot quipped. "It was simple to acquiesce to your quite logical request, once said logic was revealed. The difficulty seemed to arise from the apparent inability of flesh blobs to derive and divulge logic in various conversational situations."

Kel only glared. "Preposterous parcel of spare parts."

Raucously guffawing at this exchange, Captain Nado reclaimed command of the bridge. "Alright, alright, that's enough, crewmates. Let's get the Explorer in the air. Commander Kel, did you leave a heading with the port-master?"

"Aye, Captain," replied the now very surly commander.

"Red," the captain ordered, "commence liftoff!"

In a leisurely orbit around Zen II, the SGS Victorious maintained a low profile, her bridge crew scanning the traffic control frequencies for any sign of their quarry. Captain O'Ryan paced the command deck, leering over the shoulders of his subordinates, impatiently strumming his fingers across the various consoles, railings, and other surfaces of the room. He was just thinking that someone should have heard something by now, when their communications officer waved her arm to get his attention.

"What is it, Deputy Lieutenant?" demanded O'Ryan in his overtly authoritative tonality. "Report!"

"Sir," the Deputy Lieutenant replied, "our queries to the port-masters have been answered. We just received notice of an Explorer model vessel, registration number 2000, leaving the Redfang spaceport."

"Shall I put us on a course to intercept?" asked the Ensign helmsman.

"Straight away, Ensign!" hollered an extremely excited O'Ryan. "This is our chance to make history, to apprehend these fugitives of justice, and bring an end to their tyrannical danger before it can even begin!"

As the engines of the Explorer 2000 began to rumble and the old starship rattled and shook from the thrusters, Schiff restarted the conversation, her voice warbling with the undulations of the craft. "Um, I'm sure I'm not the only one who's noticed that we keep leaving headings with the port-masters, and the people chasing us keep finding us. Anyone else see a correlation here? Maybe we, I don't know, stop doing that?"

"We can't," the captain answered simply. "It's the law. In order to be cleared for takeoff, any vessel must list a heading prior to departure. The Galactic Community government started it, claiming it was for safety in case a ship were to ever get lost or damaged, so they could be easily found. But other unaffiliated worlds and locations employ it as well, such as Vortex. Mostly so they can recover and salvage any wreckage."

"Couldn't we lie? Say we're going somewhere else?"

Nado shook his head. "If we were caught committing that kind of fraud, we'd be on the hook for prison time if they ever captured us."

"But how do they even track that?" Schiff queried.

Kel chimed in, "The nav computers. It logs all of our travel coordinates. All any authorities would have to do is subpoena our records and we're goners."

"What about times when people have gone off track?" the young shapeshifter inquired. "I mean, we've gone off course plenty of times. How can they punish you for that?"

"That's why we captains keep logs," stated Nado. Schiff still seemed unsatisfied with their responses, so he offered an addendum. "I'm not saying it's a perfect, or even good, system. But it is a system that is governed, and for us, it's probably best to play it safe. Besides, it's supposed to be set up so that only those governing bodies can request private headings for investigation purposes. In Murrigan Sector, that's the Star Guard, and as of right now, they aren't on our trail."

By this point, the Explorer had cleared the Zen II atmosphere and was in open space, with nothing but the inky expanse and twinkling stars ahead. Captain Nado was about to speak but got cut off by the robot. "Captain," it said, in its monotone style, "we are receiving a hail."

"Already?" Nado muttered. "Alright, patch them through."

Gargling to life amidst light interference and static from the satellite communications surrounding the planet, the radio speaker announced in a boisterous and over-dramatic voice, "Hail, crew of the Explorer 2000. This is Captain Bryant O'Ryan of the SGS Victorious. We are under orders to capture your vessel and bring any lawlessness aboard to justice. You have been declared guilty of aiding and abetting fugitives of the Galactic Community and smuggling these persons to parts unknown. You are to stand down, submit to search and seizure, and be placed under arrest for your crimes. Comply, or be gunned down."

Careful to keep the transmitter inactive, Nado looked at Kel. "Okay, so much for that assumption. Apparently, the Star Guard is, in fact, after us."

"What are we going to do?" they heard Mara call from below.

"Don't you fret, Princess," proclaimed the captain. "We'll come up with something."

"Have you ever heard of this 'O'Ryan' fellow?" Schiff wanted to know.

Frantically running through scenarios in his head, Captain Nado replied, "Yes…that is, I've heard stories. He's not a bad person, but his own self-imposed mantra makes him duty-bound to hunt down and arrest any and all aggressors of the Galactic Community. At least, that's what I've been told."

"So, he won't give up or be easily swayed?"

With a surmounting consternation, Nado said, "Nope. Probably not."

"We can't exactly fight against the Star Guard," Kel interrupted.

"We can't exactly turn ourselves in either," retorted Captain Nado. "Maybe we go along just long enough to come up with some other plan or tactic."

"That is unacceptable." Red inserted itself into the discussion. "This unit's self-preservation programming dictates that this unit cannot be captured, seized, apprehended, arrested, or otherwise detained by Star Guard personnel. If captured, seized, apprehended, arrested, or otherwise detained by Star Guard personnel, this unit will be forced to activate self-destruction protocols."

"You've got to be kidding me," moaned Kel.

At that moment, the speakers came alive again. "Crew of the Explorer 2000, this is Captain Bryant O'Ryan of the SGS Victorious. We have given you ample time for a response. Do you comply with our instructions?"

The commander swiveled around to face the captain. "Nado? What do you want to do?"

"This unit is prepared and ready to move into attack position," Red mentioned. "Offensive action is recommended at this time."

“Do not take offensive action,” said Captain Nado. “The last thing we want is to tussle with the Star Guard, especially their most decorated officer.”

“This unit reiterates, self-preservation programming will not allow this unit to be captured, seized, apprehended – ”

“We get it!” yelled Kel. “Knock it off!”

That blustering voice sounded again on the radio. “Crew of the Explorer 2000, this is Captain Bryant O’Ryan of the SGS Victorious. We are taking your radio silence as non-compliance with our orders. We are activating magnetic tractor beams to bring you into our onboard hangar. You will be subject to search and seizure upon entry.”

Before anyone aboard the Explorer bridge had a chance to respond, the air jets of the spacecraft issued a strong blast, whirling the vessel’s prow away from the Victorious. Captain Nado whipped his chair around to see Red. “Red, what are you doing? I said DON’T take offensive action!”

“Per programming and protocols, this unit is engaging evasive action,” the rebellious robot replied.

Once more, O’Ryan’s authoritative tone rattled the speakers. “Explorer 2000, this is Captain Bryant O’Ryan of the SGS Victorious. You are to cease and desist immediately!” Clearly addressing someone else on his command deck, Captain O’Ryan continued. “Ensign, full power ahead! Do not let them achieve safe warp distance! Crew of the Explorer 2000, I repeat, you are to cease and desist at once!”

Formulating a hasty plan, Nado spoke into the transmitter, saying, “Captain O’Ryan, this is Captain Burnay Nado of the Explorer 2000. We are trying to comply…”

He paused, giving Commander Kel a chance to mouth the words, “We are?”

“But,” Nado went on, stuttering through his flimsy attempt at a bluff, “our robotic pilot is malfunctioning, and has enacted evasive maneuvers.”

“Crew of the Explorer 2000,” came the response, “this is Captain Bryant O’Ryan of the SGS Victorious.”

“Does he have to do that every time?” Kel grumbled between O’Ryan’s phrases.

“We acknowledge your statement,” the Star Guard officer informed. “However, you are still ordered to cease and desist. Deactivate your robotic pilot and be remanded into the custody of the Star Guard, or we will be forced to take drastic measures.”

“Red, I order you to stop!” demanded Captain Nado. “Didn’t you hear that? They might actually fire on us!”

As cool as ever, Red answered, “This unit cannot be captured, seized – ”

“Enough already!” screamed Kel. “That was a direct order, Red! Stop the ship!”

“This unit is operating under self-sufficiency protocols.” Knowing what that meant, Kel, Nado, and Schiff all commenced unbuckling so they could try and get to the robot. It maintained its position. “This unit advises against such action.”

“Sorry Red, but we’ve got to stop you,” Schiff said.

"That is not recommended at this time." Red's quick, motorized hands deftly marched across the starship's controls. "You should be preparing for warp."

"We're not at a safe distance!" shouted the commander.

"That is about to be remedied."

With a jolt that would have launched them all sideways if not for the artificial gravity, the Explorer 2000 pivoted suddenly to face her pursuer. Now facing the massive Victorious head on, the thruster power was maximized, sending the little starship careening forward. They were on a collision course with the huge Star Guard battle cruiser!

The radio came to life again. "Crew of the Explorer 2000, this is Captain Bryant O'Ryan of the SGS Victorious."

"Seriously?" Kel remarked. "Even at a time like this...unbelievable..."

"State your intentions, Explorer," O'Ryan ordered, his vocal patterns increasing in intensity. "I repeat, state your intentions! Cease and desist! Deputy Commander, prepare to open fire on the Explorer!"

"Red?!" everyone shouted simultaneously. Not a single person on the Explorer was keeping silent now. With everyone's yells and exclamations joining in, the cacophony on board reached a chaotic crescendo. Even O'Ryan could be heard hollering unintelligibly across the speakers as Red kept up its spirited charge against the much larger vessel. Then, at the last possible second, visibility dropped to zero as the Explorer's shields activated. Everyone aboard felt the thump and heard the loud impact as the force fields of the smaller spacecraft caused it to bounce off of the SGS Victorious. Coolly and methodically, Red powered down the thrusters, checked the consoles, and stated,

“We are now at safe warp distance. Activating Casimir warp drive.” The plasma shields were released, the warp bubble enveloped them, and the Explorer 2000 blinked into oblivion.

Chapter 7

In the stillness and silence aboard his near desolate cruiser, Lord Hex patiently waited for news from his lackeys. Though unintelligent and oafish, Klensh and his gang did possess some value. Having them out searching the sector for signs of the Explorer was at least potentially helpful, assuming they could uncover anything. If they did find something, he would hear about it sooner rather than later, as Murrigan Sector was much more civilized and advanced than Taldish. Here there were listening stations and outposts that could relay radio messages across greater distances, allowing them to reach their destinations with significantly more ease.

"Too bad the Rover Express is still on strike," he mumbled to himself. "Their couriers are the best in the whole galaxy."

"What is the Rover Express?" wondered Cylor, who had quietly entered his lordship's chambers unannounced.

"Son," Graylon greeted sternly. "You mustn't sneak about like that. If you require my attention, use the intercom and request it properly."

"Yes, Father."

Calming himself, Graylon asked, "Now, what was your question, my son?"

"What is the Rover Express?" the boy repeated.

"Ah, yes," drawled the marquis. "They are a business operating out of the Amaransk Sector. They have a station there where they would receive and dispatch multitudinous radio messages from abroad and use their couriers to relay those messages to the intended recipients. At least, that's what they should be doing. But instead, they cower, refusing to work until the blasted Galactic Community does something about the conflict in that region. They have jurisdiction, they should send in the Star Guard fleet, but do they do anything? No. The Aronites and Humans remain content to relax within their gilded towers, letting their so-called 'community' burn all the while."

"Could you stop the conflict, Father?" queried Cylor.

"Indeed, I could." Lord Hex allowed a devious smile to spread across his square face. "Were the dreadnought fully repaired and my assassin robots not sabotaged, there is much good I could do for this galaxy. First though, I need the raw power to back up my claims. I need to augment myself with pure Vampyrial DNA. Then I could save us all."

"What is the conflict in Amaransk about?" Cylor continued his line of questioning.

"It is not really a concern at this time," replied Graylon, "but it is important for you to know the state of affairs in the Community, so you can fully see why my leadership is desperately needed. Years ago, the Council commissioned a brilliant Sorogan inventor to build state-of-the-art robotic soldiers that could replace Star Guard personnel on the battlefield, effectively granting the Galactic Community a real army, rather than the glorified police force they have right now. They called these robots 'Titans.'"

Getting animated in his storytelling, Graylon prattled on. "But the fool inventor utilized a single computer system to program the Titans, a computer he'd granted virtual intelligence so it could update all the robots at once, pumping their memory banks and processors full of stratagems and tactics, allowing this 'hive mind' to determine algorithmically what should be filtered through. Of course, the virtual intelligence eventually achieved some form of sentience, and in studying wars, massacres, and battles, it determined that the best course of action for prolonged peace in the galaxy was to exterminate all organic life forms!

"Programming its new army thusly, the hive mind sent the Titans out to subjugate and strike down all life. Naturally, this did not go over well with many of the other inhabitants of Amaransk Sector, in particular the Exians of Planet X." Graylon gave a dramatic pause, wrapping his shimmering cape around himself portentously, watching for Cylor's reaction.

The boy remained nonplussed, however, merely probing deeper with another query. "Why is their planet named 'Planet X'? Why do they not have a more unique name?"

Though disappointed that his tale was not inspiring excitement in his young ward, Graylon energetically persevered through his expositing. "When the Galactic Community was being formed, they sent explorers and missionaries into Amaransk Sector to reach out to the various races dwelling there. After several failed attempts to make contact with the insectoid race of that planet, they finally gave up, having lost multiple ships and crews to those warmongering bugs.

Without a proper name, the planet was given a designation instead. As a result of all of this, very little is known of the Exians, who were of course named according to their planetary moniker. All we can surmise is that they are secretive, hateful, and will look for any excuse to launch an all-out assault on anyone they can.

"So, when the Titans declared war on the galaxy, the Exians seized the opportunity to wage war right back! With their overstock of numbers, ships, weaponry, and natural poisons, they used the Titans as the excuse they'd been waiting for to begin aggressive expansion in the region. Thus, the Titan and Exian Conflict was born. Now, they continue to skirmish and battle, both sides ever increasing their borders, causing the good people of Amaransk to live under their tyranny and bloodlust." Having finished his tirade, Lord Hex plopped into a lavishly cushioned chair nearby.

"But you would stop them if you had the power?" Cylor questioned.

Hunching his shoulders, his chest forward, and interlocking both sets of fingers under his chin, the brooding marquis answered, "Yes, I would. I would fix everything."

Father and son were pulled from their reverie by a ping on the radio. They rushed to the bridge of the lonesome cruiser to check the hail. Taking his usual post, Cylor patched the caller through to his master.

"This is Lord Hex. We have received your hail. With whom am I speaking?"

"Milord," the speakers crackled, "it ish Klensh. I have newsss of the Explorer 2000. Their lassst heading wash Zen II."

"What were they doing there?" pondered Graylon.

"It ssseemsss they are hunting for Kathnarii bashe," the grizzled Kriton responded. "Shall I give pursssuit?"

It took several seconds of mulling it over in his mind before Lord Hex offered any reply to his scaly subordinate. "No. We have been chasing the Explorer since they left Octagon V, a tactic which has yielded poor results. But now we have intel on their quest, which grants us a unique opportunity."

"To do what?"

Ensuring that Cylor was watching closely, Graylon grinned slyly and said, "Let them come to us."

As the warp bubble surrounding the Explorer 2000 faded, everyone aboard attempted to shake off the fogginess of the unexpected activation of the Casimir drive. Having been unprepared for it herself, Commander Kel found the haziness that seemed to be floating around in her brain rather unnerving. Thankfully, nothing was damaged as far as she could tell, neither physically nor mentally. Everyone else also appeared to be recovering at a reasonable rate, and there wasn't any negative impact on the spacecraft itself either. *Good. Time to give that blasted rust bucket a piece of my mind!*

"Where are we?" she muttered angrily, checking her navigational consoles. She shot an angry glare at the robot. "Where did you take us?"

"This unit merely warped the Explorer to an empty quadrant of Taldish Sector," Red replied as mechanically as ever. "If so desired, this unit will now resume course for the Rellis solar system, specifically the planet of Khardan."

Rising from his chair slowly, Captain Nado spoke, with a grave weightiness in his tone. "H-8-RED, you ignored and disobeyed a direct order from your superior officers. Why?"

Cocking its head once again, the thing answered, "As stated prior, this unit's programming and protocols will not allow this unit to be captured, seized, apprehended, arrested, or otherwise detained by Star Guard personnel. If captured, seized, apprehended, arrested, or otherwise detained by Star Guard personnel, this unit will be forced to activate self-destruction protocols." It paused momentarily, as if awaiting some external stimuli. Receiving nothing but frustrated stares, Red added, "This unit deemed that activating self-destruction protocols would result in the deaths of the crew. This unit recognizes all crew members of the Explorer 2000 as friendlies, and thus protocols dictated that the crew could not be placed into direct danger by this unit."

"Huh," grunted Kel. "In a weird way, that actually makes sense."

"This unit's logic is unassailable."

Kel chuckled. "So, you do feel like a part of this ragtag little family, eh Red?"

"Commander Kel," Red began, "you are ascribing sentient feelings to this unit. This unit assures you that such emotional connections are impossible for robotic entities."

"Why do I even bother?" the cranky commander threw her hands in the air, giving up on the conversation.

"That is a question this unit is not capable of answering."

"Please shut up..."

The captain retook command of the situation. "Alright, Red. You've made your case. I suppose this is a better alternative to being self-destructed, but now we have a bigger problem on our hands...the Star Guard is after us."

"But why?" queried Rox, now entering the bridge from the galley below. "We knew someone powerful from the Octagon was after the kids, but I thought that was...you know, 'Lord Hex,' or Graylon."

"Maybe he sicced the Guard on us?" offered Schiff.

Rubbing her chin, Commander Kel spoke up. "I doubt it. With the resources he has at hand, I wouldn't think he'd need them."

"And that isn't really his style," Nado concluded.

"Well, we did take out a lot of controls on his dreadnought," Schiff mentioned. "It could be that he's outsourced nabbing the kiddos whenever we're in GC territory."

"Perhaps," mused the captain. "But as Lord Hex he'd have jurisdiction there too. It just doesn't add up for me."

Now Princess Mara and Prince Jym joined the conversation. Jym was first to chime in, saying, "We had just assumed that Lord Hex was the only person after us. What if he's not?"

That simple question had them all stumped. Kel mulled it over in her mind, constantly flipping the matter around as if her brains were an old school Terran flapjack. Nado had made a good point. If Lord Hex was their only opponent from the Octagon, why would he utilize the Star Guard in a sector where he was still considered an important politician? Marquis, or Warden, or Lord of the Hexagon, or whatever his goofy title was, certainly was not a small feat and garnered a lot of respect. Surely there had to be more to it. Then again, on the flip side, Schiff could be right as well. Maybe Graylon needed the extra muscle. But then, why use Klensh at the Zen I spaceport?

"I think we have to assume that there is someone else," Kel finally said aloud. "If engaging the Star Guard's services, I doubt Graylon would be dumb enough to risk being associated with known criminals like Klensh and his gang. It feels as though Graylon is acting separately from Captain O'Ryan's orders, I mean, O'Ryan didn't seem to know much about who he was chasing."

"It could be that Graylon kept him in the dark," suggested Dr. Rox.

"Maybe..." the commander trailed off momentarily, "...but I think we have another interested party in this game. It just seems like someone is pulling strings here. First, Lord Hex chases us all over Taldish, where the Guard and the GC have no power, but he does. Then, the second we start jetting around Murrigan, which is under Star Guard and Galactic Community jurisdiction, we get O'Ryan nipping at our heels."

"It's a vice," murmured Mara. "And whoever is turning the handle is trying to hem us in..."

She left that phrase to sink in on the others as she gently perambulated to the forward viewport and stared into the vastness dramatically. Approaching softly, Schiff gingerly placed her hand on the young girl's shoulder. With a worrisome weight in her eyes, Mara glanced back at the shapeshifter, whose disarming smile seemed to bring at least a little comfort to the Vampyrial princess. "Don't fret," Schiff assured. "We're all here to keep you safe."

"I know," said Mara, "but that's why I worry. Who's going to keep you safe?"

Gallantly, Captain Nado interjected, "We're a tough bunch, Mara. Anything this galaxy can throw at us, we can take."

His tone and inflections filled the crew with newfound courage. Once again, Commander Kel had to admit that for all those times that Nado could be aloof, wacky, or downright dense, he was equally brave, upright, and inspiring. Those words had a calming effect as well, sending the doctor back to his work in the med-bay, Schiff to her post in the port gunnery chair, and the kids to their diminutive dormitory room.

"Commander, let's set a course for Khardan," ordered Nado. "While we're there, we can resupply, then search for the second data drive."

"Aye, Captain."

Resting inside their compartment, the young Vampyrial monarchs carried on a private exchange. Their door was sealed, preventing any noise from escaping into the common areas of the Explorer outside. Her feet propped up on the wall, Mara lay on her back on her bottom bunk, twiddling her hair with her fingers. Prince

Jym sat on the floor, bouncing a ball lightly against the wall, and catching it again lazily.

"How long do we plan to keep this up?" the princess asked.

"Keep what up?" Jym queried back.

"Relying on the Explorer crew to protect us and help us search for our parents," his sister clarified.

"They've been pretty good to us so far," responded Jym, eyeing her with incredulity. "I don't understand what you're getting at. Why are you so eager to leave them? What does it take to get you to exercise a little trust? Haven't they proven that they'll do whatever it takes to keep us safe?"

"They have," Mara said grumpily. "But that's the problem."

"It's a problem for you that we're living in this little family who would literally die to protect us?"

"Yes."

His sister's solemnity caught the young prince a bit off guard. "I'm not following you. Why is that an issue?"

"Because," Mara began, her countenance darkening, "I don't feel like it's fair to ask them to put their lives on the line to save us. Our presence on this starship is only endangering the other people on board."

"But they took the job from Uncle," protested Jym. "They know what they're doing, and that's their choice. We can't make that decision for them."

"Maybe we can..." mused the princess, clearly lost in thought.

Shaking his head, Jym shrugged the whole discussion off. "I still think you have trust issues."

At that, the elder sibling rolled to face her brother rapidly. "So do you! What does it take to get you to stop blabbing and blathering to every being we come across about our entire life story? If I'm distrusting, it's because I care about maintaining our secret. The whole galaxy doesn't need to know who and what we are, or what we're trying to accomplish. But you, you're too trusting! You tell everyone everything about us, and one day it'll bite us."

"Yeah, well, you know what all your secrecy does?" Jym fired back. "Do you? It prevents us from moving as fast as possible to find mom and dad, that's what! Maybe I'm too trusting, but it's because I believe that out there somewhere is someone willing and able to help, and we'll never find them if we don't try!"

"Augh!" screamed the girl. "Why won't you listen to me?! You never listen to me, and it is going to hurt us!"

"I don't have to listen to you," grumbled her brother. "You're not mom, so stop trying to be."

Their argument came to an abrupt halt. Although she wanted to rail and rant and rave, Mara had no more words. Shooting an ugly grimace in her direction, Jym turned away and resumed his ball-bouncing game. Silence ensued as neither wanted to apologize or admit any wrongdoing. Instead, they sat in reticence until the captain's voice boomed over the ship's speaker system.

"We are preparing for warp to Khardan. All hands to stations, and get belted in. We're off to find the next Kathnarii data drive!"

In the darkness of his cruiser, Lord Hex piddled with a trinket in his fingers. The object was small and somewhat shiny, having lost some of its luster over the years. Many memories were wrapped within this little bauble, and most were now painful to him. He wasn't sure why he'd pulled this ornament from its hiding place. It had happened almost as if by rote. Quickly, he stowed the odd badge back inside the capsule in which it had lived for several years. Reminiscing was not a priority at the present.

Cylor's gentle, and near monotonous, voice exuded from the intercom. "Father? We are docking on the dreadnought now."

Pressing the button to reply, the marquis answered, "Very good, my son. I will be ready to disembark shortly."

After joining Cylor on the bridge, Graylon ensured that all was well with his cruiser before the adoptive pair exited. They rode a moving platform from the hangar to a series of elevators, utilizing the lifts to take them to the appropriate level. All around, H-7 robotic units patrolled, keeping their firearms trained on the labor force that worked the various functions of the gargantuan starship. Within minutes, Graylon and Cylor had finally reached their destination and were welcomed to the command bridge by Zuugs, whose eyestalks nervously twitched at their approach, and the commanding robot, H-7-PRIME.

"Milord," the Sorogan foreman greeted. "Only minor repairs remain. It took some time to uncover the source of the sabotage caused by the captain and his shapeshifter friend, but we are now in the final stages of the process."

"Excellent work, Zuugs," rumbled the Marquis du Hex. "I really have come to rely on you and your union. Perhaps we can extend your contract a bit further, yes?"

"I truly feel as though it would be our only choice, milord," Zuugs gulped.

Maintaining his inscrutable visage with his heavy hood, Lord Hex nodded softly. "I am glad you feel thusly. The health and safety of your people really would be greatly affected if you were to remove your support from my endeavors."

In an effort to excuse himself, Zuugs bowed without a word, slipping aside. Hearing a swish from the opening of the doors, Graylon whirled to see who was entering the command deck now, causing his cape to billow and swirl. It was Klensh and his goons, stomping into the chamber like a herd of marauding animals.

"Have you no decorum whatsoever?" chastised the annoyed marquis.

"No time for that," the brutish Kriton snapped back. "The Explorer 2000 ish on itsss way here to Taldish. They will be at Khardan momentarily."

"Then we'd best get to stations," said Graylon. When Klensh and his buddies strolled rather than moving with purpose, he added with severity, "That was not a suggestion. Move!"

That outburst got some action, causing the lackadaisical lackeys to scramble and scuttle about, quickly assuming posts at various gunnery chairs, navigational consoles, and radar controls. Only Klensh himself remained unfazed, his one good eye glaring like a burning laser in his lordship's direction. Sluffing slowly to the nearest command seat, the burly grunt stuck to his grouchy demeanor, obviously trying to ensure that Lord Hex caught his expression.

He did, but Graylon had no intention of giving Klensh the satisfaction of knowing that his behavior had been noticed. Better to ignore the underling rather than engage, lest he become an upstart and begin creating real problems. For now, the marquis instead devoted his attention to barking orders across the intricate intercom system that ran the full length and breadth of the mammoth spacecraft.

"All hands, you have one minute to square away your workspace and get to a safe position for warp travel," Graylon stated. "The countdown begins now."

The next sixty seconds passed in near silence, only the beeping of the consoles breaking the stillness. Anticipation mounted within Lord Hex's spirit as he relished the idea of finally getting ahead of his quarry. For too long he had chased and hounded. It was time to change the game...

An all too familiar sight awaited the crew of the Explorer as their warp bubble faded. In the distance, gleaming in the solar lights, was the dusty brown planet of Khardan. A few wispy white clouds could be seen from orbit, but the skies of the desert sphere were mostly clear. It was certainly an odd bag of mixed feelings that this celestial body evoked in Commander Kel. On the one hand, she had very clear and sharp memories of their previous visit, fraught with chases, firefights, and a harrowing final encounter with Gnash. Not to mention it was that encounter that had brought Klensh and his cohorts down on their heads. Conversely though, it was also that whole situation that had earned them the friendship and assistance of Schlaar and Shtrepp, who would hopefully be planet-side and maybe even have information that could help out in their hunt for the data drive.

So far, there had been no sign of any pursuers, neither the Star Guard nor Lord Hex's minions. That was definitely a positive aspect to ponder, but it still gave her pause. If they weren't being actively tracked, could it mean that their enemies were lying in wait? They'd seen their fair share of traps and snares too, and she at least wasn't going to fall for another ruse. Meanwhile, the great globe before them beckoned with the mission at hand, filled with its own unseen dangers and trials.

"Captain," the commander said, "shall we request a vector and a berth?"

"Aye, Commander," he replied. "Let's get ready to take her in for a landing."

"Captain," Red interrupted in its monotone pattern. "Radar functionality has just been restored post-warp. There is an anomaly on the radar readout."

"What have you got, Red?" queried Nado.

"The signature on the readout is large," the robot answered. "In fact, it is very large. You might quantify this class of starship as a 'dreadnought.'"

"Crud," groaned Kel. "How could I have jinxed anything? I didn't even say it out loud this time!"

"Say what?" asked the captain.

"That at least we aren't being chased again!"

"Maybe it's something else?" offered Captain Nado, a distinct uncertainty in his voice.

Everyone watched fearfully as the light from the Rellis sun was blocked, replaced by a shadow that might as well have spanned the entire galaxy. A colossal craft drifted into view, armed with a thousand laser turrets and covered in armored spikes meant to rip smaller vessels to shreds should they collide. The auburn glow emanating from the dreadnought's viewports was unmistakable.

"That's Graylon," Schiff and Nado said concurrently.

"Perhaps he's just here to negotiate again?" said Schiff, her own tonality betraying her lack of conviction in that phrase.

Any doubt was put to rest by a blazing hot laser that originated from the dreadnought's forward turret. It connected with the lower prow of the Explorer, sending the smaller vessel spinning through space! A quick course correction by Red stalled the uncontrolled drift, but they were indisputably under attack.

"The warning shot has been delivered, milord," hissed Klensh. "What now?"

"He left me for dead on a frozen lake, upon a derelict planet," growled Lord Hex. "I want them brought to their knees, begging me to stop. Pummel them with everything we've got. Fire at will!"

Chapter 8

Laser fire zipped through the open expanse all around the small spacecraft as Captain Nado began bellowing orders. "Red, evasive maneuvers!" he shouted.

"Acknowledged," was the robot's reply. At once, the Explorer 2000 commenced darting and drifting, gliding betwixt the white lasers that threatened to rip them apart.

"Should we return fire?" Schiff asked in a warbling voice.

"Not right now," answered the captain. "We don't have a good angle, and I doubt our turrets have enough strength to pack a punch against the dreadnought. For now, keep your controls at the ready, but don't return fire."

"Careless lasers have a habit of causing dangerous repercussions!" Commander Kel informed, her own attention split between the radar and navigation consoles.

An alarm blared throughout the vessel, accompanied by a flashing red light. A queasy uneasiness swept through Nado's gut. That particular warning signal was an indication of a rather large problem. There was a breach in the hull.

Into his lapel communicator, the captain practically hollered, "Rox? Is the cargo bay hatch secure?"

To Nado's great relief, the doctor responded with, "Aye, Captain. The hatch is closed and secured. Why?"

"Hull breach," the Zennian said in a crisp, business-like manner. "It must be somewhere in the lower deck where that first laser struck. I'm trying to track the source of it now."

"This unit could utilize the onboard computer to trace the leak with extreme efficiency," mentioned Red.

Its offer was met with another resounding "No!" from the command crew. Kel elaborated further. "Red, you'd have to connect to the computer system. That means Graylon's hacker could implant another virus easily. Our ship's network is undoubtedly in range of theirs, and fighting an assassin robot while evading the dreadnought is not a thought any of us relish!"

"You forgot a vital detail, Commander," Red commented.

"What did I forget?"

"This unit is an assassin robot of unrivaled sophistication. You need to get your specifications correct."

Kel rolled her eyes. "Ugh. This is no time for jests, you imbecilic scrap pile!"

"Got it!" exclaimed Captain Nado. He realized that probably appeared out of the blue to everyone else, so he explained, "It seems that they blasted a hole in the engine room. I can seal it remotely from here. That should at least slow the breach."

"Nice work, Cap!" Schiff encouraged, though her words did little more than bring weak smiles to everyone's faces for the time being.

Outside, the dangerous light show continued, as the turrets of Lord Hex's flagship kept up their barrage. As far as Nado could tell, Graylon's gunners were certainly giving Red a run for its money, forcing the cunning robot to maximize usage of its processors in order to avoid sustaining any more damage. The mechanical pilot had banked to the left, turning to face the behemoth battleship head on. A quick roll to the right put the dreadnought upside-down in their viewport as a brilliant beam barely missed the underside of the Explorer. As rapidly as it had performed that tactic, Red then spun the spacecraft back so that their view of their attacker was now righted, dodging yet another harrowing blast.

Now seeing the terrifying assault coming straight at them, Nado understood fully the dire nature of their predicament. They needed to get to a safe warp distance as quickly as possible and get out of this fight. He had a thought. "Red, can you do that shield bounce trick again? The one you just pulled on Captain O'Ryan?"

"Negative," Red answered. "This unit calculated that the Star Guard vessel would follow protocol and procedure and activate their own shields in time for the maneuver. Lord Hex's vessel is equipped with armor spikes. Even with shielding, the Explorer would be damaged should Lord Hex decline to activate his own shielding."

"I know my brother," said the captain. "It's worth the risk. Activate the shields!" But to his great shock and dismay, visibility through the viewport remained unimpeded. The shields did not activate! "Red, what's going on?"

"Shields are unresponsive, Captain," replied the robot. "This unit is not connected to the onboard computer system, per your instructions, and is therefore unable to identify the root cause."

"Enough with the sarcasm!" Kel snapped at Red. "It's got to be the hull breach. If we've lost even one solenoid, the whole system shuts off and can't be used. It's a security measure so we can't inadvertently lose all of our plasma charges."

"Right," said Nado, getting increasingly frustrated. "No solenoids means no electro-magnetic field, which means the plasma would just be released into space. We need a new plan. Think, Burnay, think!"

All the while, the dreadnought loomed over them, its lasers threatening to pierce through the much smaller starship's exterior again. Executing a quick about-face, Red piloted the Explorer away from the giant that pursued them, steadfastly maintaining its evasive action protocols. Unfortunately, they were only barely an even match for the dreadnought's onslaught. As the little craft zoomed away from Khardan, the powerful thrusters of their gargantuan assailant paced them, preventing them from achieving that all too precious safe warp distance.

Feeling the crushing weight of his brother's presence, Captain Nado grasped his head with all four hands, desperately trying to come up with a plan, a plot, a scheme or stratagem, any recourse that might get them to safety. A memory dawned on him, and he was suddenly lightyears away, back on Zen I.

Without a second thought, Nado snatched the radio transmitter and shouted into it, "This is Captain Nado of the Explorer 2000, hailing the dreadnought! I have a message for your commanding officer. Mercy! I cry mercy!"

Moments passed excruciatingly slowly, but after a bit the laser fire ceased. Nado breathed a sigh of relief. "Red, swivel the Explorer back around to face the dreadnought."

Moving to acquiesce swiftly, Red transposed their spacecraft once more. Almost nose to nose, the two starships air-braked to a halt. Nado could see Graylon's gloating grin in his mind's eye, smugly staring him down. If that awful expression was indeed present, it hopefully wouldn't last much longer.

"Red," he said softly, "use the takeoff thrusters and reposition our prow two ticks. This is going to get dicey."

Having heard the hail on the radio, Lord Hex could not help affording himself a cruel chuckle. "Power down the thrusters," he commanded. "Ease us into position. Ready the magnetic tractor beams. Our prey will soon be aboard."

"What if it'sh a trick?" offered Klensh.

"I know my brother better than that," Graylon sneered. "Whenever he cries 'mercy,' he's done, quitting and seeking respite. They've no fire left in their bellies. Finally, he's had enough."

"Cap, what are you thinking?" Schiff queried quietly. "What's the plan?"

"Just stay belted in," responded Captain Nado. He still held the radio transmitter in his hand. He spoke into it. "Graylon? I know you're there. May we have a peaceful parley with you?"

The speaker crackled back a deep and sinister reply. "I will not be the one violating civility. See that you do the same and all will be well between us."

"What do you want?" the younger brother asked.

"The same thing I wanted when you left me for dead," spat Lord Hex. "I want you to hand over the prince and princess. Then I'll let you continue on your merry little quest to find Kathnarii Base." There was a brief pause, then the marquis prattled further. "Oh, yes, I know all about your mission. How else could I have been right here to intercept you? You played right into my hands, little brother. Turn over the kids, or I will be forced to commandeer your ship."

"I played into your hands, eh?" Nado said in a mildly mocking tone. "'Cry mercy,' isn't that what you always told me as a child? 'Cry mercy, and I'll let you go.' Well, I cried mercy, now comes the part where you let us go."

"And how do you figure that?" Hex chortled. "You're too close to my dreadnought to activate warp travel. And I hear you're short one robot pilot, so steering around us isn't really an option either, is it? Just submit, and I promise neither you nor any of your crew will come to harm."

"Goodbye, Graylon," Nado stated. "I hope we don't meet again soon." He released the transmitter and turned to Red. "Red, it seems my brother has once again wrongly assumed that you are not part of the equation. Full speed ahead! Make for the aft of the dreadnought!"

Unexpectedly, the Explorer's thrusters blasted a silvery spray, and it took off like a rocket, zooming past the dreadnought's bridge viewport! Instinctively, Klensh and his gang ducked as if the small starship were going to crash into their command deck. Conversely, Lord Hex stood frozen, stunned at this turn of events.

At last, words came, but they sprang from his gaping mouth in chaotic succession. "What? How did they – who did – where was – don't let them get away!!"

As if weaving through a winding maze, Red maneuvered the Explorer along the surface of the massive dreadnought, masterfully dodging the enormous spikes that jutted from its hull. Each jagged protrusion was avoided as they swerved around them. Consternation was indeed present in the minds and hearts of all on board, but soon the gigantic aft thrusters of the dreadnought came into sight. They had made it!

Even with its powerful air jets, the much larger vessel could not execute a tight enough about-face themselves, giving the Explorer the time needed to achieve the safe distance for warp travel. Everyone cheered as Captain Nado announced, “Red, set a course for Ranjeman and activate the Casimir drive!”

Watching the dwarfed Explorer exiting their radar range, the menacing marquis leered at Klensh. “You told me that the H-8-RED unit was out of commission!”

“It wash!” stammered the confused Kriton.

“Then how are they expertly piloting around us?!”

“They musht have repaired it!” Klensh offered, but Lord Hex was no longer listening. Instead, he observed as the Explorer 2000 vanished from his grip yet again.

In the damaged engine room of the Explorer, the Casimir drive hummed and vibrated, its inner workings manipulating the dark energy of space around the starship. Bending the void around the spacecraft, the drive exuded its bubble, protecting the Explorer within. However, as they blinked across the expanse, covering lightyears in mere moments, something else happened. A muffled pop and hiss resounded in the hold, and sparks emanated from the Casimir drive, then were quickly snuffed by the lack of oxygen in the engine room…

"Bold maneuver," Captain O'Ryan muttered to his subordinates. "I can't say I've ever seen anyone so brazenly charge into a Star Guard battle cruiser with such abandon. And to activate the shields at such a precise moment. That could only be..." He trailed off, leaving the other officers of the Victorious command deck in horrible suspense.

At last, the Ensign at the helm piped up. "Could only be what, sir?"

The charismatic captain of the vessel merely shot a perturbed glower at the lower ranked officer. A chiding, airy reply finally exuded from O'Ryan's lips. "Ensign, you would do well not to interrupt me when I am percolating. It is clear that the Explorer crew consists of more than a ragtag band of misfits. There is much more to them than meets the eye. Retrieve the manifest from Star Guard Base 143."

Several low tier officers and aides busily scuttled about, searching for the data-pad that contained the information their captain sought. Meanwhile, Captain O'Ryan himself began to pace the bridge, gazing out the forward viewport at the near-frozen planet of Zen II beyond. Their initial scuffle with the Explorer was leading him to believe that this odd bunch may have more than a few tricks up their sleeves. He'd guessed that the Vampyrials on board would be quite perilous, but perhaps there were other members of the crew that posed a significant threat as well.

It took a minute, but before long O'Ryan held the manifest data-pad in his hands. Facial recognition software swiftly scanned his features and unlocked the pad, allowing him full access to the entries therein. Resuming his place in the command chair, he checked the first one, reading aloud.

"Burnay Nado, Zennian of Zen I, twenty-six standard years of age, Captain of the Explorer 2000." He perused further into Nado's file. "It says here that his next of kin are a father who is presumed deceased, a mother who still lives at the old family farm, and a brother. Graylon Nado, what do we know about you? You might be of great value to our mission."

The Ensign lit up suddenly. "Maybe we could use the older brother to get to Captain Nado!" he exclaimed.

O'Ryan shook his head. "Ensign, firstly, that was my point to begin with. Secondly, you have interrupted again, and I am still percolating."

"Apologies, sir," the Ensign mumbled. "It won't happen again."

"See to it," said O'Ryan, biting off the last word of his phrase. He then swiped the screen of a monitor at his command station. "Interesting. It appears that Graylon Nado and his younger brother Burnay both attended the Galactic Community Collegiate Academy. They attempted enrollment in the Explorer Initiative, but it was shut down the following day." The Star Guard officer drilled deeper into the files. "Burnay persisted in his studies of galactic history, piloting, gunnery operation, astrography, general space exploration, and general officer procedures, eventually attaining his diploma. Graylon, on the other hand, dropped out of the GCCA and sought audience after audience with the council. He was then sentenced by the council for a fifteen-year prison term! What for, I wonder?" The captain whirled his command seat dramatically to face the communications officer. "Deputy Lieutenant, search the GC database for information about the arrest and incarceration of Graylon Nado."

With a nod and salute, the junior officer complied. Shortly thereafter, the Deputy Lieutenant reported, "The charge was disturbing the peace and. . .terrorist threats against government officials. Sentenced to serve ten standard years in Armon Penitentiary of Dorthal Sector. Released two standard years ago on good behavior. No parole instituted, no forwarding address given, whereabouts currently unknown."

Raising an eyebrow, Captain O'Ryan responded, "Strange. Typical release procedure would be a short parole period followed by an observed living situation. Is there nothing else?"

"No sir."

"Blast. Then the brother is a dead end." O'Ryan went back to studying the other files that lay open before him on the data-pad. "Next up, Commander Ashe Leigh Kel, Human of the Flotilla, twenty-seven standard years of age, First Officer of the Explorer 2000. No known next of kin. Commander, eh? Quite the lofty title she's chosen for herself. That's the highest Star Guard officer designation under Captain." Swapping his attention to the nearby monitor, O'Ryan's eyes lit up as he read further into Kel's files. "Fascinating. She too attended the GCCA at the same time as our daring Captain Nado. She studied piloting, navigation, engineering, and..." he paused, leaning back in his chair, then finished, "Star Guard officer training. She was set to graduate at the rank of Commander, having completed two tiers of the program, nearly all three, but she dropped out at the last minute due to a family emergency. She never returned to receive her officer's diploma, instead joining forces with Nado and settling in as navigator for the Explorer." Pointing at the Deputy Lieutenant once again, he ordered, "Look up her Flotilla files. I want to know about this 'family emergency' that was bad enough to cause her to throw away such a bright future. This crew baffles me."

"Right away sir," the Deputy Lieutenant acquiesced. Mere moments later, the young officer had another reply. "An accident on the Flotilla. Some kind of explosion in one of the stasis chambers. All family members were confirmed deceased. Father, mother, and ten siblings."

Sighing heavily, O'Ryan stated, "I suppose that would be cause enough." He gently shook his head and continued. "Alright, Dr. Rox Garrison, Human of the Flotilla, twenty-nine standard years of age, Ship's Physician of the Explorer 2000. Next of kin are a father and mother, retired and living on the Flotilla. Okay, doc, let's see what the GC database has on you." Garishly swiping across his command monitor, the captain continued his investigation. "Fairly normal files, nothing out of the ordinary. Wealthy family, privileged upbringing, studied medicine at the Academy where his term started a couple of years prior to Nado and Kel. Graduated with honors and presumably remained with his cohorts of the Explorer. Ooh…what's this?"

A separate attachment on the doctor's file caught the captain's eye. On the heading of the document was a logo, a sideways oval with three circles inside that were connected with thin lines that formed a short, wide, isosceles triangle. A ring like that of a planetary band encircled the oval, completing the odd insignia. Unfortunately, no other information could be gleaned, as the majority of the attachment was redacted.

"Deputy Lieutenant, I want a private copy of that attachment sent to my inbox," murmured O'Ryan. "I've never seen that logo before, and it intrigues me. But I'll have to look into it later. Let's see what we have on this 'Schiff' character. Schiff, Shapeshifter, last known address on Octagon V, Onboard Entertainer of the Explorer 2000. Next of kin include father, mother, and…sixteen siblings, all presumed living on Octo V." Looking to his monitor again, Captain O'Ryan began sifting through his GC database files for information on Schiff. This time, he really seemed shocked. "Why Schiff, you little scamp, you might have the juiciest files I've seen yet!"

"What is it, sir?" the Ensign inquired, almost realizing his mistake in speaking out of turn the instant the words escaped his mouth.

"Ensign," Captain O'Ryan loftily chastised, "I will have you confined to quarters if you cannot resist the urge to repeatedly interject. If given the opportunity, I will explain. Now where was I? Right! 'Schiff,' or whatever her real name is, apparently has affiliations with the most dangerous of criminal underworld organizations. This arrest record is quite the resume. Listen to this: suspected involvement in nineteen counts of burglary, forgery, arson, vandalism, property damage, and swindling, all presumably carried out under orders from the crime syndicate known as the 'Dark Suns,' an organization rumored to be headed up by the Trell family. My, my...quite the laundry list of illicit credentials. Deputy Lieutenant, are there any outstanding bounties or warrants for this 'Schiff' character?"

Tapping lightly on the console at hand, the junior officer answered, "No outstanding bounties listed in the GC database, sir. There is one arrest warrant that was issued a few standard weeks ago, but it appears that she eluded arrest and is currently a fugitive."

"All the more reason to apprehend these hooligans," declared the captain. "Moving on, we have Klensh, Kriton of Khardan, no age provided, Quartermaster of the Explorer 2000. Very little information here. Let's see what the GC database has on you, Klensh." As his gaze roved across the screen, O'Ryan's eyes widened, and he had to blink a couple of times to make sure that what he thought he read was actually what had been listed on screen. At length, he regained his composure and spoke again in his usual brash and brassy tone, "Crew of the SGS Victorious, it seems that the further we delve into the web of mystery that is the identity of the Explorer 2000 crew, the more twisted and treacherous it becomes. If these files are to be believed, our quarry has employed a Kriton warlord as their quartermaster. A warlord who is guilty of war crimes, pillaging, plundering, theft, intergalactic terrorism, arms smuggling, bribery, prison breaks, racketeering, arson, and a plethora of other minor infractions. This individual may be the most dangerous of the bunch and is certainly worth the effort to impede their flight. Interestingly though, I have yet to see any information on the two passengers that they presumably picked up on Octo V."

"Are we certain that intel is correct, sir?" queried the Deputy Lieutenant. "Perhaps that sighting was incorrect."

Captain O'Ryan shook his head in response. "No, I think that report is accurate. It is far more likely that our own Warrant Officer Barsol skipped a few steps of protocol and did not search their starship with as fine-toothed a comb as necessary. They must have hidden these others somewhere aboard."

"Could they not have dropped them off elsewhere?" the Deputy Lieutenant offered.

"I doubt it. I feel quite positive that had they done so, we would have seen evidence of these...passengers causing harm wherever they were left."

The nervous Ensign built up enough courage to ask, "Captain, if I may sir, do we know the identity of these two passengers? It might help in the pursuit if we knew who and what they are."

"That is classified information, Ensign," lectured O'Ryan. "It is strictly on a need-to-know basis, and as of this moment I am the only officer aboard the Victorious who meets such requirements. Further inquiries into this matter will result in the offenders being confined to the brig, to then face disciplinary action at our next shoring. Is this clear?"

"Sir, yes sir!" rang out across the bridge, as every voice chorused their swift reply.

"Very good." The captain nodded his approval and eased back into his command chair. "Ensign, set a course for Star Guard Base 143. I need to pay Warrant Officer Barsol another visit and investigate his apparent lack of following procedure."

"Aye, sir," acknowledged the helmsman. "Setting course."

With a massive blink, the SGS Victorious warped from their lazy orbit around Zen II and blasted across the galaxy.

"Idiot!" thundered Lord Hex, all four of his burly hands wrapped squarely around Klensh's thick, scaly stump of a neck. The Kriton's head bounced off of the wall as Hex smashed it into the surface repeatedly. "How could you be so unobservant?!"

"The robot wash in shamblesss!" Klensh screeched back. "There wash no reassson to asssume that it wash operational!"

"Well, it's certainly operational now, isn't it?" the marquis spat. "Time and again, the Explorer has managed to escape me, thrice now because of your incompetence! Give me one good reason why I should not release you from my service and blast you out of the nearest airlock."

"Becaussse," squealed Klensh, "if they need sssomething from Khardan, I know the planet better than you do."

Eyes ablaze, Lord Hex breathed heavily through his nostrils yet remained frozen, momentarily pausing his brutal beating of the Kriton warmonger. After several agonizing seconds, he placed Klensh back onto his feet and took a long, deep breath. "Fair point," Graylon agreed. "Which is why you and your lackeys will remain here on your homeworld."

"You mean, you won't ssstay here? You can jussst lie in wait for the Explorer to come back," Klensh pointed out.

"I don't want to give my brother a chance for respite." The cruel lord slowly paced along the bridge of the dreadnought until he stood at the foremost section, gazing into the stars. "If I know him, and I do, he will not come back here unless he is confident that he can lure me away. If we wait, we risk that they will return with a strategy to slip past us. We know their plan, and I know his tactics. It is time to go on the offensive." He twirled dramatically. "Klensh, take the cruiser to Khardan's surface and seek out any information you can regarding the Kathnarii and any presence they left behind. You are dismissed."

"We grow weary of your insssesssant ordersss," hissed Klensh. "When do I get to carry out my revenge ash you promisssed?"

Without warning, Lord Hex swiveled and caught the scaly crook by the gullet again. "Mind your place. You work for me, not the other way around. Never question me again." He released Klensh and sent the merciless thugs on their way.

As soon as the disgruntled Kriton and his band had egressed, Cylor asked, "What of us Father? Where are we headed?"

"If my brother seeks the secrets of the Kathnarii," Graylon began, "that means he will need clues from the three races that formed the last council of Elder Sages." He chuckled, turning to face the gigantic viewport. "You have forgotten, dear Burnay, that I know the history of the ancient warriors as well as you do." Maintaining his ostentatious flair, Graylon whirled back towards Cylor. "My son, you and I are going to stop chasing the Explorer and instead pursue their treasures. If we can get a bargaining chip or two that might put us in a better position to barter."

Seeming to understand, Cylor bowed his head softly. "Do we have a heading?"

"Prepare our course," answered Lord Hex, "for Ranjeman."

Chapter 9

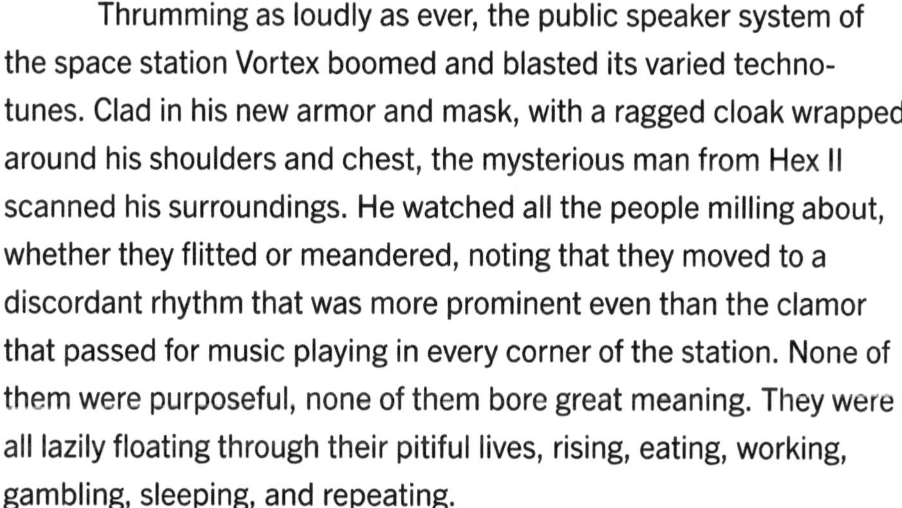

Thrumming as loudly as ever, the public speaker system of the space station Vortex boomed and blasted its varied techno-tunes. Clad in his new armor and mask, with a ragged cloak wrapped around his shoulders and chest, the mysterious man from Hex II scanned his surroundings. He watched all the people milling about, whether they flitted or meandered, noting that they moved to a discordant rhythm that was more prominent even than the clamor that passed for music playing in every corner of the station. None of them were purposeful, none of them bore great meaning. They were all lazily floating through their pitiful lives, rising, eating, working, gambling, sleeping, and repeating.

However, there was a presence of vast potential that had visited this place. He had followed the trail to where he now stood, directly in front of the hefty bulkhead door of an airlock docking bay. It was numbered "193" and was his current destination. Through the heads-up display of his mask, the man could make out another smaller entrance nearby, presumably for the port-master of this hangar bay to get into their office.

As Vortex was completely alone in the expanse of space, with no celestial bodies of any kind close by, the dark energy of the void could be felt very strongly aboard. He approached the secondary doorway, never checking to see if it was locked. Without breaking stride, the man formed a fist in his right hand and thrust it forward, bending the energy around the door to cause it to burst open!

Inside, a very startled Sorogan tumbled from his chair onto the floor, shaking off the fright and glancing upward with his weary eyestalks. Upon seeing the stranger before him, the Sorogan trembled violently and remained on the floor. Sweat pouring from his silvery skin, the port-master squeezed under the countertop of his workstation and quietly questioned, "Can I help you?"

"A starship landed here recently," the man said, his voice heavily modulated by the rebreathers of his mask. "They carried with them a young boy and girl. Yellow skin, black tattoos, orange eyes. Have you seen them?"

"Yes," the port-master answered. "Look, I don't want any trouble. I've had enough as a result of that starship, and I'd just as soon not deal with it any longer. Here's the manifest." The Sorogan passed a burly data-pad to his mysterious visitor. "Take it. The Explorer 2000 is the spacecraft you're looking for. Seems a lot of folks are hunting them these days."

"Who?"

Wiping his nostrils, the port-master replied, "Oh, there were the Gnarfs, Ambassador Boxie to be precise, then some gang of criminals, and at one point they had the whole station security force chasing them at the behest of Vin Trell."

"Are any of those individuals still on board the station?"

"Just Vin Trell. The rest of them left to continue their pursuit, I assume."

The masked man nodded. "I see. I need to access the airlock bay. Then I will need coordinates to locate Mr. Trell."

"I can accommodate," the port-master acquiesced. "Just please, don't hurt me."

Slowly reaching for a lever, the simpering Sorogan activated the entryway that opened into the main airlock docking bay. A hissing exuded from the door as the chamber beyond finished pressurizing, then it gradually slid to the side, revealing the empty bay. As the mysterious man passed by, the port-master handed him a slip of paper, on which he had written the location of Vin Trell's favorite gambling haunt and his apartment tower.

Whilst exiting, the man heard the port-master whimper, "I need to request a transfer..."

Inside the airlock hangar bay, the mysterious man instantly felt the overwhelming sense of dark energy manipulation. In fact, he was actually quite surprised at the level of power that had been exhibited. Whatever happened here, the girl must have exerted an incredible amount of force, but it was also clear that her abilities were untrained. At least, at the time of this particular use of power, she was inexperienced. Nonetheless, a confrontation could be difficult, especially if he had to face both siblings simultaneously.

Having garnered what he needed from the docking bay, the masked individual silently slipped from the large chamber and headed in the direction of the apartment complex noted on the scrap of paper from the port-master. He checked the surrounding area, quickly determining his heading. It wasn't far...

Standing in the center of Vin's extravagant apartment, Gren Trell stroked his well-manicured goatee as his silvery hair wafted gently in the lightly circulating air. The gentleman crime lord swirled some liquid around in his chalice, as his golden-haired son scrambled around. The younger Trell frantically searched for something, eventually pulling some papers from a small lockbox.

"I knew it was around here somewhere," he blurted. "One moment, Father, and I'll have this unlocked."

"Take your time," said the elder Trell in a calculated tone. "I'm only losing...," he paused to think, "approximately...twelve bits per hour by having to come here to personally oversee your antics. Truly riveting 'father, son' time."

Holding aloft a set of papers triumphantly, Vin exclaimed, "Found them!"

His stern father only returned a hard glare. "That does not resemble a cloaking device, son. Looks an awful lot more like a stack of documents."

"These are better than a single device," argued the younger Lorian. "With these schematics, you could craft dozens of them. Think of it! Your own personal fleet, invisible to radar tracking."

Gren Trell methodically paced toward his son. "And how much money do you suppose it will cost to manufacture these devices? How much to pay for workers and resources? How much to silence those involved in such an illicit project? How much?"

Hanging his head in defeat, Vin replied, "I understand your point, Father."

It appeared that Gren had more to say, but he was interrupted by a proximity alert at the door. "Are you expecting visitors?"

"No," answered Vin. "Nobody."

"Call for your guards," his father instructed. "Have them respond."

Speaking into an ornate intercom, the young Lorian ordered, "Guards, come to the parlor." Shortly thereafter, his four burly Fangorian mercenaries filled the room. As they entered, Vin continued, "Man the door. Inform whoever is there that we aren't accepting any callers at this time."

"Is there a threat?" asked the leader, a grizzled veteran with plasma burns that resembled patches of mange spread across his face.

"No, it's probably a solicitor or a creditor – ," Vin started to say.

"Threat or not, treat it as such," the elder Lorian cut him off. Clearly resenting that action, Vin bristled, but Gren's commanding eyes caused the younger man to back down.

One of the guards dared a question. "What if it's someone important?"

"I don't care if it's the Yildi themselves!" Vin berated him. "Tell them to come back later."

Obeying swiftly, the mercenaries readied their plasma rifles and took up positions around the entrance, two on each side. Using hand motions to direct, the leader of the pack indicated for one of them to open the door while the rest stood at the ready. Slowly, cautiously, the first guard unlocked the reinforced entry, while the leader drew a breath to speak. Not a word escaped his gnarled lips, however, as the door was gripped by a hand from the outside. It forced the portal completely wide, and the owner of the hand shot their other fist forward, sending the mercenaries sprawling across the foyer with a blast of energy! Unsheathing a crystalline sword and a sleek plasma pistol, a masked man entered, his cloak flapping in the breeze created by the station's powerful circulation fans.

Watching in horror, Vin shouted at his men, "Up! Up, you louts! Stop him!"

In obvious pain, the four Fangorian mercenaries rose from the floor and took aim with their rifles as the stranger merely stared at them through his steely mask. A shot rang out as the pack leader fired a plasma bolt at the intruder, only to have it deflected by a twirl of the mysterious man's blade. Instead of penetrating the man's armor and burning his flesh, the plasma bolt was embedded into the foyer wall, scorching the surface.

Before any of them had a chance to shoot next, the trespasser returned fire with his pistol, hitting the Fangorian leader in the left shoulder. Almost simultaneously, the masked man flipped his right wrist, flinging his crystal sword at another mercenary guard. Instinctively, the guard raised his rifle to protect himself. Ringing resounded throughout the room as the sword impacted the guard's weapon, knocking it from his grasp. Not missing a step, the intruder followed this up by racing toward the other two guards and ducking under their clumsy attempts to blast him with more plasma bolts. Leaning back, the man dropped to his knees and slid across the smooth flooring, utilizing his own firearm to shoot the trigger hands of each of his assailants. Howling in misery, the two let their weapons clatter to the floor.

By now, the leader was recovering from his shoulder injury and awkwardly tried to operate his rifle with one arm. Seeing this, the mysterious stranger sprang from his knees, going airborne from a burst of energy that sent a minor shockwave through the apartment. While in midair, the anonymous attacker spun about, seeming to defy gravity, and fired two more times with his pistol. Receiving a blast to his right shoulder, the mercenary leader crumpled in agony. The second shot hit the first guard in the foot as he stooped to retrieve his lost firearm, causing him to lose his footing and fall face first on the floor.

Upon landing, the stranger then squatted low, spinning on the ball of his right foot with his left leg outstretched, tripping the last two guards. Swiftly and nimbly, the man used his momentum to launch himself into a roll across the foyer, snatching his lost blade in the process. A roar emanated from the opposite side of the chamber as the guard leader charged at the man, despite his immense pain. As unflappable as ever, the mysterious man ran toward the nearest wall as his pursuer closed in, and in two swift steps he ascended the surface, performing a dexterous backflip to land behind his attacker. Feeling a piercing sting in his back that spread all the way through his abdomen, the pack leader glanced down to see the pointed tip of the crystalline sword protruding from his midsection. As the blade was removed, the mangy Fangorian collapsed.

Scrambling for their own guns again, the remaining guards were shocked when the man vehemently waved his arm in a wide sweep, and their weapons were inexplicably slung by an invisible force in the direction of the doorway. Seeing all his guards so easily overcome, fear and dread filled Vin Trell's entire being and he stumbled backward, dropping the cloaking schematics on the low table near his lounge. His father, on the other hand, only appeared to be mildly bothered by all of it.

With that crystal blade now aimed in their vicinity, Gren remarked, "Alright, you've made yourself clear. There is no need for further bloodshed. You obviously won't be deterred from whatever it is you desire, so what is it you seek?"

"You are Vin Trell?" queried the man.

"Hardly!" laughed the elder Lorian. "No, that would be this simpering whelp behind me. But he is not the one with the power here. You may address me."

"I seek the ones who travel aboard the Explorer 2000," stated the intruder. "It was my understanding that you sought them at one time as well."

"My son did, yes."

"Do they harbor a small boy and girl?"

Gren pursed his lips. "As far as we know, that seems to be the case. It was the children I believe that were being hunted by the Gnarfs and their enigmatic master."

"Gnarfs?"

"Yes," Gren sighed. "The Gnarfs were employed by Lord Hex to kidnap the young ones. That is the extent of our knowledge."

The man nodded. "I know the Gnarfs. But who is this 'Lord Hex'?"

Offering a wry smile, the elegant Lorian explained, "The Marquis du Hex, Warden of the Hexagon system. You haven't heard of him? He's a rather well-positioned politician."

"I am not familiar with these titles. What do they mean?"

"Have you been living on an asteroid?" chuckled Gren. "Lord Hex both rules over and protects the Hexagon, keeping it preserved from outsiders, and outsiders safe from its perils."

There was a moment of muteness from the masked man, but he soon broke that silence by growling, "No one may rule the Hexagon but my master. Not even I am worthy of that level of prestige. Nevertheless, Lord Hex will soon face his own comeuppance for such presumptuousness. For now, you have given me enough." He glimpsed down at the papers on the table. His analytical mind quickly deduced what they were. "Almost enough. I will be taking these as well," he finished, sheathing his sword and snatching the documents with his free hand, pistol still trained on the Trells. Backing out, the man speedily egressed from the apartment, disappearing out the damaged door.

A great sigh of relief exuded from Vin, who then hit the floor himself, nearly fainting. In disgust, Gren shook his head at his son's lack of gumption. "You never cease to amaze me with your ever-increasing levels of disappointment," he groused.

Vin hung his head in shame. "I'm sorry about the cloaking schematics."

"Forget the schematics," snapped Gren, proceeding to issue commands. "I want to know more about our mysterious attacker.

That display was an absurd amount of power for any being. This was obviously no random event."

"Shall I track his movements on the station?" offered Vin. "If he leaves, I can find out where he goes."

The older Lorian was quick and decisive with his answer. "No. I will have another more capable agent perform that task. For now, I must return to Noxus to see to other family business there."

"What should I do?" queried his son.

Staring at Vin with an expression that made the younger man's heart drop, Gren Trell wryly uttered, "Stay here and do what you do best. Gamble away all my hard-earned profits."

With that, the gentleman crime lord spun on his heels, allowing his extravagant white cloak to billow, and exited the apartment. It was now despairingly quiet, the guards having retreated, the visitor disappeared, and now Gren himself gone. Alone, Vin plopped dejectedly onto his lounge and began pouring another drink for himself.

As the verdant world of Ranjeman filled the viewport, the Explorer 2000 crew noted the vast fleet of hunter class warships that surrounded the globe in every orbit. Clearly the Ranjeman people were incredibly security minded, guarding the secrets of their jungles and forests zealously, even religiously. Their huntsman's lifestyle was well documented by the Galactic Community records, however, the specifics of their beliefs and practices remained a mystery. This was reason for caution, as no one was quite sure how the Ranjemans would react to the arrival of the Explorer.

Mere moments later, a sigh of relief proceeded from Kel's mouth as they were granted access to the surface, gently gliding past the watchful blockade. Citing repair and resupply as their cause for visitation, Nado's smooth talking convinced the feline folk commanders to allow them entry. Soon, they were directed to a berth within a spaceport that was buried deep in the equatorial jungles. Massive tree limbs supported the catwalks and platforms that formed the port, while the traffic towers and administration buildings protruded from the tops and sides of the trees themselves. Many of the giant plants had hollowed sections, specifically carved to act as elevators and stairways for these structures.

With a hiss and a groan, the bulkhead at the Explorer's aft lowered, and the crew disembarked. Awaiting them was a world rich with foliage of varying shades, ranging from dark, sage greens, to bright yellows and oranges. Dotting the canopy were also branches sporting reddish leaves, and more than a few fir trees added their bristly needles to the landscape.

A quick surveillance told Kel they would have a long repair time ahead of them, as items of a mechanical nature would be in short supply here. "I suppose I'll see what I can scrounge up," she snorted. "It'll take a hot minute to get everything assembled and fixed."

"I can help you," offered Rox. "Maybe with two sets of hands we can get it all done a little faster."

His genuine and genteel phrase was greatly appreciated by the commander, but all she could give in response was a tired, but accepting, smile. He reciprocated her expression, giving her a knowing nod. Meanwhile, Captain Nado and Schiff were laying out plans of their own as the kids stood quietly by, taking in the sights and sounds of the untamed world around them.

"Someone in the port might have information about the Kathnarii," the captain was suggesting. "Though it's doubtful they'd be willing to share it with off-worlders…"

As he trailed off, Schiff piped up. "But if one of us didn't look like an off-worlder, perhaps they would be more inclined to give helpful knowledge."

"Good idea," Nado agreed. "Alright, check out the local watering holes and see what you can dig up. I can take Mara and Jym with me to do a little shopping – "

Kel cut him off quickly. "Emphasis on ***little***," she said, pointing sharply at the big Zennian. "Only the necessities. No novelty purchases."

"Psh," he jovially dismissed. "I seem to recall that a certain 'novelty purchase,' as you put it, bailed us out of a tight spot on the Star Guard base."

"Nado, I'm serious," the commander reiterated. "We've used most of the Gonian's stipend already. We can't afford to blow it all."

"Understood, Commander." The captain returned her staid demeanor. "We'll restock rations, water for the recycler units, and fuel."

After a solemn nod, the groups headed in their separate directions. Kel watched the children leave with the captain, as Schiff skipped merrily in the direction of the nearby village that also hung from the gigantic branches and tree trunks. She nodded to Rox, and the two of them made their way towards what appeared to be the most promising locale to find parts and tools for repair. In the meantime, they left H-8-RED to guard the Explorer in their absence.

On approach, the mechanics' shop didn't fill Kel with much confidence that they would be able to procure everything they needed. Inside though, the place was a veritable playground of spare parts and junk piles. Amidst exclamations of, "Oh, I can use this," and, "Yes, that will do," followed by murmurings of, "I guess I can make that work," the commander wound her way betwixt all the bins and shelves. Her mind was whirling with plans and blueprints, a mashup of repair manuals and jury-rigging ideas.

She was yanked from her internal machinations by a statement from the doctor. "It's good to see you excited about something," he remarked.

"Huh?" Kel shook her head. "Oh, sorry, I was trying to figure out how to weld the hull breach closed and get those busted shield solenoids functioning again."

"I could see the wheels turning," replied Rox. "But I don't recall you studying any of this at the academy. Where did you learn all your mechanical and robotics skills?"

Staring at the assortment of items before her, the commander quietly answered, "My parents. Dad was a lead repair technician on the flotilla, and Mom taught advanced robotics in the schools."

"Are you still in touch with them?"

Kel picked up a spanning tool and held it close to her chest, a pensive look in her eyes. "It's not something I like to talk about."

"I understand," said Rox. "Family can be hard to discuss. We can just focus on our work."

She nodded in response. As they continued to gather supplies and drag everything back to the Explorer, Kel held the doctor's kind words in her heart. Even as they began their various repair tasks, she appreciated his restraint in not pressing the matter. Maybe one day I'll tell him, she thought. But not right now.

Hours later, the crew reconvened aboard their vessel, gathered in a tight conference inside the galley. After storing and securing the new supplies, and completing the much needed repairs, everyone took their seats as Schiff reported, "Alright, I had to dig a bit, but eventually I came across a band of hunters that told me about 'The Great Temple,' a structure located several leagues from here in the eastern jungles. There is a landing pad close by, and they've already radioed ahead to inform the guards that challengers are on their way."

"What kind of opposition should we expect?" asked Commander Kel.

"They said only two challengers could enter at a time," the slender shapeshifter replied. "And they would have to face off against two other challengers. That's the only way to uncover the 'secrets of the Ranjeman Kathnarii,' as my chatty informant...," she looked for the right word, but it didn't come. "Informed." Schiff paused again. "So, I guess we need to decide who's going as the challengers?"

"I'm going," Captain Nado declared heroically. "If anyone is putting themselves in harm's way, it'll be me."

"One of us should accompany you," interjected Princess Mara, a grim resolve in her tone. "It's only fair. I mean, this whole thing is because of us."

"I should do it," said Jym. "If we can't use our powers, at least my skill at swordplay isn't hampered."

Though frowning, Mara nodded her agreement. Nado rose from his chair at the head of the table and announced, "Then it's decided. The prince and I will take on the dangers of this Great Temple and secure whatever knowledge of the Kathnarii lies within."

"We can take the Puddle Jumper to the landing pad," the commander stated. "From there, you and Jym can hike through the forest to the temple. We'll be on standby, Captain. Just ping us on the communicators if things go wrong."

"Will do, Commander. Let's move out."

Not long thereafter, Commander Kel and Princess Mara, who insisted on accompanying her brother, had transported Nado and Jym to the landing pad that was their destination and dropped the pair in the deep, dark forests. As they trudged through the darkened woods of the Ranjeman surface, Captain Nado and Prince Jym found themselves constantly waving oversized insectoids from their faces and pushing large fronds and branches out of their path. Pools of mud and treacherous swamps threatened to impede their trek, but the two pressed onward, following the map point that Schiff had provided. Peering past the foliage and staring at a concave spot in the canopy, Nado could just make out their destination, as the temple's viridian apex was barely visible above the dense forest.

Amidst panting breaths, Jym voiced a question. "Nado? Remember when we were on Khardan and had to fight Gnash and his gang?"

"Yep," was the captain's focused reply. "Kind of an odd thing to mention at this juncture. Why bring it up now?"

"I wanted to know, how did it feel to take down the bad guy?" The boy's tone increased in excitement as he continued.

"Why do you ask?"

Jym shrugged. "I don't know, I just wonder if I'll have what it takes in the moment if I have to defeat enemies too. I couldn't do anything to General Hämm after our duel, and things are only getting more intense. My sister says I'm too trusting and caring and need to be more hardened. So, tell me, how do you muster what it takes?"

Nado thought long and hard. "Please don't glorify the act of harming or. . .killing another person, even if it's someone who threatens your own life. What I did to Gnash still doesn't sit well with me, and I have endeavored not to take another life since, no matter what they threaten."

"What if it's Graylon?"

That query almost stopped Nado in his tracks. He paused momentarily, but ultimately sloughed off the question and plodded forward. "We'll deal with that when the time comes. Hopefully we keep ahead of him and don't have to face him."

Within minutes they had cleared the jungle at last, stepping into a wide, open space of lush grass. Looming in the distance was the massive Kathnarii temple, a visage of mystery and danger. A contingent of Ranjeman guards stood at hand, the leader of which approached cautiously.

"You are the challengers of the Great Temple?" she asked solemnly.

"We are," answered the captain. "We are ready to proceed with whatever may lay within."

"Not yet," the huntress retorted. "No one enters the Great Temple unless they are facing challengers."

Jym looked at the hunters gathered around. "We'll be going against them?"

"Not quite," uttered the guard captain. "Your challengers arrived a short while ago." She gestured to a sharp corner of the temple edifice, and out strode two figures. Nado and Jym could only stare in shock as the deep, resonating voice of Lord Hex echoed throughout the glen.

"Hello, Burnay."

Chapter 10

Captain Nado's words were filled with dismay as he finally spoke to his imposing elder brother. "Graylon...what are you doing here?"

"Is it not obvious?" quipped the Marquis du Hex. "Wherever you try to hide these children, I will be there to seize them. It was inevitable that you would end up here in your search for the secrets of the Kathnarii Order." Lord Hex stopped his monologue temporarily, clearly savoring the look on his sibling's face. "I told you, I know all about your hunt for Kathnarii Base. I knew you would come here when I confronted you at Khardan. I know you better than you know yourself, Burnay."

Noticing the smaller individual that accompanied Graylon, the captain gestured in the boy's direction. "And who is this?"

The marquis followed his brother's indication. "Forgive my manners. Burnay, say hello to your nephew, my son Cylor."

At the mention of his name, the small being flexed all four of his own arms, his augmentations glowing faintly as he did. Natural black tattoos covering the boy's body were an almost identical match to

Prince Jym's, while Cylor's gray skin tones reflected those of Graylon and Burnay Nado. Shadowy eyes glared back at Captain Nado and Prince Jym from under a furrowed brow, Cylor's dark expression one of severe determination.

"I figured it was high time I stopped chasing from behind," prattled Graylon, "and started striving to get ahead, so I could cut you off at the pass. I don't know why you seek the Kathnarii, but if that's what you want then that's what I will steal from under you."

"But why?" questioned Burnay.

"I obviously haven't been successful in snatching the Vampyrials from you by force," responded Graylon. "Therefore, it stands to reason that the better course of action is to find something with which to bargain."

Breathing heavier all the while, Captain Nado prepared to answer his brother's snide remarks but was halted by the lead huntress. "Enough talk!" she ordered. "If both parties are ready, it is time to enter the Great Temple and engage with the many challenges that lay within. Are you ready?"

"Ready," grunted the captain.

"Ready," echoed Lord Hex.

"Then let us begin." The Ranjeman woman swiftly and deftly trotted to the grand archway that acted as the primary entrance to the marbled, palace-like building. "I am Li'Nora, lead huntress of the Temple Guardians, last descendants of the Dumrii. I will be acting as your master of ceremonies for the upcoming competitions. Follow me."

In quiet obeisance, both pairs trailed after their moderator as she led the way inside the dim temple. Despite the present company,

Nado couldn't help but admire the architecture of the massive pillars that upheld the high towers, stretching skyward and decorated so that their rooftops resembled huge fronds. The bulk of the structure sprawled further under the jungle canopy, hidden by the deepening woods. It made it impossible to determine just how extensive the temple really was.

Before he could ruminate further however, Li'Nora interrupted Nado's thoughts. "The Dumrii were warriors of cunning. So, the competitions are centered around this theme. Three separate games designed to test the three aspects of the cunning warrior." She leapt atop a small dais in the center of the main chamber as torches suddenly blazed to life, lighting up the tile mosaics that depicted scenes of hunts and battles all around. "Aspect number one: the cunning warrior is courageous. Aspect number two: the cunning warrior is strategic. Aspect number three: the cunning warrior is brutal. Fulfill these aspects, and you will achieve the ultimate goal of understanding what makes a true Dumrii.

"The general rules of the Great Temple are quite simple. Firstly, the competitors are never to engage in any altercation outside of those allowed by the rules of each game. Secondly, competitors cannot leave the temple once the games are in progress. Finally, any decisions made in the games cannot be altered or changed once they have been made. To attempt to undo one's decision in the field is to falter in one's resolve, a sign of weakness and not the way of the Dumrii, especially not the Kathnarii." Li' Nora began to pace on her platform. "Your first challenge is the Purrat Kique, the Game of Courage. In the next chamber, there are multiple holes in one wall. Hidden somewhere is the key that will let you pass to the next challenge. You have to find it to proceed. Those who reach through the holes in the wall must brave whatever dangers may be on the other side. Perhaps a predator will rip your arm from your torso! Or perhaps. . .nothing will happen at all. Remember, courage is the key to advancing through this round. Let us proceed."

Shouldering her highly ornamental bow, Li'Nora vaulted from the dais with a twirl and a flip, alighting nimbly on the tiled floor almost silently. As if on their own, the nearly four-meter-tall bronzy double doors ahead of them swung open, revealing a short staircase that led down into a new room. It was smaller and far less ornamental than the previous chamber, and the wall opposite the entrance did indeed feature a series of holes, beyond which no light could be seen.

As they approached the daunting wall of mystery that lay before them, Li'Nora gave one final instruction. "Oh, yes. I forgot to mention that there is a time limit to this challenge."

She pulled a nearby lever, activating ancient gears and pulleys that issued grinding and clunking noises. With these obnoxious sounds pervading the previously serene atmosphere, the competitors all covered their ears. It became quickly evident that the cacophony was due to the ceiling and side walls of this chamber beginning to move. They were closing in! Spikes protruded from fine pinholes, adding even more danger to their task. Captain Nado and Lord Hex both spun around to shoot angry glares at their referee, who only smiled coyly in return.

"Courage is always best tested under duress," she said coolly. "No time to waste then, is there? Find the key."

Grasping hold of one of Cylor's arms with an iron grip, Lord Hex grumbled, "Well, you heard her. Get to it! Start checking those holes for the key."

Though obviously hesitant, the boy acquiesced. Meanwhile, Prince Jym sighed heavily and declared, “Guess we'd better do the same, huh?”

“Not yet,” Captain Nado halted him. “Something about the way she worded the rules feels off to me. ‘Courage is the key,’ she said.”

“We don't exactly have a lot of time to sort through all of that. We've got to find that key and get out of here before we're turned into courage soup!” The young monarch began to head for the wall of holes. “Holler at me if you figure it out, I'll go ahead and start searching.”

“Wait!” called Nado. “No need for that.” He smiled slyly and narrowed his eyes. “I think I know where the key is.” Turning, the clever captain confidently strode to their master of ceremonies. “Li'Nora? Hand over the key.”

A snarl formed across the Ranjeman huntress' lips. “You dare to make demands of your moderator? Are you that foolish?”

“No,” the captain stated with utmost surety. “I'm that courageous. You said we had to find the key, and that courage is the key. Blindly sticking one's hand in a hole is not courage. Being willing to stand out and appear foolish though, that is courageous. And if I'm not mistaken, the key is in the breast pocket of your vest, close to your heart, the wellspring of courage.”

The scowl on the woman's face faded into a soft, fanged grin, as she stuck two spindly fingers into her pocket. Upon withdrawing them, she revealed that there was indeed a skeleton key made of bone that had been concealed therein. Lowering her clawed hand, she presented the object to Captain Nado with a nod of respect. She then flipped the lever back, returning the spikes, walls, and ceiling to their proper place.

"Well done," Li'Nora remarked. "You understand that courage involves wit, and not just blind bravery. Though there were some in this challenge who did not even perform blind bravery very well." She eyed Graylon, who sneered back in response. "But on to the next competition. This is the Purrat Hetch, the Game of Strategy."

With a quick opening of her palm, Li'Nora indicated for Captain Nado to return the skeleton key. Using it, she accessed the hallway that led into the succeeding room. As they entered, all of the contenders gazed in wonder at the intricacy of this spacious arena. On either end of the chamber there was a raised platform with some kind of primitive control panel on it. Dominating the center of this room was a series of barriers and block towers, some several meters tall, creating a labyrinth of sorts. The flooring here was made up of large tiles that were each around one and a half meters squared. At the base of each platform, a colored tile rested, one blue and the other red.

Not missing a beat, Li'Nora launched into her explanation of this game. "Two of you will act as the players in this challenge. The other two will act as the game pieces. Those who are acting as game pieces will start on the colored tiles, one on red, the other on blue. The 'players' will utilize their controls to move their 'pieces' around the board, navigating the various obstacles to get their 'piece' into an advantageous position that they might attack the other.

"You are only allowed one action per turn, and each action must be taken within five seconds. You may choose to move your 'piece' any number of spaces in one direction, provided they are not impeded by an obstruction. You may change which direction your 'piece' is facing, allowing them to turn ninety degrees to the left or right. Instead of moving your 'piece,' there is also the option of moving an obstacle on the board. Or, if you feel you are in the correct location, you may fire the weapon that your 'piece' possesses. Bear in mind, there are also additional traps and pitfalls that are unseen that your 'piece' can activate, so be careful with your movements.

"Lastly, all of the traps are non-lethal, so there is no cause for concern or alarm in that regard. Does everyone understand? I would hate to have to repeat myself."

The captain nodded forcefully. "Understood."

"Likewise," oozed Lord Hex.

"Good. Then we shall begin," proclaimed their Ranjeman arbiter. "Choose your players and pieces."

"Cylor," the Marquis du Hex uttered, "I think it best that I act as player for this particular endeavor. You shall act as the game piece. Don't worry my son, I will keep you out of harm's way."

This statement prompted Captain Nado to turn to Jym. "If Graylon is calling the shots over there, then I should probably go head-to-head with him. Are you good being the game piece?"

"Not a problem," the brave Vampyrial prince replied. "We can take them."

"To your starting places!" shouted Li'Nora.

A rumbling exuded from the arena as the raised platforms lowered to allow the Nado brothers to step aboard and assume their places at the controls. Prince Jym took up his position on the blue tile, while Cylor stepped onto the red one. As soon as all the participants had taken their places, Li'Nora rang a loud, clanging gong, and the game commenced!

"Red acts first," she announced.

With that, Graylon made his first move with a couple of taps on his panel. Upon doing so, a line of red light issued from the tiles below, showing Cylor what he was supposed to follow. Up next was Captain Nado, who activated blue lighting for Jym. Back and forth, little by little, the two chased each other's pieces around the board.

"You can't win, Burnay," Graylon called out. "I told you, I know you better than you know yourself. I taught you how to play every strategy game we ever owned. This is a battle you will lose every time."

Frustratingly, no comebacks would pop into Nado's head. He knew he'd think of something, probably hours later, and kick himself for not saying it. In this moment, however, it was likely best to shrug off the taunts anyway. Let Graylon babble like a fool. The captain had to keep a clear head and protect his ward. It was his turn, so he repositioned Prince Jym on the floor again. This time though, as Jym followed the blue trail, one of the tiles dropped, and the boy disappeared beneath the game board.

"Jym?!" shouted Captain Nado. "Jym?! Can you hear me?"

"I'm okay," came a muffled response. "There's a bunch of tunnels down here. Just figure out how to get me out of here!"

"I'm on it!" declared the captain, busying himself with his controls. "Maybe there's an exit hidden under one of the other board components."

Seeing the unfortunate turn of events, Lord Hex chuckled to himself, taking his own turn and seizing the opportunity to move Cylor closer to Jym's departure point. In so doing however, he walked his own game piece into a second trapdoor, losing sight of the augmented child. "Blast," he grumbled. "Not to worry son, I'll get you back up here."

Glaring across the playing field at one another, the brothers now started repositioning the obstacles on the board here and there, searching for the elusive exit from the trapdoor tunnels. Meanwhile, Prince Jym found himself crouching and slinking through a crawl space beneath the arena, hearing the sounds of the large, heavy objects shifting above. He rounded a corner and nearly yelped, coming face to face with the other boy, Cylor.

Startled, the prince stumbled back, but Cylor only stood his ground and did not advance. Giving his opponent a once-over, Jym noted the various augmentations that dotted the young man's body. There were several small metallic plates fastened to the top of Cylor's head, and while his upper arms were fairly clear and looked strong and healthy, his lower arms were nearly covered by wires and tubing. He wore a specially designed black vest with matching pants and boots but carried no other paraphernalia.

"Hi," stammered Jym, unsure what else to do. "I'm Jym."

"I am Cylor," the cyborg boy replied.

Easing into a sitting position, Jym continued. "We might be down here for a minute while they look for the exit. Want to take a seat?" With a brief nod, Cylor silently agreed and also sat. The prince kept up the conversation. "So, you're Graylon's son?"

"Not entirely," Cylor answered. "I was not spawned from a union of mother and father like you, but Lord Hex is nonetheless my progenitor. I would not have survived the clone pod without his intervention."

"You're a clone?"

"Yes. I thought my verbiage made that clear."

Jym chuckled a bit. "Sorry, I'm just fascinated, that's all. Who were you cloned after?"

"Lord Hex added his own DNA to my makeup," explained Cylor. "Other than that, I am uncertain of my origins."

"Those tattoos look like mine," Jym observed. "You must have some Vampyrial lineage."

"I do."

"So, Vampyrial and Zennian...neat. What about your mechanical parts? Why do you have those?"

Looking at his arms in ponderance, Cylor responded softly, "I was unstable. The second set of arms didn't form properly and were weak when the process completed. Father said I would need augments to assist. As for the ones on my head, there were too many soft spots on my skull. The machinery and equipment used in my resuscitation were rather antiquated for the process."

"Do they hurt?" Jym wanted to know.

"Yes. Always. But it is necessary, and they are helpful with my computer hacking."

"So, that was you who hacked our robot?"

"Yes."

The prince sighed sympathetically. "You know, I believe that the people who claim to be family ought to love and care for us, not purposefully hurt us. There might be a way to heal you."

"But I am your enemy," Cylor said. "Why would you help me?"

"Because I don't think we have to be enemies," replied Jym. "What do you say? Would you rather be friends?"

"I think I would like that." Though it was awkward and a bit strange to see, a gentle smile brightened Cylor's face.

"Alright." Jym paused a moment to listen to the noises above, as the magnetically controlled labyrinth shifted overhead. "As soon as our teammates find a way out, we'll go. But let's make a truce not to attack if one of us ends up in an advantageous position. Sound good?"

"That does sound good."

As if on cue, at that moment they heard Nado's booming voice calling, "Jym! I found an exit! Head to your left and look for the opening!"

Overlapping the captain's final words were the thunderous commands of Graylon. "Cylor, my son! Turn and head towards your starting place! There is another open trapdoor and ladder!"

"See you on the other side," encouraged Jym, giving Cylor a grand grin. The other boy reciprocated the expression, and the two made their way out. As they reached the surface of the arena once again, Jym could see that he was in line to attack Cylor. The young cyborg boy wouldn't even see it coming.

"It's our turn," proclaimed Captain Nado. "Jym, attack!" But the young prince did nothing. "Attack! Hurry!" Still, Jym didn't budge. They were almost out of time. "What's the matter? Jym, this is the only way to get to Kathnarii Base!"

"Time's up!" yelled Li'Nora. "Red team, take your turn."

Both "game pieces" were lined up, with not a single thing separating them. Lord Hex didn't waste a nanosecond. "Cylor, attack!"

Locking eyes with his opponent, Prince Jym gave a solemn nod. He felt relief when his counterpart nodded back. In an instant though, everything the young monarch was feeling shattered into shards of confusion, crushing despair, and utter betrayal as Cylor thrust all four arms forward, manipulating a shockwave of dark energy across the playing field! Forced to react quickly, Jym instinctively threw his own hands up, trying to ward off the blast with an energy manipulation of his own. With great fright and dismay, the prince realized he was outmatched power for power, as Cylor's shockwave overcame him and launched the young prince into the far wall. Landing with a thud, the boy's heart seemed even heavier than his body.

Though his ears were ringing, Jym could hear Captain Nado speaking to him as he helped the young prince to his feet. "Jym, are you alright? What happened? We could've won!"

Shaking off his bewilderment, Prince Jym answered, "We made an agreement. I thought he wanted to be friends."

After a long sigh, Nado reservedly said, "It's okay. We'll just have to win the final challenge."

"Well done, Cylor," they heard Graylon congratulating. "Excellent use of subterfuge."

This game was ended and Li'Nora beckoned, so they all made their way into the chamber that housed the last game. There was little more to this room than a short, round barrier that formed the sort of ring one might use for a show of pugilism. Upon entering, the huntress described the guidelines of this third competition. "This is the only remaining challenge for you. The Purrat Reowl, the Game of Brutality. The rules are quite simple. This is intended to be a one-on-one fistfight. The first to be rendered unconscious, or to surrender, loses. Choose your champion and choose. . .cunningly."

Mustering all his gumption, Captain Nado approached his elder brother. "Graylon, if this is supposed to be a man-to-man fight, it only makes sense that you and I be the ones to face off. There's no reason to put the boys in further danger. Agreed?"

"I agree," Graylon responded. "There's no reason to put the boys into further danger."

"Then let's get to it."

Stepping into the conversation, Li'Nora asked, "Have you decided who will undergo this challenge?"

"We have," answered the captain.

"Assume your posts," the Ranjeman instructed curtly.

Following their referee's commands, Captain Nado quickly doffed his duster, bandoliers, belts, and weaponry. After rolling all four shoulders, he bowed his head and closed his eyes, taking a deep breath as if preparing for a plunge off a cliff. This was it, a showdown between him and Graylon, just the two of them. It was the right thing to do. Though he didn't want to, Nado knew he had to deal with his brother alone. The captain turned and entered the ring, only then raising his square chin to level his gaze at his opponent. To his shock, Cylor stood before him on the far side of the ring.

"Graylon, what is this?" the brawny Zennian inquired of his sibling. "I thought we agreed that you and I would fight."

"Did we?" mocked Graylon. "I believe what was stated was that there was no reason to place the young men in harm's way. That's what I agreed to. So, what will it be, Burnay? Surely you don't intend to harm your own nephew, do you?"

Glaring hard, the captain replied, "You know I won't fight a child."

"You forfeit, then?" A cruel grin spread across Lord Hex's broad face.

"You cheated!"

"The weak in mind and will always say such things." Graylon leaned forward. "Now say it. Say you give up!"

Exchanging a depressive look with Prince Jym, Captain Nado murmured, "I give up," and exited the ring.

"The fight is declared!" announced Li'Nora. She addressed Graylon. "You truly have the mind and spirit of a strategic and brutal warrior. Today, you are the victors, and to the victors go the spoils. Follow me, there is one last chamber to visit."

A hidden doorway on the eastern wall opened, revealing a staircase winding upward beyond. Proudly, Graylon led Cylor up the stairs, while Nado and Jym trudged dejectedly behind. They had lost the challenge, but maybe Graylon didn't know yet what they were after. Maybe they could still slip the data drive out from under him in his braggadocious bravado.

One more hidden panel slid aside with the crunching of stone on stone, and they found themselves entering an expansive room that featured multiple glassless windows that allowed for a nice breeze from the outside air. The chamber itself was filled with all manner of armaments. Ancient armor on stands, spears and bows mounted on the walls, a few tomes written by bygone battle-masters, and a few trinkets made from bone and encrusted with gemstones. One thing really stood out to Nado though. Under a dome of glass rested an unassuming data drive. This could be their chance.

"Welcome to our relic room," Li'Nora said warmly. "The winners of today's games may choose one item to take with them. A souvenir and reminder of what it means to be counted among the Dumrii."

As optimistic as Nado had been, he lost all hope when he saw that Graylon's eyes locked onto the data drive. "I'll take that," declared the malicious marquis.

Li'Nora also glanced at the drive. "I'm sorry, but that item is not available for requisition. I cannot let you take it."

"Pity," muttered Lord Hex. "Cylor? Dispatch her."

"Father?" the boy questioned. "You wish me to kill her? Is that necessary?"

"Don't question me boy, just do it!" exclaimed his father. Shocked by the sudden change in the man's demeanor, Cylor immediately complied.

A scream that was swiftly muffled barely escaped Li'Nora's throat as she was violently slammed against the wall by Cylor's power. Her head banged into the stone with a crack and her body slumped lifelessly to the floor. In the meantime, Graylon waltzed to the glass case and smashed it, snatching the data drive from within. With a grand flourish, he whirled to face Nado and Jym, who were caught off guard by this sudden turn of events.

"Alright, Burnay," Graylon began, "I now have the drive you sought. But I'm willing to trade right here, right now. The data drive for the Vampyrial boy."

"You know I'll never agree to that!" shouted the captain. Out of the corner of his eye, he noted a hefty tree branch near one of the windows. Grabbing hold of the young prince, Captain Nado darted for the opening. "Come on Jym, run! Run! Let's get out of here while we can!"

"What about Li'Nora?" questioned Jym.

"There's nothing we can do," answered the captain, dread and heaviness in his tone. "She's already dead, Jym. Come on!"

With a mighty leap, Captain Nado lofted both of them through the window, grasping the tree branch with his other arms. The limb was strong enough to hold them, but still flexible enough to lower them almost to the ground, where they immediately copped a heel and booked it for the tree line ahead. As they fled, Jym asked, "Why didn't we stay and fight?"

"Against Graylon and Cylor?" panted Nado. "I'm not sure we have the firepower today. Let's just get back to the landing pad!"

Above their pounding footsteps, they could hear Lord Hex hollering after them, "Run all you like, Burnay! If it's Kathnarii Base you want, you have no other recourse but to get this data drive! No matter where you run or hide, eventually you'll have to come running back to me! And then we shall have our reckoning! Sooner or later, you'll have to face me again, Burnay! You'll have to face me!"

His scornful laughter continued to echo throughout the whole forest, haunting their every fleeing step…

Chapter 11

Squawking and howling occasionally sounded throughout the dense jungle, carrying across the landing pad where the Puddle Jumper rested. Commander Kel and Princess Mara had left the sliding side doors open to allow a breeze to filter through the tiny vessel, but the hot winds did little except to wreak havoc on their hair. Conversation had been short and limited, as merely the act of speaking in this climate made their mouths feel like sand. As bad as it was on Ranjeman, Kel wasn't looking forward to going back to the brutal deserts of Khardan. Be that as it may, however, Khardan was their next stop. As soon as Nado and Jym returned with the data drive here, it would be time to brave whatever dangers lay in wait between them and the third Kathnarii drive.

A shout in the distance pulled the commander back to the present. It was muffled from the thick foliage, but it certainly boomed like Captain Nado's bombastic tones. Both she and Mara strained their ears to hear what the voice was saying.

"Start the engines!" bellowed the captain, as he and the prince burst from the shrubs and low-hanging branches at the edge of the landing pad clearing. "We need to get back to the ship while we still can!"

"On it, Captain," Kel responded, quickly taking her seat and belting in. Once the boys had flopped aboard, wheezing and sweating profusely, she asked, "What's going on? Is everything okay?"

"Did you get the data drive?" Mara inquired.

Her brother shook his head. "We couldn't. We lost it."

"Lost it?" the princess repeated incredulously. "What do you mean you lost it?"

This time it was Captain Nado who answered. "Someone beat us at the challenges."

"Cheating Ranjemans," muttered the commander. "They rigged the games, didn't they?"

"Not them," Nado heaved, clutching his chest with both right arms. "Graylon."

"What?" Now it was Commander Kel's turn to be incredulous. "How did he know we'd even be here?"

"He knows we're after Kathnarii Base," groused the captain. "He knows the legends as well as I do. Our only hope is to get to Khardan and find the last data drive before he does."

"What do we do about the one that he has in his possession now?" Princess Mara quietly questioned.

"Don't fret, Princess," proclaimed Captain Nado. "I said it before, I'll say it again. By Trock Taran, we're going to uncover the secrets of Kathnarii Base, and we will find your parents!" He calmed himself, feeling somewhat sheepish. "I just don't know how yet..."

Despite the captain's bravado, Kel could sense his anger and frustration mounting beneath the surface. These run-ins with Graylon were taking a heavy toll on his demeanor. It was building too. She'd first seen it after their battle with Klensh on Zen I, then again when they fled from the dreadnought at Khardan. Seeing Nado in this sort of state was all new territory for the commander.

Silence enveloped the fuselage of the Puddle Jumper, as they all fell to quiet ponderings and musings. Constant humming from the shuttle's powerful jet engines became the only sound in anyone's ears, propelling the little craft over the thick canopy of Ranjeman that passed rapidly below. After a couple of hours, Commander Kel had piloted them back to the Explorer, landing the Puddle Jumper inside the cargo bay once again with expert skill. They alighted gently and quickly departed the cramped vessel , making their way to the upper deck.

"Schiff?" called Captain Nado. "Dr. Rox? Red! Everyone report to the war room for a conference." Minutes later they had assembled, taking their usual places around the galley table. Once the crew was gathered in their seats, Nado relayed the events that had occurred at the temple, careful to exclude the part about Jym's misplaced trust in Cylor. "At this juncture, I'll have to confront Graylon eventually to get the last data drive so we can complete the star map," he concluded.

"You mean we'll have to face Graylon," corrected Kel. "We're a team. We work together."

The captain shook his head. "He's my brother, my problem. But we need to move on to the next order of business. Where do we go from here?"

"We either go toe-to-toe with Lord Hex," inserted Princess Mara, having clearly slipped into another moody slump, "or we go for the final data drive on Khardan. Not much else to do."

"It's your parents we're looking for," Dr. Rox said softly. "What would you like to do?"

Mara harrumphed a reply. "If it's just the two of them, perhaps we could take the drive by force. We've overcome Lord Hex before, we can do it again."

Her brother disagreed. "Last time, we surprised him. This time around, he'd be expecting us. We'd get trounced."

"I can defeat them," she murmured.

"You didn't see how much energy Cylor was able to expend," Jym debated. "He might be even stronger than we are! Not to mention he's Graylon's hacker that took over Red. I hope I don't have to face him again..."

"I can defeat them," Mara insisted. "I know I can."

"That may be," interjected the doctor, "but I still think it's best that the two of you avoid using your powers for now. Just the little expenditure you utilized to stop Red back on the farm was enough to put you into a temporary catatonic state. Imagine how bad it would be if you had to manipulate the amount of energy required to overcome both Graylon and Cylor. I'm not sure that's best."

"Because it would be too dangerous?" queried the girl.

"I believe so, yes."

The princess nodded solemnly. "I understand."

"Not to change subjects too drastically," Commander Kel remarked, "but what do you think the fallout will be concerning the death of a temple guardian? Li'Nora was a high-ranking member of that faction, right? Could we be blamed?"

Rubbing his square chin, the captain gave a grim answer. "With the resources Graylon has in this sector, that's a distinct possibility. He could absolutely pin Li'Nora's death on us."

"Oof," Schiff phonated. "Then we definitely don't want to stick around here. Ranjeman justice can be pretty nasty." All eyes turned to her momentarily. Schiff chuckled nervously before stating, "Don't ask how I know."

"What do they do?" queried Prince Jym.

"Well, all Ranjemans revere the hunt," Schiff started to explain, "so most of their law enforcement is based around that idea as well. They have justiciars who can act as judge, jury, and executioner who would form a posse to hunt down the culprits. Those who are caught quickly face a swift death. Those who run and cost the posse more time hunting only increase their hunger for the hunt. That scenario usually ends in the captured prey being flayed and skinned alive, then put on display outside the justiciars' offices..." Now, not only were all eyes on Schiff, but all mouths were agape. "Again, don't ask how I know."

"Huh," huffed Nado. "No, we certainly don't want to stick around for that. All in favor of getting prepped to depart for Khardan?"

Most of the crew raised their hands. As Kel scanned the room, she saw that only one raised hand was absent. Princess Mara had not elected to make the vote unanimous. Feeling very empathetic towards the young girl, Kel focused on the princess' faraway expression as Captain Nado rather clumsily offered the other option.

"Um, okay," he stammered. "I figured that would be undisputed. All in favor of fighting Graylon for the Dumrii data drive?" No hands were raised at all, not even Mara's. "Princess? Did you want to vote on the matter?"

"Oh," the little Vampyrial uttered. "I abstain from the vote, I guess."

"Are you sure?"

Merely nodding back in response, Mara retreated into herself. It was an emotional tactic that Kel knew quite well, one that she herself employed often. Something else was very obviously on the girl's mind, something that gave her great consternation.

Nado's deep voice broke Kel's concentration as he boomed, "Then it's settled. Red, start working on the bridge controls and get them ready for takeoff."

"Affirmative, Captain," the robot readily replied, immediately exiting the galley to assume its duties.

The captain continued giving orders. "Rox, take care of the med-bay supplies. Schiff, secure the cargo hold. Commander, let's you and I get the navigational consoles and gunnery chairs checked, then do a final sweep of the engine room. Mara and Jym, help Schiff in the cargo hold. This should only take a few minutes. Crew of the Explorer 2000, dismissed!"

As they all rose and commenced heading in their various directions to complete their assigned tasks, Commander Kel stole a moment to grab Schiff's attention. "Hey Schiff?"

"Yeah?" the cheerful shapeshifter answered.

"Keep an eye on Mara, will you?"

Schiff glanced at the princess as the girl gloomily descended the cargo bay ladder. "Of course." She smiled reassuringly at Kel. "I see it too."

Feeling that their young ward was in good hands, the commander bustled after the captain to work on getting the Explorer ready for liftoff.

A dark and dismal room, the interrogation chamber aboard Star Guard Base 143 was foreboding and uninviting. It had, of course, been designed that way, as no interrogator wanted to grill a suspect in a warm, cozy den. Being on the other side of the table though, was a new concept for Warrant Officer Barsol. He felt incredibly uneasy as he waited anxiously for the arrival of his interviewer. Stories of Captain Bryant O'Ryan's ability to get confessions and clues and answers had become legendary, and now permeated the officer's thoughts. Barsol wasn't generally given to fits of nervous energy, but facing O'Ryan in this sinister setting was unsettling to say the least.

Tension only mounted further when the swishing of the magnetic sliding door echoed in the chamber. Striding into the room,

O'Ryan's muscular form seemed almost to march in military style, like a drill instructor about to berate his underlings. But no bellowing or browbeating exuded from the Star Guard captain's throat. There was no yelling, no screaming, no angry tirade that threatened to shatter the two-way mirror. Instead, the trim superior officer leaned onto the table, placing both hands on the surface. Though open palmed, O'Ryan put all his weight on his fingertips, arching his fingers so that they resembled spindly legged insectoids.

Having made his intimidating presence known, the man spoke in a low, monotonous voice, "Warrant Officer Barsol, I asked you this the last time I was here, and I will now ask it again. When you inspected the Explorer 2000, did you check every nook and cranny on board?"

"Every location we knew to check, we checked," the Zennian replied, trying to sound as respectful as he possibly could. Hopefully, Captain O'Ryan would take notice of that.

"Did they have a robot?"

Barsol swallowed hard before answering. "Yes sir, they did."

"Then why was that not mentioned on the manifest?"

"It was defunct, non-operational. It appeared to be missing its primary processor."

"I see." O'Ryan now pulled away from the table and began pacing the floor. "So, because it was inoperative, you assumed it was to be listed as...what did your report say? Ah yes, 'miscellaneous hardware,' I believe were your words."

Thinking it best to remain silent, Barsol kept his mouth shut. In situations like these, he had learned from suspects that it was far better to rely on silence rather than trying to offer too many explanations which inevitably led to talking oneself into a corner. Let O'Ryan lead this meeting and do the talking. Quick, simple answers were the right course of action.

"I'm curious Barsol," the gallant O'Ryan mused as he continued to perambulate across the room, "what else did you incorrectly list? Perhaps your manifest report of the Explorer 2000 is riddled with inaccuracies. Is that a possibility?"

"I suppose so," Barsol gulped.

"You suppose? You're not sure if your own report is accurate to the best of your knowledge?"

"I mean...I don't know..."

Captain O'Ryan stopped him. "Warrant Officer, we have reason to believe that these individuals are harboring incredibly dangerous fugitives, and that they have an intergalactic terrorist in their employ. Now all you can tell me is that you don't know the accuracy of your manifest that you filed, is that right? The best you can offer is that you 'suppose' there may be inconsistencies, correct?"

"Sir, I – "

Once again, O'Ryan quickly cut him off. "Is it possible, Barsol, that as I suggested prior, you decided to waive formalities in favor of racial camaraderie? A fellow Zennian asked you to look the other way, avert your gaze for just a moment, and you caved. Isn't that what happened?"

It was all too evident to Barsol now that the tales of Captain O'Ryan's prowess as an interrogator were not exaggerated or hyperbolic in the slightest. Charisma seemed to excrete from the man's pores as he spoke, whether for persuasion or intimidation, giving the captain an aura of captivation. No matter what he said, Barsol wanted to agree, even though it meant the end of his career as a lawman. Feeling he had little other choice, the warrant officer lowered his face, his countenance seeming to drop as low as the flooring, and mumbled, "Yes sir. That is more or less what happened."

"More or less? Define 'more or less,' Warrant Officer Barsol."

"We conducted the crew and passenger manifest per protocol," replied the deflated Zennian. "The search of the vessel was done in haste at the request of the vessel's captain."

"I see," O'Ryan sighed. "I do thank you, Barsol, for your honesty. It shows real integrity, something that is desperately needed, yet severely lacking, in these times."

"Am I to be court-martialed, sir?"

"No, not at the moment anyway," answered the Star Guard captain, a certain garish joviality returning to his manner. "I am inclined to keep this incident between the two of us. Provided, of course, that you are willing to assist me in another matter, one that requires absolute secrecy."

Barsol was utterly lost. "What is it you want me to do, sir?"

"As it happens, the Explorer 2000 evaded me at Zen II, outmaneuvering the Victorious with a stunning stratagem. It was a move only a robotic pilot could execute so precisely. A robotic pilot that, I remind you, you failed to mention in your report, Warrant Officer." O'Ryan halted to send a knowing stare in Barsol's vicinity.

He then went on, saying, "Regardless, the only heading left behind by the Explorer was the planet Khardan, deep in Taldish Sector where, as you are aware, the Star Guard has no jurisdiction. I cannot take the Victorious, as she is a spacecraft of the Star Guard, and by extension, the Galactic Community. Entering any space controlled by any one of the many warmongering factions in that sector would be considered an act of war, something the Galactic Community undoubtedly wishes to avoid. Do I have your full attention, Warrant Officer Barsol?"

Snapping to attention, the junior officer sat straight up and gave a quick nod. "Yes sir."

"Good," said O'Ryan, resuming his monologue. "The dangerous fugitives aboard the Explorer are enough of a threat that I have been given a special assignment from the Community Council to track them down and apprehend them, dead or alive. Unfortunately, I can only perform that task if the Explorer remains in GC space. They did not.

"Due to our last confrontation, they are no doubt aware of the fact that the authorities of the GC desire to arrest them. Thus, they are staying out of GC space, and out of Star Guard jurisdiction. Are you following, Warrant Officer Barsol?"

Though he was barely comprehending the captain's line of thinking, he was managing to at least somewhat keep up. "Yes sir."

"Good. As long as the Explorer avoids GC space, the Victorious will be unable to overtake her. It stands to reason, then, that we must alter our course, so to speak. I am going to pursue a new tactic to detain and capture the crew of the elusive Explorer, and I want you to help me carry out this plan. In exchange, we will keep this little mishap with the manifest report under wraps. Is that clear?"

"Yes sir." Barsol wanted to be relieved about the whole matter, but O'Ryan still hadn't quite laid out how he intended for Barsol to help. "Though, if I may sir, you still haven't answered my original question. What is it exactly that you want me to do?"

"No point in beating around the bush anymore, I suppose," responded the ostentatious O'Ryan. "I am going to charter a private craft to taxi me to Khardan. I need a support officer to go with me as backup. There, we will find and arrest the persons of interest that the Council is after."

"But sir," Barsol protested, "You said it yourself. We have no jurisdiction to arrest them on Khardan."

"That is correct, Warrant Officer Barsol," the captain affirmed, "however, we will only be there as escorts of the person who will actually perform the arrest. You see, I am setting in motion a plan as we speak to utilize a portion of my savings to list an official bounty for the crew of the Explorer 2000. The price is high enough that it should attract quite the menagerie of bounty hunters, mercenaries, and scoundrels. I've also requisitioned a courier to relay a message I recorded to one hunter in particular."

"Who?"

"You may have heard of this one," replied O'Ryan, flamboyantly gesturing with his hands as he spoke. "No one has ever seen her face, or heard her true voice, as her identity is shrouded beneath the blackened visor of her helmet. Sporting a powerful jetpack, a .44 magnum carbine for range, and matching plasma throwers on each wrist, she is a force to be reckoned with. Her distinct rose-gold and onyx body armor is said to be able to absorb most attacks, and gives her an edge in martial combat, a fighting style with which she is just as deadly as anything else in her arsenal."

Barsol was shocked. “Mauve? You want to hire Mauve? Sir, she has a reputation for violence and ruthlessness.”

“Given the enemies we are up against, that may be necessary, Warrant Officer Barsol,” O’Ryan explained. “Did the name ‘Klensh’ not come up in any databases when you entered your report? Right, I forgot, the manifest did not quite make it all the way to a database entry. You filed it locally on your data-pad.

“Let me extrapolate, Warrant Officer. Klensh is a Kriton warlord who is guilty of dozens of crimes across multiple sectors. He is the intergalactic terrorist of whom I spoke earlier. So, I hope you’ll forgive me for deciding to resort to more extreme measures. If he is allied with the fugitives of the Council, then we are in a dire situation.”

I understand, sir,” the warrant officer muttered, “but Mauve’s not quite on friendly terms with the Star Guard. What makes you think she’ll work with us?”

Captain O’Ryan chuckled and shook his head. “Because of the price, Barsol. I’m offering to pay her handsomely, and as part of my pre-recorded message, I made sure to include the fact that others will be seeking this contract as well. The offer has an expiration date, as you and I will be in a hurry to have this rabble extradited back to Dorthal Sector as expediently as possible. Mauve will accept the bounty, I assure you. And if she doesn’t, we’ll take the next best bid.”

“Sir, are you sure this is sanctioned? I mean, this sounds like you want to assume the role of a vigilante. That’s not upholding the law, it’s acting as if you’re above it.”

“I understand your concern, Warrant Officer Barsol. Nevertheless, justice must prevail, and these outlaws must be brought to face it.” Still strutting about the small chamber, Captain O’Ryan circled behind Barsol's chair and grasped the back of it with both hands. "Besides, given your recent circumvention of protocol, I hardly think you have grounds to lecture anyone on acting above the law. Rest assured Barsol, I would not be considering such drastic action were it not of utmost import.

"Remember our creed, Warrant Officer: 'To defend the poor and fatherless, to do justice to the afflicted and needy, and to deliver the innocent from the hand of the wicked.' That is a concept not bound by jurisdiction or borders."

With a deep sigh, Barsol inquired, "Sir, if these fugitives are as hazardous to the galaxy as you claim, why were they not under a closer watch when they were on the Octagon? Who are they?"

Leaning over the back of the chair, so close that Barsol could feel his breath, Captain O'Ryan dramatically whispered, "Vampyrials, Warrant Officer Barsol. Vampyrials."

Chapter 12

Evening sounds from the Ranjeman jungle filtered through the open airlock bulkhead at the aft of the Explorer 2000. Amidst hoots and howls came the occasional public announcement from the traffic tower. Schiff tried to complete her work while keeping a watchful eye on the outside spaceport. Meanwhile, the young Vampyrial monarchs sorted and cleaned in silence, Mara due to moodiness, Jym due to fatigue from his adventures in the temple.

After several minutes of this uncommunicativeness, the princess at last broke the silence with a quiet question. "What happened at the temple? Captain Nado didn't tell us everything, did he?"

"Why do you say that?" asked Jym.

"Because I could sense that he wasn't being entirely honest," Mara replied bitterly. "When retelling the part about the strategy challenge, he left out details. He just said that Lord Hex and Cylor won the competition, but he never said how."

"Why didn't you bring this up before?" Jym wanted to know. "Why ask me and not Captain Nado?"

"He won't give me a straight answer," she stated. "But you will. And I'll know if you're lying too."

The prince rolled his eyes. "Fine. I fell through a trapdoor into a subsection of the chamber under the magnetic flooring. While I was down there, Cylor also fell through another trapdoor. We met up, and I tried to make friends. I thought I could help him."

"What would make you think that's a good idea?" his sister scolded. "Didn't you learn your lesson after what happened with Boxie?"

"I had a hunch that Cylor was just a kid like us." Jym turned his back, his frustration rising. "It seemed like he was in pain and wanted help. So, that's what I tried to do. Do you have a problem with me trying to help people?"

"It isn't that," chided Mara. "I've told you, you're too trusting. You can't go around opening yourself up to everyone we meet! It leaves us vulnerable, and now hopefully you can see for yourself how it has jeopardized our mission to find Mom and Dad. Seriously, I don't know what possesses you to do these things."

"I just got this vibe from him," Jym tried to explain. "You know, a feeling. A feeling that he was in trouble. I figured you of all people would understand that."

"A vibe?" Mara spat, with a fierce gleam in her eyes. "No, you don't get vibes. You don't get 'feelings' or 'hunches' or anything else. That's me! I get the vibes and the feelings and the hunches. That's my thing, not yours! It's your job to use your powers to knock anyone who tries to get in our way, silly!" Her voice rose more and more in intensity as her rant persisted. "We've been over this and over this! This is why I told you back when we were staying with Uncle that it's my job to decide who we talk to and how much we say. You can say 'you're not my mom' to me all you want, but the fact of the matter is someone has to look out for you, because you prove time and again that you can't look after yourself, and you certainly can't be trusted with deciding with whom we ought to interact!"

"At least I try!" Jym fired back. "I try to make friends, I try to be kindhearted, I try to be a good person. I'm trying to show the people of this galaxy that we aren't the bad guys! That we want to help, and not just blast them with our powers every chance we get."

"Are you saying I'm not a good person?" The perturbed princess glared hard. "I am a good person. I'm not a monster!"

"Phooey," her brother snorted. "If it hadn't been for my willingness to talk to the crew when we first met, we wouldn't even be here."

"We shouldn't be here! We're putting their lives in danger every day that we stay aboard!"

"Do you really think we can do this by ourselves?"

Princess Mara's breathing became shallow and quick. "We are only making them more of a target. And Nado is making you even more trusting than you were before. Face it Jym, your naivete cost us a valuable piece of information related to finding our parents!"

"You say I'm too trusting?" the prince argued. "What about you? All you trust in are your own powers, nothing else. If it weren't for me, we wouldn't be anywhere close to figuring out where our parents are. Face it Mara, if we listened only to you, we'd never find them. And it would be all your fault!"

"SHUT UP!!" screamed Mara, a burst of energy escaping from her tiny body. The blast shook the entire starship, launching Prince Jym across the room. Crates and boxes were toppled, supplies spilled onto the honeycombed flooring, even the Puddle Jumper shifted a couple of meters. Frightened by her own display, Mara tumbled backward and tripped. She picked herself up, turned around, and sprinted from the bay into the cool darkness of night.

Above, on board the bridge, Commander Kel could hear the princess' screech, though it was muffled to the point that she couldn't understand the exact words. She too felt the spacecraft quake and shiver, nearly losing her balance. Shooting a glance at Captain Nado, Kel could see that he'd had to reach out with all four arms to keep from toppling. They shared a concerned glance between them, then the pair hurried from the command center and shimmied down into the cargo bay. The two arrived in time to observe Schiff assisting Prince Jym by removing him from a pile of debris. Shortly thereafter, they were all joined by Dr. Rox and Red, who surveyed the carnage of the supplies strewn about the area.

A quick perusal of the bay left one burning question in Kel's mind. "Where is Mara?"

Following Schiff's indication, everyone peered out the airlock door. Captain Nado clearly didn't want to waste any time as he ordered, "Fan out and search. Red, activate your scanners."

"Acknowledged, Captain," replied Red.

"We've got to find her."

Looming in the forward viewport of the Drakewing was the planet Urkasak, homeworld of the Gnarfs. Bright blue oceans to the north and south almost perfectly framed the halo of green that ringed the equator. Though the globe was indeed beautiful, the pilot of the small spacecraft knew all too well that its inhabitants were less so. Further, it appeared that the splendor of Urkasak's nature was marred by an enormous brown blotch, around which even the clouds of the upper atmosphere bubbled and swirled like a boiling stew. It was an odd sight to be sure, but not something that the enigmatic entity who piloted the craft was unable to identify.

Steering his Drakewing closer to the muddy spot on the planet's façade, the mysterious man studied it closer. Yes, it was indeed the result of an orbital laser. The aftereffects were unmistakable. A strange sense of both pride and trepidation now entered his mind. If his master's memories served correctly, he had once toyed with the idea of such a formidable technology, but it had proven to be more of a long-term project than intended. Too many extra generators were needed to power the weapon, requiring a spacecraft of such colossal construction that he never had the resources to build.

Of course, that meant someone else had completed the task. Someone out there in the void had perfected the design of a dreadnought and had outfitted it with one of the most devastating technological arsenals ever dreamt about. Regardless, the strength of the Vampyrial people was not to be trifled with, no matter what weaponry anyone might boast. Right now, the mission of finding the children was of singular importance.

For the time being, the man veered toward the surface of Urkasak. He had been able to sense the dark energy traces left behind by the girl's usage of her powers and confirm that they must have come to this planet at some point. Hopefully, the Gnarfs would yield more answers in his quest...

Long shadows danced across the surplus of stacked up crates and totes scattered across the treetop spaceport. Light shone from humongous jar-shaped fixtures that appeared to be filled with luminous insectoids that glowed a brilliant yellow. These were hung from low hanging branches all around the suspended structures, creating the shadows in which Princess Mara now hid. Her initial dead sprint from the Explorer had slowly devolved into a jog, then a trot, down to a brisk walk, and now a dejected plod as she moved from one dark hiding place to the next.

Discovering a small container that acted nicely as a seat, the princess plopped onto it roughly, resting her elbows on her knees and her head in her hands. For a while, she simply stared off into the black silhouetted forests ahead of her, taking in the sights and sounds of the wildlife within. Cawing and croaking could be heard, but as the minutes passed and the night waxed on, the cacophony gradually subsided.

Other sounds also surrounded the little Vampyrial girl. There were dock workers, busily hefting and hauling the various supplies that had been heaped into hastily sorted piles. Periodically, the public announcement system blared, most often in the Ranjeman language, a hissing, purring type of speech with which Mara was entirely unfamiliar. After what seemed like an eternity, another noise caught the girl's attention and caused her to jolt a bit.

"Hey kiddo!" Schiff's chipper tones rang out. "Everyone's out looking for you. What are you doing out here all alone?"

Mara heaved a heavy sigh. "I was attempting to run away."

"Why?" the nimble shapeshifter questioned.

"Because I don't belong with you guys."

"What makes you think that?"

"You saw what just happened!"

Schiff shrugged. "Eh, you had an emotional outburst. Everyone gets angry and lashes out from time to time."

"Yeah, but if it happens to me, I apparently turn things upside-down..." Mara trailed off, leaving her face buried in her palms.

"Sometimes rage gets the better of you," said Schiff, "no matter how controlled you try to be."

"If I let that happen, too many people could get hurt," retorted the princess. "You saw what I did to my own brother."

With compassion and kindness practically etched on her face, Schiff leaned down and lifted Mara's downtrodden countenance. "It was an accident. Give yourself some grace."

"I can't."

"Why not?"

This time, the princess took her time to respond. "Because Jym was right. As much as I may want to deny it, as badly as I wish for it not to be true, I can't escape our grandfather's legacy. He was a monster..." Princess Mara finally raised her gaze to meet Schiff's with tears streaming down her cheeks, "...and so am I."

"Mara," declared Schiff, firmly yet with gentility, "you can't let someone else's actions dictate who you are. I've seen the merit of your own action. Actions that tell me that you choose to be a kind, caring, loving, protective person. Those are not the traits of a monster."

Through tears now turned joyful, Princess Mara offered Schiff a trembling, yet pleasant, expression. She then proceeded to leap from her spot and throw her arms around Schiff's waist in a firm hug. Giving her own soft smile, Schiff happily returned the sentiment, holding the little princess tightly. For several seconds they simply stood in a warm embrace, Mara's face pressed against Schiff's shoulder. The evening air had begun to turn cold, but they held each other, blocking the chilly breeze.

After they had stood in silence for a while, Schiff finally remarked, "We'd better go and find the rest of the crew and get back to the Explorer."

"Not so fast," growled a nearby shadow. Whirling to look, both girls could perceive something odd about the menacing shade. It slithered and writhed, taking shape bit by bit until it rose into a sleek and fit form. Bearing long claws, pointed ears, and eyes like yellow orbs that glowed faintly in the dark, the creature sported a sinister visage. The being stepped forward into the light, revealing itself to be a Ranjeman in a black leather jerkin that draped to its knees.

A gold pauldron fashioned like a feathered wing gleamed upon his right shoulder, while a composite longbow fitted with a computerized targeting system was slung over his left.

"Who are you?" Princess Mara queried.

"Justiciar," whispered Schiff. "An Ascendant Justiciar at that."

"I thought you might be members of the Explorer crew," the justiciar snarled. "I only had to wait a minute or so to confirm."

"What do you want?" Schiff demanded.

"It was reported to us by the estimable Lord Hex that your crewmates were responsible for the death of one of the Great Temple guardians," informed the Ranjeman. "I have a whole posse poised to hunt every one of you down. We will have justice."

"Huh," Schiff nervously chuckled. "Commander Kel was right. How's that for calling them?"

A horrible, guttural yowl exploded from the justiciar's fanged maw as he jaunted toward the girls, claws outstretched! In a moment of fright and horrification, Schiff stiffened her body, and a flash of light enveloped her and Mara. Instantaneously, they were transported from the path of the deadly deemster and reappeared several meters away. Righting herself quickly and regaining her bearings, Princess Mara stretched out her hand in the justiciar's vicinity, readying her dark energy mastery.

"Not now, Mara!" shouted Schiff, lowering the princess' outstretched arm. "I can't have you falling unconscious. Let's just get back to the ship!"

Darting back in the direction from which they had both come, they spotted a pair of black-clad Ranjemans patrolling the catwalk.

Having heard the commotion of their compatriot, these two joined the hunt by retrieving their own longbows and sprinting pell-mell after their prey.

"Yeesh!" Schiff shrieked, yanking the princess by the arm in a new heading. They broke to the left, aiming for a secondary catwalk that wound around an enormous tree trunk, eventually winding back to their previous path. Whistling arrows whipped past their heads, barely missing by only a few millimeters. Electrified tips stuck fast in the bark of the massive foliage, betraying their functionality with popping and crackling.

Daring a glance over her shoulder, Schiff saw all three of their pursuers rapidly overtaking them. The Ascendant Justiciar hissed orders at the other two, who quickly chattered back a response. Their silver pauldrons flashed every time they ran underneath the lighting jars, giving the illusion that they themselves were electrified. Thinking quickly, Schiff grabbed a low hanging branch and pulled, bending it backward as she fled. When the limb was at its highest tension, she released and let it swing vehemently back towards the justiciars. Though they all managed to dodge her rather telegraphed attack, it did slow them down for a few seconds. This gave her and the princess an opportunity to create some additional distance from their harrowing hunters.

"Can't you blink us again?" asked Mara, huffing and puffing as they ran.

"Instinctively, it works," Schiff moaned, "but if I try and make it happen, it doesn't! Head through there!"

Ahead of them, the catwalk on which Mara and Schiff were making their escape entered an arboreal tunnel. Nearly out of breath, the duo dashed inside. As the justiciars raced in after them, the two subordinate vigilantes each clambered up the sides of the passageway, climbing to the apex. As they neared the end of the verdurous corridor, another figure stepped into their path.

"What now?" groaned Schiff.

At that exact moment, the justiciars pounced from the ceiling and attempted to land atop the fleeing girls, while their leader readied a shot with his composite bow. Now watching behind, neither Princess Mara nor Schiff were paying attention to the individual in front of them. Thankfully, a vocalization alerted them, and they twirled their faces forward in time to see a familiar, and very welcome, sight. "Greetings." It was H-8-RED! "Duck, please."

With extreme rapidity and ease, Red laid hold of the two girls and swept them out of the way. It followed this by twisting its arms around and delivering a powerhouse punch to the gut of each Ranjeman. A quick dodge to the right and Red swiftly sidestepped the Ascendant's incoming arrow, simultaneously reaching across its body and catching the projectile with its right hand. Using its momentum to carry itself into a spin, Red whirled in a complete circuit, twirling the arrow in its fingers with fine finesse. At the end of its rotation, the robot raised its right hand, having repositioned the arrow to be thrown like a spear. A precise flip of its wrist sent the electrified missile straight back to its origin, thudding into the Ascendant's left shoulder with a thunk! Shortly thereafter, the arrow began to sizzle as blue streaks of intermittent light arced across the justiciar leader's body.

"Logic dictates we should retreat to the Explorer," informed Red. "This unit will contact the officers and report our position."

"Works for me!" exclaimed Schiff. "There are probably more of these guys on the way."

Scooping the shapeshifter and the princess onto its shoulders, Red turned and hightailed it, following the path from which it had come. This way wrapped around the spaceport a bit longer than the first direction the girls had tried to run in, but it eventually led them to the landing pad of the Explorer 2000. While they continued their escape, Red radioed ahead via its built-in communicator to regroup the remainder of the crew at the bulkhead ramp.

Mara expected to see the starship much as she had left it, but to her dismay this was not the case. There were no less than a half dozen Ranjeman justiciars skirmishing with her friends, with at least four more prowling the outskirts of the fray. One of them, armed with a bone dagger and a riot shield, charged Captain Nado. The burly Zennian caught his attacker by the shield arm, slung the beast over his head, and slammed him onto the flooring. In one swift motion, Nado had disarmed his opponent of his shield and used it to bash another incoming foe!

Meanwhile, Commander Kel evaded a claw swipe to the chest, then batted that Ranjeman's arm aside. She proceeded to land a shot to her adversary's ribcage and was turning to run when the justiciar grabbed her fist and held it fast. A second attacker galloped on all fours at the commander, closing in with tremendous speed. Acting quickly, Kel leaned backward just enough to swing her right foot up, extending it forcefully into her grappler's abdomen. He let go and tumbled over, but the galloper was still on the move. Without losing her stride, Commander Kel swung her right foot back, catching the second Ranjeman on the jaw with a mule kick.

Suddenly, more arrows sang through the night air as the Ascendant and his two sidekicks arrived. With a long-legged gait, Red reached the aft of their spacecraft and dropped off Mara and Schiff.

It retrieved its trusty plasma carbine from the cargo bay and uttered, "Activating assassination protocols," before lining up a shot.

As if she had supernatural hearing, Commander Kel called out, "Red! No assassinations! Non-lethal attacks only! I don't want more Ranjeman deaths on our heads!"

"Very well," answered the malcontent machine, a hint of mordant melancholy in its tone. "Deactivating assassination protocols. Activating hand-to-hand programs."

The thing then sped from the cargo bay into the fight, bowling over three justiciars along the way. It blocked a roundhouse kick from one Ranjeman, catching her leg. Using this captured foe as a blunt weapon, Red swung her to the left into two more oncoming fighters. Unfortunately, even more were creeping toward them, so Schiff mustered all her courage and blinked outside the Explorer. She first grabbed onto Captain Nado and Commander Kel, teleporting them to the safety of the cargo bay. A second blink had Red aboard, while the justiciars slunk ever closer.

Then, a motorized roaring rang out in the bay as Prince Jym stepped forward, wielding his chainsaw sword! He sliced three incoming arrows from the air, making a heroic stand at the top of the airlock ramp. Revving the chainsaw a couple more times, he waved his blade back and forth, as if daring one of the justiciars to advance.

"Red, get us off the ground," ordered Nado.

"Acknowledged, Captain." The robot briskly whirled and scrambled up to the bridge.

Their standoff deadlocked, the justiciars had no choice but to let the Explorer 2000 lift off slowly. The heat from the thrusters caused the Ranjemans to fall back, allowing Captain Nado to close the airlock doors. Breathing hard, everyone raced to the upper deck, assuming their usual posts.

As they hurried, Schiff said to Kel, "No idea how you knew, but it looks like you called it."

"Wish I hadn't," panted the commander, rolling her eyes. "I guess Graylon's tactics are just too predictable..."

Once everyone was seated, Nado gave the command. "Red, get us out of here."

Rumbling and jolting, the Explorer 2000 climbed through the Ranjeman atmosphere, clearing the night clouds and reaching open space, where the fleet of warships still roamed. Before they had a chance for respite, Red made an announcement. "Captain, we are receiving a hail."

"Patch it through."

The radio speakers crackled, and a woman's garbled, mewing voice spewed forth. "This is Ascendant Ki'Vet. Your vessel is to be grounded immediately, and you will all face Ranjeman justice for the death of Guardian Li'Nora!"

Through the viewport they all saw several of the Ranjeman spacecraft begin to shift in order to block the Explorer's escape. Having deactivated the radio transmitter, Captain Nado started computing targeting data on his console. After a few moments, he turned to face the rest of the bridge crew.

"Schiff, man the guns!" bellowed the captain.

"Are you nuts?" Kel quipped. "We can't run a blockade! Those are warships, and we're in an Explorer class. We'll be ripped to pieces!"

Undeterred, the courageous captain inquired, "Red, can we pull off the 'shield bounce' maneuver now that the hull breach is repaired?"

"Performing calculations," answered their automaton pilot. After a couple seconds of silence, it reported, "That would be ill advised, Captain. That maneuver works well against a single target. The Ranjeman fleet is too vast and numerous for such an endeavor."

"Blast!" Captain Nado stared out the forward viewport with sheer determination. "Then I guess we'll have to do this the old-fashioned way. Schiff, aim two ticks left and three ticks upward. Lay down cover fire!"

"Whee!" the cheery shapeshifter squealed, letting a beam of white-hot energy loose on the closest warship. The shot knocked the enemy craft out of its orbit, sending it reeling end over end into space. Additional Ranjeman spacecraft utilized their air jets to swivel towards the Explorer, but Captain Nado's expert gunning kept them at bay. After only a couple more volleys with the laser turrets, he and Schiff had opened a hole.

"Commander Kel, set our course for Khardan space," the captain instructed. "I'd like to be out of range of planetary or orbital radar."

"Aye, Captain," replied the commander dutifully.

Nado addressed the robot next, narrowing his eyes and grinning slyly. "Red, punch it!"

Streaming a silvery spray, the Explorer's thrusters emitted a burst of energy, causing the small starship to surge further into the vast arena of the expanse around them. Multiple Ranjeman vessels zipped past as the Explorer 2000 rushed beyond them, leaving the justiciar hunters far behind.

Once the Explorer had reached safe warp distance, Nado gave the command. "Red, activate the warp drive!"

Down below, in the belly of the little starship, the Casimir warp drive hummed and thrummed. For the moment, it seemed to be doing its job. Unbeknownst to the crew, however, it also spluttered and sparked, a popping and hissing exuding from deep within…

Chapter 13

Warping into existence just outside the orbital range of Khardan, the Explorer 2000 arrived in the blink of an eye. Breathing a sigh of relief and leaning back in her chair, Commander Kel took a moment to unwind after their stressful flight from Ranjeman. Hopefully, they'd never need to return to that verdant world, otherwise they'd likely be arrested and skinned, and have their pelts hung on display.

Kel heard Schiff chittering, "What's the plan, Cap?"

"For the time being, we're not in radar range," answered the captain, sounding invigorated by their most recent misadventure. "That means we can utilize the warp decelerator to slip past Graylon's sensors, and anyone else who might be searching for us. Provided Princess Mara is willing and able to use her dark energy manipulation like last time."

"Not a problem!" the girl called out from the galley, evidently able to overhear the conversation.

"Then it's settled!" proclaimed Captain Nado.

"Are you sure Graylon is even here?" Schiff wondered.

Staring out the viewport into the stars beyond, the captain took a resolute stance and clasped both sets of hands behind his back. "He knows what we're after, and he is relentless. Am I sure he's here?" He turned back toward the crew. "I am most certain of it."

It was eerily quiet on the bridge of the dreadnought, which orbited Khardan like a drifting blimp. Anyone unfamiliar with the vessel might initially presume the mammoth craft to be a spiky, black cloud that had escaped the upper atmosphere of the planet below. On board, Zuugs' union workers buzzed about, continuing to make repairs while H-7 overseers kept a constant vigil, themselves being monitored by H-7-PRIME. Cylor stayed busy on the bridge, manning the radar and scanning for any sign of the Explorer.

Standing as still as a statue, Lord Hex monitored the entire process from his command deck that overlooked the whole control center. All four of his meaty mitts gripped the railing that encircled his observation post. With cape and cowl once again concealing his features, Hex's menacing aura seemed to fill the whole chamber.

Dutifully keeping an eye on the radar consoles, Cylor asked, "Father, are you sure the Explorer crew will come here? We defeated them rather soundly on Ranjeman."

"I do not appreciate being questioned, boy." Hex's response caught Cylor off guard as it reverberated throughout the room. "Tell me, son, do you know what a dribb is?" The boy shook his head to answer. Hex continued, "A dribb is a little predatory animal on

Zen I that scavenges for small prey. They also have a propensity for stealing bright objects for their dens. If you want to trap one, you hide something shiny in a long, thin tube tethered to the ground. The dribb will attempt to grab the object, but by forming a fist, it ensnares its own appendage in the tubing." Hex paused momentarily to ensure Cylor was comprehending. The young man was listening intently, so he went on. "When it comes to causes he assumes are righteous, my brother is like a dribb with a shiny object. Once he has it, he refuses to let go, and therein lies his weakness. Am I sure he will come?" The malicious marquis stood erect, clasping both sets of hands behind his back as he gazed out the forward viewport intensely. "I am most certain of it."

Within about fifteen minutes, Captain Nado had assembled his crew into their positions for the warp deceleration maneuver. Having left Kel, Schiff, and Red in command of the bridge, he himself, along with Dr. Rox, took up posts in the cargo bay to ensure Mara's safety. Buckled in as best as they could manage, they'd decided to use supply totes as seating and ratchet straps as seatbelts. They made sure Princess Mara was also secured at the entrance to the engine room where she had greatest control over the dark energy manipulator inside the warp drive. As backup, Prince Jym was belted down close to his sister.

"Everyone's in place," the captain reported into his lapel communicator. "Commander Kel, set our course. Red, ready the deceleration device. Standby to activate the warp drive."

"Aye, Captain," replied Kel. "Course is set."

"Acknowledged," the robot confirmed. "Deceleration device is ready."

Captain Nado nodded to the kids, who responded back with nods of their own. With their permission having been granted, the brave Zennian gave the order. "Red, activate the warp drive!"

Extending their fingertips, both children could clearly feel the energy vibrating within the vessel. Ever watchful, Nado and Rox kept their respective gazes locked on the young Vampyrials. They could tell when Mara had to intervene and assist the decelerator as her body stiffened and her face twisted into a wincing grimace. Jym reached out and gently took her hand, which appeared to calm the princess. The captain and doctor were both able to observe Jym taking on Mara's pained expression as he resolvedly held her hand.

Dr. Rox stole a glance at Nado. "Did he just do what I think he just did?"

"He absorbed her pain," said an astounded Captain Nado.

Mercifully, the process was finished in a few seconds. "It's over," whispered Princess Mara. Her brother only gave a tight smile as a reply.

Almost simultaneously, Red's mechanical tones rang through the captain's communicator. "Captain, we have breached the planet's atmosphere through warp. Deceleration is complete."

"Commander Kel," said Nado, "find us a vector and a berth. Let's head for the same outpost spaceport as our last visit. At least we know that area. Maybe that barkeep will have some information we can use."

"Um," Kel's voice trilled back, "Captain, do you remember how well that went for us last time? How about we let Schiff do her thing like on Ranjeman?"

"I did a thing?" they heard Schiff say in the background.

"You shifted into a Ranjeman and dug up info on the Kathnarii data drive," answered an exasperated Kel.

"Oh, yeah! I did do that! But I don't think a Ranjeman would fit in too well on the Kriton homeworld."

An audible pop! could be heard through both the communicator and the cargo hatch as Kel smacked her own forehead. "Schiff, you would shift into Kriton form."

"Oh...right, got it!"

Displaying a broad grin, Captain Nado laughed, "Let's just get to the spaceport landing pad and go from there."

A few minutes later they were all taking in a familiar sight. The sparse port was still just as dusty, dirty, and dingy as ever, but at least the wreckage from their previous stopover had been cleared away. There was no evidence remaining from their battle with Gnash and his gang. Signaling for the rest of the crew to follow him, Captain Nado started for the scant grouping of buildings that formed the port town.

Ensconced in the crags and foothills of a rocky mountain range, the tiny town enjoyed the warm desert sun in the daytime, and was shielded from the cold, barren winds of the night. Everyone recognized the domed structures with long staircases inside that gave way to massive underground burrows in which the Kritons lived. Commander Kel watched the hunter's lodge where she'd exchanged blows with Schlaar and Shtrepp with a wary eye. She also caught that Captain

Nado was giving no small amount of attention to the entrance of the sizable superstore where he had been assaulted.

As they neared the center of town, Schiff spoke up. "Are we not concerned that Graylon might be waiting for us?"

"If he was, I think we'd have heard from him by now," replied Nado. "He's the gloating type. On top of that, if he knew we were here, he'd have Klensh and company attacking us. I think the kids with the decelerator trick gave him the slip."

"Let's hope so," interjected the commander. "Otherwise, we're walking into another trap."

"Fair point," agreed the captain. "Red, Dr. Rox, how about you take the kids back to the Explorer while Schiff, Kel, and I have a look around."

"We want to help," said Mara.

"Yeah, I mean, it's our parents we're looking for," added Jym.

Captain Nado knelt to one knee to get on eye level with the two young monarchs. "I get that. I just want to be sure you guys get the chance to find them. Last time, we had to flee from a nasty gang of mercs and crooks. I don't want you to be hurt."

"We'll hunker down while they snoop around," Dr. Rox joined in. "Once they know where to go, we can go together."

"And this time," Kel reiterated, "we all go. No one left behind, no one diving into danger by themselves. Understood?"

With a good-natured roll of the eyes, Nado jested, "Yes, mother."

"I'm serious." The commander frowned at him. "You're not expendable. Or invincible."

Mustering a bit more solemnity, the captain acquiesced. "Okay, okay. Understood, Commander."

Though somewhat disgruntled, the kids agreed and walked back to the Explorer with Rox and Red. After watching them safely board their vessel, Captain Nado rolled all of his shoulders while Commander Kel cracked her knuckles. Schiff tilted her head to either side, popping her neck. She proceeded to throw a few mock punches in the air, huffing sharply with each swing of her fists. It was only then that she noticed Nado and Kel staring.

"I thought we were getting tough," the sheepish shapeshifter muttered.

Nado smiled. "We were. Come on, let's go."

Navigating around the little swirling dust devils and the bouncing tumbleweeds, the trio marched into town. To their left, on the northern edge of the settlement, was the sandy old cantina they'd ducked into on their previous trip to Khardan. Tromping down the staircase like he owned the joint, Captain Nado entered the main room of the establishment. Kel could tell he was about to announce their need for assistance, so she halted him before he had the opportunity to oust himself.

"Captain," she quickly blurted, "how about we have a look around, see if there are any familiar…uh, friendly…faces in the crowd." It was only an attempt to keep the big Zennian from blaring their arrival as he had done prior, and seemed to have worked for the time being.

"Not a bad idea, Commander." Nado surveyed the saloon. Kel was just preparing to offer another suggestion when the captain loudly stated, "Oh, look! There are two friendly faces over there!"

Kel was stunned. "Wait, seriously?"

"Over there. It's Schlaar and Shtrepp!" Nado replied, hurrying in their direction. He brazenly snatched an unused chair from another table nearby as he approached, thumping it at the table of their Kriton allies. "Fancy seeing the two of you here," Captain Nado happily proclaimed. "What are the odds of us running into each other again?"

Also shocked, Schlaar could only stammer, "Pleashe, don't ever bring up thoshe oddsss with me. . ."

"You're either very lucky," said Shtrepp, "or very unlucky, depending on the sssituation."

"I see the two of you made it off Vortex safely," the captain noted. "What about Buddy? Is he safe as well?"

"After you left, neither Vin nor Klensh were interesssted in chasssing ush." Shtrepp shrugged and cocked her head to one side. "But what are you doing back on Khardan? You should be laying low from Vin and the Gnarfsss."

Joining them at the table, Commander Kel and Schiff also stole a couple of vacant stools to add to the gaggle. Kel answered, "I know, but we're on the hunt for the kids' parents. Our only lead is Kathnarii Base. We're here to see if we can find the data drive of the last Kriton Kathnarii Sage. Is there any chance that you two know anything about the legend?"

Both Kritons exchanged a look, then Shtrepp responded, "Many of our people know a little of the hissstory. The broodlingsss of the Na'Kosh clan now live in the mountainsss of Ghishnik and have sssworn off the bloodthirsssty waysss of their forerunnersss."

"They live quiet livesss," Schlaar informed, now picking up the tale. "We can give you directionsss to their village where you can find the clan chieftain. He can likely tell you more."

"You won't go with us?" queried Schiff.

"We cannot," Shtrepp responded. "We have...presssssing mattersss that musht be handled here."

"Sssorry," shrugged Schlaar. "That'sss really all we can do for you."

"You've done more than enough," said Kel. "Thank you for all your help. Besides, Lord Hex is also after these data drives, and we wouldn't want you to get in trouble with him."

The Kriton pair looked surprised. Schlaar was the first to reply. "Lord Hex ish a powerful enemy. I am torn, for I wish we could help you, but am alssso glad that we will not be confronting such a great foe."

"But we do wish you the besht of luck," his female compatriot mentioned. "You should hurry. You do not want to be wandering in the mountainsss after nightfall."

"You'll need thessse," hissed Schlaar. The burly Kriton fellow indicated for Commander Kel to start writing. After she had produced a diminutive data-pad and stylus, he had her jot some coordinates down. "Go here, and you'll find what you need."

"Again, dear friends, we thank you for everything you've done," said Captain Nado. "Looks like we have a trek ahead of us. We'll bid you a fond farewell, and I hope the odds of seeing you once more remain unchanged."

Everyone smiled and chuckled a little at the captain's quip, then the Explorer crew members rose to leave. As they prepared to depart, Schiff gave one last parting wave to the Kriton duo, then deftly skipped up the stairs after Nado and Kel. There was no need to linger in this simple spaceport town, so they made a beeline for their spacecraft, the coordinates from Schlaar prepped to guide the way to the final Kathnarii drive.

Meanwhile, back inside the cantina, the two scaly-skinned former enforcers finished sipping their beverages quietly. With downcast countenance, both stared at the bottom of their respective glasses with dismay. As they did so, the curtain at the rear of the barroom was swept aside by a cloaked figure that slunk to their table. A brown hood atop the robe obscured the person's face, but his unambiguous albino snout stuck out from underneath.

"Well done," the individual congratulated in a hoarse, gravelly voice, speaking in the Kriton language. "They'll be right where I want them now."

"We did as you demanded, Klensh," Shtrepp growled, also speaking the native tongue. "Now what about our hatchlings? You will leave them be, yes?"

Klensh sneered from within his cowl, showing his slimy fangs. "As you have performed properly in your task, I will not report your unholy union to the kingpins. In the meantime, you are to have no further communication with the Explorer 2000, am I understood?" The other Kritons nodded to the affirmative. Klensh continued to flap his jaws. "Good. See to it that you don't forget. If I find out you have violated this oath, I will not hesitate. Either I or one of my associates will notify the kingpins."

With that, Klensh backed away, slithering behind the curtain once again to rejoin his gruesome gang. The tech wizard Pyrian of the group voiced a question. "Seems the Explorer made it planet-side. Are you ready to radio Lord Hex?"

"No," grumbled their Kriton leader. "I am done being bossssssed around by hish high and mighty lordship. Today, we hunt the Explorer oursssselvesss."

"Couldn't we at least have given them false information?"

"They're too sssmart to accept anything but the truth," snapped Klensh. "And Schlaar and Shtrepp are too dumb to tell a convincing lie. Thish wash the only way. Now we gather our gear and prep for the fight we've been anticipating. No more holding back, no more avoiding harming the captain or the kidsss. Thish time, we make them all bleed!"

Pacing his raised deck, Lord Hex grew ever more impatient with each passing minute. They should be here by now. Perhaps his ruse with the justiciars on Ranjeman was too much for his brother to handle. Did he make a mistake? Had he given them more than they could withstand?

Or had the Explorer crew survived, as he expected they would, and somehow slipped past him? What if Klensh had decided to keep their arrival a secret from him? A million questions pumped through Graylon's skull, each opening the door to yet another.

He had to silence these doubts. "Cylor," Hex commanded, "set a course for Ranjeman. We need to make sure that my plan succeeded. The justiciars were only meant to slow Burnay down. I don't want him captured by those barbarians."

"Are you certain, Father?" asked the boy. "The prince had much strength stored within. If his sister is similar, they would be more than a match for the savages. If we leave now, we run the risk that they will sneak past you, as you have feared – "

"Do not imply that I fear anything!" roared the marquis, leaning over the railing with bombastic ire. "And do not make me say this again. Never question me. To Ranjeman, NOW!!"

Quietly and demurely, Cylor obeyed his father's wrathful mandate. Following a few taps on the varied keyboards that surrounded the young man, the dreadnought creaked and groaned as it shifted in space. Soon thereafter, the prow was angled toward the correct heading, and the colossal craft slowly began to become wrapped in an enormous warp bubble.

In a flash, the gigantic vessel blinked out of view. All the while, the tension stayed thick between father and son on the bridge. Not daring to look Lord Hex in the eye, Cylor maintained focus on the dreadnought's controls, unsure what he had done wrong.

Several hours passed between the conversation at the saloon and the flight to the Ghishnik mountains. Rather than trying to cram everyone inside the Puddle Jumper, the captain and commander instead elected to fly the Explorer itself across the barren dunes to the location provided by Schlaar. It was simple enough to inform the traffic controllers of their destination and obtain clearance for liftoff. They would use up a bit more fuel by flying the Explorer inside the atmosphere like a passenger shuttle, but it was easier than any other option.

Upon arrival, there were many open plateaus on the stony ridges, but none of them were within close proximity to the Na'Kosh village. No matter where they landed, there would undoubtedly be a rocky hike. Kel and Red worked to find the best locale and brought the Explorer to rest on a mostly level peak.

A few minutes later, the commander was digging through supplies in the cargo bay, hoping to find something that they could employ to assist in the climb across the ridgeline. Tossing things around inside one container, she grumped, "Of all the items he could have wasted money on, why didn't he buy anything that would be usable for this?"

"I did," the captain's booming voice announced. "Ta-da!"

Startled, Commander Kel jolted upright, to see Captain Nado holding several sets of climber's gear in his four hefty hands. "Where were you keeping those?" the commander interrogated.

Now he looked embarrassed. "I didn't want you to think I had wasted money, so I hid all of it in my quarters. . ."

Offering a wry smile, Kel chuckled, "Definitely not a waste. Come on, let's get geared up and get started on this trek."

Not long after, every single one of them was bedecked in an array of straps, ropes, belts, clips, and cleats. After ensuring the Explorer was secured for their absence, Captain Nado led the expedition up the face of the rugged ridges. Slowly, bit by bit, hour after hour, they cautiously climbed the great mountain, maintaining an easterly aim. Constantly on the lookout for safe passages and hewn trails, the captain and commander eventually got the entire group to their destination.

Dusk was just beginning to settle when they breached the final peak, the bright sun of Khardan turning a deep orange and sending streaks of purple across the desert sky. Nestled in the escarpments below they could make out a ring of scattered domes with a large burn pit at the heart. On the far eastern end of the community sat a slightly bigger stone and mud yurt, probably that of the village leader.

An ocean of bright stars lighting the indigo sky heralded the fall of night, causing the hikers to activate their flashlights. In a few minutes, they had at last entered the diminutive settlement. The Kritons here were all dressed in simple muslin and canvas outfits, donning heavy leather coats as the evening winds turned cold. A bonfire was lit in the huge firepit by some folk, while others hustled away upon seeing the intruders. They returned shortly, with two individuals who were obviously the heads of the tribe.

One was bedizened in an elaborate headdress made of bone and hide, while the other, who was younger and significantly larger, wore armor fashioned from enormous animal skulls and ribs. The elder was first to speak. "I am Curik, elder and clan patron of the Na'Kosh. What bringsss outsssiderssss to our landssss?"

“Ssspeak before we rend you in half,” threatened the big brute, brandishing a plasma rifle in one massive claw and a spiky spine sword in the other.

“We are here on peaceful terms,” Captain Nado began, but was not allowed to finish his thought.

“Many before you have sssaid the sssame,” growled the gargantuan Kriton guard. “What makesss you any different?”

“We’re only here to ask about the wisdom of the Kathnarii,” Commander Kel offered, trying to diffuse the escalating situation. Unfortunately, she didn’t seem to help much.

“We’ve heard that before too,” the well-armed watchman retorted. “Give me a reassson not to blasht the lot of you into oblivion!” He grinned a toothy smirk. “Better yet, give me a reassson to do it.”

“Easssy, Mukeh,” the old one quelled his young aide. “Let ush sssee what they have to sssay firsht. Then we will determine whether or not they are fit meat for the fire.”

Stepping forward, the prince and princess stood bravely before the two Kritons. Encouragingly, Mara prodded Jym to talk, but the lad held back, allowing his expression to sink toward the ground. With sweet softness, the princess held her brother’s hand with her right and lifted his chin with her left.

“You were right,” she whispered to him. Then aloud she said, “My brother and I seek the Kathnarii data drives. We believe they are the only way to find our missing mom and dad. They’re lost…and so are we.”

Several seconds of silence passed uncomfortably as Curik and Mukeh merely stared unsettlingly at the crew. Finally, Curik broke the awkward muteness by saying, "In all my time ash warden over the sssecretsss that the Na'Kosh Ssssage left behind, I have never heard anyone utter sssuch an honesht thing. Typically, we hear 'I am worthy,' or 'I am ssstrong,' or 'I dessserve to know.' But you have told the truth, which ish that you are lacking and in need. We will help you."

"But mashter – ," Mukeh started to protest.

"Enough," said the elder. "I have decreed it. It shall be done." He addressed the crew again. "In exchange, you will complete a tashk for ush. In the sssame cavesss in which the data drive ish hidden, there you will find our village heating core. It warmsss the burrowsss underneath our yurtsss when the mountain growsss cold. The shielding on the rear of it ish meant to reflect the heat back to ush, but recently it hash become broken. The heat now drawsss the attention of the great girth wormsss, who hibernate around it. Fix our core, and the data drive ish yoursss to keep."

"We accept," the captain approved. "The Explorer crew is always happy to help in times of need. Just point us in the direction of the danger."

Kel rolled her eyes. "Yep, danger, that's what we love the most...apparently."

At that very moment, the ground beneath them began to shake. Gradually, the tremor intensified until it had developed into a full-on quake. Desperate for balance, the crew reached for anything to steady themselves, while the townsfolk fled from the firepit, running for cover in their homes. Only Curik and Mukeh stayed above ground, readying themselves for an attack. Near the bonfire, the ground exploded, and a long, tubular creature burst forth!

"What is that thing?" Schiff screamed.

"Girth worm," grunted Mukeh. "Prepare for battle!"

Chapter 14

REEEEEEECH!! Wretched screeching pierced the tranquil evening as their unwelcome guest appeared. Ejecting through the displaced soil, the girth worm launched a throng of Kritons across the area, catching one in its open throat. The thing swayed around with elongated tendrils protruding from its beaked maw, stretching skyward as if reaching for the stars and moons. Its body bulged as the poor victim caught in its gaping mouth was swallowed whole. Sensing there was more prey to digest, the monster doubled over and tunneled back under the ground, sending shockwaves out in ripples.

"Sssplit up!" roared Mukeh, sprinting south and motioning for Curik to go east. "Girth wormsss hunt by vibration!"

"Red, get the kids!" Captain Nado shouted, dashing off in a separate direction.

Computing hundreds of tactics and stratagems in its processors in a flash, the robot complied. "Acknowledged, Captain." It then proceeded to pick up both Vampyrial children, one in each arm, and bounded in the direction of a close-knit grouping of mud yurts on the western side of the burn pit. In one effortless leap, Red sailed toward the edifice of one building and kicked off it, propelling itself and the young monarchs to the topmost section of the domed roof next door. After setting the kids down, Red retrieved its plasma carbine, slung across its back, and readied the weapon.

Meanwhile, Captain Nado and Schiff darted in a westward route, weaving around the smattering of domes and listening carefully for the telltale sounds of the monster tunneling. At the same time, Kel and Rox headed north, making for the large outcropping of rock spires that extended from the mountain's peak, forming the settlement's northern border.

Too many villagers still scrambled for shelter and safety, causing chaos within the little township. Keeping an eye from its rooftop perch though, Red was able to at least perform some reconnaissance, scanning for seismic activity. "This unit detects unusual geological interference five meters north of the village center," it reported. "It is moving slowly, hunting."

"Here that, Commander?" the captain spoke into his communicator. "Sounds like it's headed your way."

"We'll be ready," she answered.

There was no time for any further exchange of words, however, as the creature broke through the surface once more. Shooting forth its tentacular tongues, the girth worm reached for Dr. Rox. For its effort, the thing only received two burning projectiles from Commander Kel's plasma pistol. Roaring in pain, the worm recoiled, but only for a moment before it barreled at them again!

"Look out!" shouted Rox, shoving Kel to the ground as the worm's sharp beak careened over their heads.

Having caught nothing but a mouthful of rocks, the girth worm pulled away, shook its head in frustration, and dove beneath the dirt again. For several seconds, Rox and Kel dared not even breathe. When it seemed that the monster was no longer targeting them, the commander murmured, "Um, doctor. I think it's gone. You can get off me now."

"Sorry," he stuttered, quickly rising and offering his hand to help her up. "I was just...that is, I figured..."

"Hey," she said. "Thanks."

Giving a curt nod in response, Dr. Rox lifted the commander to her feet and the two ran to the center of the village. They arrived just in time to see the gargantuan grub breach the ground, spraying rocks and loose dirt across the village center. This time it was after Nado and Schiff, who had doubled back when they heard the attack on the doctor and commander. With a short shriek, the nimble shapeshifter blinked herself and the captain to the opposite side of the firepit, buying Nado enough time to shower the worm with plasma bolts. Unfortunately, it appeared that his assault was in vain, as not one single bolt penetrated the creature's thick hide.

Turning toward Captain Nado, the girth worm spewed forth its terrible tendrils in an attempt to ensnare him. Though rather speedy himself, the brawny Zennian was caught off guard by the monster's speed and dexterity. As the snapping, slimy mouth of the girth worm came within mere centimeters of the captain's head, it was suddenly thrown off course by an incredible blow from Mukeh, who had circled around to assist.

"YAH!" the Kriton defender bellowed as he struck the beast. His sword swipe hit with enough vehemence to push the worm aside and cause it to sway with dizziness. "Make noissse!" he instructed. "We musht disssorient it!"

Everyone immediately commenced screaming, shouting, banging surfaces, stomping feet, clapping hands, and anything else they could conceive in the moment to create a clamor. It seemed to be working, as the girth worm screeched again, moving back and forth as if unsure which way to go.

Without hesitation, Princess Mara gave it a direction. She reached for the ground, leaning over the curve of the dome, and the soil beneath her arm began to quaver. This was the enticement the worm needed, and it slithered close to where the children and Red were positioned on their rooftop. Blood dripped from the princess' nose, and as the creature reared up in front of them, she blacked out and began sliding down the curvature of the structure towards the waiting tendrils of the monster's gullet.

In an effort to save his sister, Prince Jym skidded to her and grabbed the collar of her dress, trying desperately to pull her to safety. But her momentum had already picked up too much speed, and he was pulled along. Though they were all already making an uproar, the rest of the crew increased their output of volume, hoping to get the worm's attention. It, however, could clearly now sense how close the princess had gotten, and wasn't about to lose its meal.

"We've got to make more noise!" shouted the commander, firing her pistol into the air.

The captain, on the other hand, had a new plan. Racing to aid the kids, he stole a burning log from the firepit and with it started hammering away at the giant animal's tail end. Though squealing in pain and anger, the girth worm stubbornly stuck to its task, shooting its tongues out and snatching Mara's legs.

"Everyone, get over here!" boomed Captain Nado. "Help!"

With that, he jumped with all his might, planting both cleated feet into the monster's backside. Dr. Rox and Commander Kel dashed over to join in, while Schiff blinked several meters overhead and dropped her full weight, as little as it was, onto the worm's tail as well. Even Mukeh and Curik added their strength to the endeavor. Once they had all piled atop the great beast's back end, it released Mara and stood erect, its gaping maw open to the moonlight. Flipping dexterously, Red vaulted onto the girth worm's beak, positioning its feet on the creature's split jaw. Aiming straight down, the automated assassin fired three shots in rapid succession right into the thing's throat.

Retching and writhing, the girth worm convulsed and shook, spitting up peach colored goop all over. After its initial thrashing about, the worm eventually subsided, slowing to an awkward waver. Then it violently slammed to the ground with an enormous and definitive *THUD!* Everyone breathed a sigh of relief as the night went silent once more.

Kel wiped her brow. "Whew. Well, at least now we know we can take on one of these bad boys if we need to."

"Ha!" Mukeh guffawed. "You think that wash one of the great girth wormsss?"

"I did," muttered Kel, "until you laughed like that."

"That wash only the larval form," informed the large Kriton, sending a condescending glare at the crew. "That wash jusht a baby."

Captain Nado gulped. "Oh, boy."

Dim yellow lighting accented the lazy haze that hung in the air inside the run-down establishment, casting a sickly glow across the vapors. Tucked away in the recesses of the Octagon V space station, the joint had certainly seen better times. As Captain O'Ryan and Barsol walked through the doorway, they had to duck under the drooping neon signage that read "Olshen's." On entry, their senses were immediately assaulted by the stench that clung to the gaseous fog. Their boots squelched on the sticky floor while they meandered between the varied tables and booths that were haphazardly arranged. Both still in uniform at O'Ryan's behest, they approached the shot glass littered bar.

Before either of them had the chance to utter anything, the Baldin barman saw them coming. In a flat, squat voice that almost perfectly encapsulated his appearance, the fellow grunted, "Star Guard? What brings you here? We haven't had any complaints that I know of, and no illegal activity. You got a warrant? Because no one searches my place without a warrant!"

"Easy friend," the confident captain calmed. "We're just here to meet someone. This is not a spot inspection. Are you the proprietor?"

"I am," said the Baldin. "This place is my namesake."

"Could be worse names, I suppose," O'Ryan joshed good-naturedly.

Olshen's bulgy eyes squinted a bit, a half-hearted grin teasing the corners of his wide mouth. "I suppose so. Could be named after my brother, Ickshen. I always said I had the best name."

Captain O'Ryan gave a wink and a nod. "A moniker that proves you were your mother's favorite."

"You got that right!" the short, dumpy barkeeper laughed. "Poor Ickshen. What a weird guy. Likes to breathe nebuladon fumes through a goofy mask. Never takes the blasted thing off!" Olshen wagged his head. "But I'm digressing. You're alright blue star. What can I do for you?"

"We're here to meet a rather unsavory character," O'Ryan informed. "A bounty hunter by the name of Mauve. She sent me a message to find her here."

Gesturing with his bulbous orbs, Olshen pointed them to the rear of his place of business. "Out back, in the cage. Fights are sanctioned, in case you're wondering. Got all my permits and licenses in order."

"No need, my friend," replied the captain with a carefree wave. "Carry on."

With that, he and Barsol wound through the scattered seating until they reached the infamous rear door. Beyond, they could just barely perceive the muffled sounds of cheering and chattering, the loud, obnoxious kinds one might hear at a sporting event. The door itself had been reinforced with noise dampening foam and was solid metal. Pushing past it, Barsol was nearly knocked backward from the sheer volume of the chaos within.

A multitudinous crowd surrounded one lone, plasti-steel, chain link cage. It was comprised largely of Gonians, a few Baldins, a couple of Aronites at a high stakes table, and an assortment of Humans. Several Gonians operated the betting booth, and the whole place felt strange and foreign to Barsol. It felt out of date, barbaric, even primitive.

Conversely, O'Ryan appeared to have no trouble at all, watching the cage fight with intense interest. Inside the ring, a Fangorian and a Zennian were double-teaming a single combatant who wore rose-gold and onyx armor. Her face was obscured by a sleek, black visor, while her mane of charcoal hair stuck out of the back of her helmet and whipped around in a frenzy as she fought.

"That's her," O'Ryan pointed out. "That's Mauve."

It was evidently nearing the end of the match, as the tag-teamers were fairly battered and bruised. Both were panting hard, the Fangorian's tongue hanging from his mouth in a slobbery mess, the Zennian coated in sweat and nursing a developing shiner on his left eye. Signaling to each other, the two burly brutes charged simultaneously at their opponent. The Zennian swung all four fists in rapid succession, while the Fangorian swiped with his claws, baring his fangs for a bite attack.

Like they were in slow motion, Mauve nimbly leapt atop the Zennian's outstretched fists, dancing from one fist to the next as if she were merely climbing the stairs! Upon reaching the topmost fist, Mauve somersaulted through the air, righting herself mid-flip and extending her feet into the back of the Zennian. The force of the kick sent him crashing into his Fangorian comrade, whose claws and teeth connected with the Zennian instead. As if defying the laws of gravity, Mauve gracefully drifted to the floor, watching her challengers collapse, utterly defeated and humiliated.

The scene went crazy as money changed hands, arguments broke out, and everyone rushed the betting booth. Amidst the hubbub, Mauve silently exited the cage and weaved betwixt the swarm of bettors toward the door. She stopped in her tracks when her visor turned to face squarely at O'Ryan. After a brief pause, the bounty hunter gradually made her way forward.

Once she had reached them, the Star Guard captain offered her a handshake. Mauve, however, only gave a brief glance downward. Raising her gaze, she cocked her head to the right, obviously rebuffing O'Ryan's friendly gesture.

"Understood," stated the captain. "How about we step outside and talk business?"

Motioning with her right hand toward the exit, Mauve indicated her approval of that suggestion. The trio egressed and found an unoccupied booth in the main restaurant area. Captain O'Ryan took one of the booth benches, while Mauve took the other, leaving Barsol to grab an unused chair from a vacant table.

"I see no reason for formalities," O'Ryan started, "and you, Miss Mauve, don't seem to care for them anyway. Shall we cut to the chase?"

Mauve gave a curt nod to the affirmative.

"Very well." The loquacious officer leaned closer. "Do you have a vessel here, fueled and ready for takeoff?"

Mauve nodded again.

"Do you have any issues pursuing this bounty into Taldish Sector?"

This time a headshake to the negative.

"Do you have any further pressing matters here?"

Another headshake.

"Then I guess we go and hunt down my bounty, yes?"

Mauve gave a long, slow, steady nod. Barsol couldn't be sure, but she seemed overly eager for the task.

"Mukeh, ssstop dragging your heelsss," Curik lectured as they ascended the peaks of Ghishnik, leading the Explorer crew along. "I cannot finish the journey up the mountain trail. You musht take them the resht of the way."

"Elder," the big Mukeh protested, using their own language, "they are outsiders and not worthy of this opportunity."

"We have been over this," reprimanded the elder. "We cannot spare our own for such a mission. And the shield must be repaired, or we will not survive the cold season. You will show them the way to the mouth of the cave. If they do not return, I will consider your alternative proposal of...temporarily relocating the tribe."

"Good enough," mumbled the gruff guardian. He then spoke to the crew. "For the remainder of the trek, you will all follow me. Thish ish ash far ash Curik can go."

"Right behind you, Mukeh," Captain Nado assured.

"Let'sss hope you can keep up," quipped the Kriton, pivoting hard and jogging along the rocky trail. Though caught by surprise, the Explorer crew all fell in line and proceeded to trot after him. It took approximately another hour, but eventually they stopped at a point along the trail that was nearly at the summit.

"Here we are," Mukeh stated. "Thish ish the cave that will take you to the heating core. Beware, lesht you find yourssselvesss a girth worm sssnack. Do you sssee thish emblem?" He motioned at a carving on the rock wall that resembled a crude depiction of fire. "That ish the sssign for the heating core. They are poshted throughout the cave. Follow them to the core and repair the shielding. When you are finished, look for thish sssymbol." He now indicated another marking of a three-fingered claw. "That will lead you to the data drive. Good luck."

With those final snarled instructions, the muscly Kriton quickly turned away and briskly huffed down the trail they had just ascended. After watching him go, the entire crew faced the dark, black cavity that opened before them. Jagged outcroppings at the top and bottom of the cave entrance gave the illusion that they were walking into the very mouth of the alp. While the prince and princess grasped each other's hands, Captain Nado and Commander Kel courageously stepped forward.

"What do we do about the girth worms?" the cautious commander wondered.

"I guess we'll deal with them when we get there," answered the captain, shining his flashlight inside the gaping cave. Nothing but the faint echoes of their own voices could be heard within. "But I am open to suggestions."

"Mukeh and Curik said they hunt by vibrations, right?" Kel mused. "We definitely need to keep our mouths shut and stay silent. I wonder if there's a way to muffle our footsteps."

"Maybe we can help," offered Princess Mara.

"How would that work?" questioned Nado. Though they were outside the orifice, his deep tones were already resonating in the massive caverns.

Mara quietly replied, "First off, I know you can't really help it, but your voice is too loud. Secondly, Jym and I can possibly manipulate the fields of dark energy inside and sort of mimic what the artificial gravity generator on the Explorer does. We'll create a gravity field of dark energy around your feet while we walk. That should at least lessen your weight on the ground inside, wouldn't it?"

"I don't know about that," warned the doctor. "You still haven't mastered your abilities, and they take quite the toll. I'm worried what that could do to your health."

"We can do it." Prince Jym tightened his grip on his sister's hand. "We discovered when we did the deceleration trick that we can kind of...share power. I can absorb some of her strain. You saw it happen. I didn't even mean to do it, it just sort of happened."

"I still don't like it," murmured Rox.

Kel took his hand. "Neither do I. But they're tough, they can do it. And if anything does go wrong, you and I will be right there to deal with it. Okay?"

"If you say it's a good idea," conceded Rox, "then I trust your judgment."

"I didn't say it was a good idea," Kel corrected. "But it's the only one we've got."

"That's the plan," declared Captain Nado. "We stick together and take our time. We'll take as many breaks as we must for the kids. I'll go first, Schiff you stay near Mara and Jym so you can blink them to safety if we run into trouble. Red, keep your scanners active for signs of life down here. I don't want any surprises. Kel and Rox, watch the kiddos and alert me if they look like they need a rest. Are we ready?"

There were no questions or objections. Nado beamed at his crew. "Let's go save the day."

Into the winding passages beyond they wandered, with the prince and princess warding their every footfall. Kel immediately noticed the odd sensation of walking on pillows. Thankfully, she was able to adapt to the feeling quickly, and it appeared the rest of the party did so as well.

Carefully and cautiously edging their way onward and downward, the crew practically tiptoed deeper and deeper into the caverns, keeping a vigilant lookout for the fire emblem carvings. They were only minutes into their journey when Mara's nose began to bleed heavily. Rox moved to intervene, but before he could do anything, Prince Jym stepped in and firmly took hold of the princess' quivering palm. Almost instantaneously, the nosebleed slowed, and a light trickle seeped from the prince's nostrils instead. Giving the doctor a steady nod, Jym held his sister strongly and proceeded on, though this did little to assuage Rox's concerns.

Sensing his consternation, Commander Kel placed a gentle hand on Dr. Rox's shoulder, meeting his fearful gaze with her own expression of hopeful determination. It obviously wasn't the doctor's preference, but he indicated that he was willing to allow them to continue. With Captain Nado's guidance, they plunged further and further into the bowels of the mountain.

It had been nearly two hours of methodical plodding, with multiple rests for the kids at Rox's insistence, before they reached their destination. At last, the group entered a cavernous shaft wherein the humongous heating core hung from the roof of the cave, suspended by a series of steel cables. An enormous, metallic shield, bent to wrap around the core in a half-cylinder, was positioned to reflect all heat from the core up toward the surface.

Everyone could feel the warmth exuding from the elephantine element as it radiated throughout the entire chamber. Commander Kel could clearly tell that the reflector shield was not properly calibrated and needed adjustment. She started for the core, but was halted by Red, whose attention had been captured by something far beneath. Upon following its stare, Kel understood why the robot had paused.

Below, in the lowest section of the shaft, creatures the size of star cruisers lined the cave walls, wrapping around in seemingly endless spirals. Quiet rumbles were the only noise the massive monsters made, deep breathing from their hibernating slumber. Seeing the unbelievably large girth worms, Schiff very nearly let out a gasp, but caught herself.

After exchanging knowing looks, the crew set to work. Kel prepped her tools with Red's assistance, while Nado and Schiff kept watch. The doctor remained focused on the children, who strained hard to maintain their artificial gravity field around everyone's feet. Agonizing minutes passed as the commander painstakingly repaired the shielding. To her astonishment, the apparatus was rather ingenious. Above the machine, a lone vent straight to the surface allowed luxonite panels like those from a starship to absorb solar energy, powering the gigantic electric coils inside. By concentrating all the heat from the core via the reflector shield, the heat reacted with the Khardan mineral deposits inside the mountain to carry the warmth directly to the village burrows.

She had little time to appreciate this marvel of engineering though, as the repair was fairly simple for someone with her knowledge. A quick rearrangement of the pulley system that upheld the shield was the only job necessary. The toughest part of it all had been trying to mouth which tools she required to a robot that relied more on aural input for communication than visual. *Worthless waste of wires and wattage!* she fussed in her mind. But now the job was complete. On to the next task of locating the last Kathnarii data drive. *And not getting devoured by giant worms…*

Seven sour individuals stood at the top of the mountain path, also staring into the inky darkness of the cave system. They too studied the carvings, and their albino Kriton leader had a pretty good idea of where to go. In their wake, they left behind a beaten and bloody Mukeh, and an injured Curik. Armed for war, the grisly gang marched inside, weapons in their hands, and evil purpose in their shadowy hearts.

Chapter 15

With his Drakewing now on the planet's surface, the pilot stared at the devastation wrought by the incredibly destructive weapon that had been unleashed on Urkasak. Little remained of what appeared to have been the once rich and thriving capitol. It was in shambles, but the palace still stood. There were no guards or military to speak of on patrol, though. No one was walking the streets, no one was out in the open. Though primitive, the Gnarfs had quite successfully evacuated and abandoned this place.

In the distance, he could see where the laser had struck. A large swath of the otherwise lush landscape was scorched and dead. Ash covered debris littered the area, and nothing that was once constructed there had stayed intact.

Movement to his left caught the mysterious man's attention. Someone was in the palace. He headed that way, stealthily moving from shadow to shadow after his quarry. It turned out to be a Gnarf palace guard, who tromped along the main entryway until he reached the throne room. Pausing in the anterior hall that preceded the king's chamber, the man waited with an ear aimed upward, trained to hear whatever dialogue may be uttered. He did not have to wait long.

"Sire," the guard grunted. "The other kings have spurned your orders. They say the banishment of General Hämm has left the armada in a weakened state. They will not add their own sky-beasts to your search for the Hex-man."

"Fools!" another individual blasted back. "I am still High King Bë-Konn of Urkasak. They must bow to my will! After the Hex-man's devastation, we have to retaliate. It is of vital importance that we show no mercy for his treachery."

"That is what I told them, sire," replied the guard. "They said they are convening in the Kingsmeet in ten cycles."

King Bë-Konn roared furiously. "A Kingsmeet?! They will elect a new high king, that is what they plan to do. That wench Boxie, and that flabby Flogg have no doubt planted these seeds of rebellion. Treason! That's what this is. I will crush them under my fist!" This last word the king placed significant emphasis upon, slamming said fist on the arm of his throne with a mighty wallop. "Ready all the remaining guards. We may have to defend the palace from these interlopers. That Explorer 2000 caused quite the ruckus and disruption to my planet."

That was the cue the enigmatic stranger had been waiting to hear. Slipping out of the shadows, he waltzed confidently into the throne room. Inside he spotted four beefy sentries in the corners of the chamber, the one lone guard near the throne, and the sanctimonious sovereign slumped in his ornate chair.

"Who are you to barge in here?" demanded Bë-Konn. "Identify yourself!" When the man remained silent, the king snorted, "Guards! Seize him!"

Using a mere flick of each wrist, the intruder took control of the dark energy fields present on this planet's surface. Both sets of guards that stood at attention in the corners were flung into the walls, bouncing off and flopping to the floor. As they laid there, each one was practically motionless except for the jiggling belly fat that made them all look like ugly piles of bronzy jelly.

Now breathing hard, the man approached the throne of the high king, who stared in horror at this trespasser. "Another trickster," he grumbled. "How many of you are there? You were all supposed to be dead!"

"I was," the man stated. "But I have been. . .revived. I need to know more about these 'trickster gods' of yours. How many have you seen?"

"I am High King Bë-Konn of the Gnarfs! Who are you to even dare to ask questions of me, as if I were some thug to be interrogated and intimidated? I should have you clapped in manacles and dragged to the cells!"

"You would only try it once." He said this with so much conviction that Bë-Konn actually shuddered. "I do not wish to expel any more of my abilities today, and I am certain that your subordinates do not wish to be dead. How about answering my question? How many 'trickster gods' like me have you seen?"

Nostrils flaring in fury, the portly ruler responded, "There were two children on that Explorer beast when they came here. We had been commissioned by the Hex-man to capture them and deliver them to him. He is another of the tricksters, vile and two-faced."

"Tell me savage, what did these children look like?" the intruder interrogated. "How powerful did they seem?"

"Strong enough to defeat my general," huffed the king. "As for appearance, they were yellowish and pale, with black hair, glowing orange eyes, and black tattoos. Good enough description for you?"

"So," mused the man, "my initial assessment was correct. They are indeed the pureblood progenies of the traitors. I wonder how they survived all this time. Must have been via stasis pods."

Bë-Konn looked confused. "Was that directed at me? You speak in riddles, trickster."

"Never mind," the stranger dismissed. "What of the rest of this Explorer 2000 crew? What capabilities do they possess?"

"I have heard that their captain is cunning," Bë-Konn responded reluctantly. "They have a shapeshifter among them as well, and an assassin robot. Two of the god-race travel with them, and they are intelligent beings. No other powers that I could see, though."

"Interesting." Left in silence for a few precious moments, the mysterious man pondered this news. "Then that means their progenitors are not with them. The offspring survived, but the parents did not. Or they are missing, separated, possibly searching to be reunited." He paused in his assessments, then voiced another pressing, burning question. "Who is this 'Hex-man'? I would know more of him."

"He is the Warden of the Hexagon, wielder of sky-fire, and bringer of the desolation that you see outside my palace." It was now Bë-Konn's turn to breathe heavier. "He must be made to pay for what he has done."

"This Hex-man," the mysterious man began, "why does he seek the children?"

"I do not know. He only said he wanted them and offered to pay us well for this service. But they are as tricksy as he is, and they escaped from us. As payment for this failure, we received. . .well, you can see for yourself what we received."

Something else in this place seemed off to the man. He was quite positive that the children did not pass through this room. Their energy trails had gone cold. There was another, however, that had spent much time here. A separate signature, that of someone older and stronger, more well versed in the art of energy manipulation. This "Hex-man" perhaps?

"Did the Hex-man exercise any power in this room?" asked the man.

"Yes," answered the brutish Bë-Konn. "It was from here that he summoned the fires from the heavens that engulfed our people."

"And to clarify, for some unknown reason he wants those kids?"

"Wants?" scoffed the Gnarf king. "No, it is more than that. He desires, covets, craves the thought of capturing them. Wherever you find the Hex-man, those trickster spawn will likely not be far away. He pursues them, chases them with every ounce of strength."

"You said you had a search party out looking for the Hex-man, did you not?" The masked face of the imposing individual stared penetratingly at High King Bë-Konn.

"I do. Why?"

"Where was the last known location of the Hex-man?"

Obviously wishing to avoid offering an answer, the corpulent king squirmed and twisted in his seat. "Ranjeman. He was last sighted there."

"Ranjeman?" the man repeated. "Why would they have gone there? Thank you, High King Bë-Konn of the Gnarfs. You have been most helpful and forthcoming."

As the strange fellow started to leave, the High King gave one last authoritative command, "Now, idiot! While his back is turned! Strike!"

The guard's clumsy, half-hearted attempt to stab the man in the back as he exited was easily overcome as the intruder met the Gnarf's blade with his own. He then shot the Gnarf sentry in the foot and knee with his plasma pistol, faster than the bloated brutes could even think. Keeping a wary eye trained on the remainder of hostiles in the area, the man dipped inside the shade once more, disappearing from their view entirely.

It was only a short jaunt to return to his landing zone, where the man swiftly boarded the Drakewing and took to the stars. If this "Hex-man," or Lord Hex, or Warden, or whatever he was could lead him to the children, then he would have to find Hex. Following the clue to Ranjeman was a better lead than aimlessly dithering around in space trying to home in on the kids' energy trails. There was no telling how easy it would be to simply get lost, or wander endlessly, in the void. He would go to Ranjeman, confront this Lord Hex character if he was still there, and finish his mission to apprehend the prince and princess.

Closer and closer, bit by bit, the crew of the Explorer 2000 trekked through the subterranean world. At certain intervals along the way, whenever pausing to take a rest, they stopped to take in the wondrous sights of the cave system, with its rivulets and underground lakes, its own internal mountains and valleys formed by stalagmites, and the varied animal life forms that dwelt therein. An entire alien ecosystem contained within this one environment. The galaxy was a truly wondrous place to behold, and Commander Kel made the conscious decision to enjoy this excursion as much as she could, given the hazardous beasts slumbering in the caverns all around them.

Continuing to maintain their dead silence, the whole lot of them crept slowly along, tunnel after tunnel, trying to remain cautious and avoid awakening any of the great girth worms. All the while, Mara and Jym used their abilities to soften and absorb everyone's steps so as to mitigate the vibrations coming from their spelunking. Even working together, however, they were both showing signs of exhaustion and the blood trails from their noses hadn't decreased.

At this point, despite being forced to remain mute, Rox was making no attempt to hide his disapproval of the whole situation. Though she agreed with him, Commander Kel didn't have any other ideas for muffling their movement either. It was all on the kids, and that was something that gave her extreme anxiety. It wasn't that she feared leaving their fate in the hands of these two tiny people. No, she trusted them with that. She was afraid that they might overdo it and cause irreparable harm to themselves by pushing too hard. She was afraid of losing them. They had all become such a close-knit unit in the past several weeks and bonded as a family. That was something the commander hadn't experienced in many years, and in spite of the danger around them, the necessity for their quietness was bringing all this to mind.

With little other choice but to grapple with these thoughts, Kel allowed her memories to flow. She remembered her mom, kind and sweet, but with a firmness that came only from years of teaching in the school system. They had become best friends when Kel was a teenager, and she had often happily anticipated a grown up "girls' night out" with her mother. Her dad, whose ability to keep working in the wee hours of night made all the kids joke that he was probably cybernetically enhanced with his own UPS batteries. His freneticism sometimes came across as gruffness, but he always showered his children and his wife with love and adoration.

Then there were the siblings. Scott the debater, who dreamt of joining one of the ministries. Reva the baker, with aspirations to have galactic renowned pastries. Chryss the scientist, whose greatest desire was to further the research of particle acceleration. Mira the nurse, with a hope to heal the universe. Newton the chef, always experimenting with new meals and flavors. The twins, Tom and Tim, who couldn't have been more different. Tom was a music prodigy while all Tim ever talked about was being a Flotilla Protection Agent. Hollis the artist, whose sketches, drawings, and paintings captured the imaginations of all who looked at them. The two youngest ones, Angel and Brooke, were still too little to have developed any real hopes and dreams in that way, though both were full of imaginative stories and games. They were all young when it had happened… too young. Staring purposefully at the two young wards that were in her charge now, Commander Kel vowed to herself that it would not happen again. Never.

A wave from Captain Nado pulled her from these reflections. He was getting very animated. They must be close to the data drive. With the beams of their flashlights bouncing off the cave walls, he led them into a small crevice marked with the three-fingered claw. Everyone, even the kids, had to turn sideways to slide inside. Only Schiff managed it easier than the rest, taking the form of a tiny mammal.

Things were even more difficult for the prince and princess in here, as they now had to keep a constant watch on the vertical surfaces too, in case anyone bumped into anything. Taking note, Captain Nado maintained a slow and steady pace, careful not to overwork the young monarchs. The blood from Mara's nose had gotten worse, and there was only so much that Jym could do to relieve it. In the darkness, Kel could make out Rox's silhouetted head shaking worriedly at the captain, who also took note of that. Nado gently gestured with his hand to stop and rest. For a couple of minutes, they all stood perfectly still, allowing Mara to cease using her abilities for a time. She formed trembling fists, struggling to control her breathing. Using his own small penlight, Dr. Rox checked her eyes.

"Very glassy," he mouthed to Kel, overexaggerating the movements with his lips so as to ensure she understood. "She might pass out."

The now incredibly concerned commander rolled her own eyes in fear and frustration. Not at the princess of course, she was doing her best, as was her brother, but her annoyance was at the situation itself. *Girth worms,* she thought. *It had to be girth worms. And they just have to hunt by vibration, don't they? Oy...*

As Princess Mara stood desperately trying to still her body and lungs, Prince Jym gave her hand a light squeeze. Weakly lifting her head, she met his hopeful gaze. "You can do it," he mouthed. "Almost there."

Mara returned a determined nod and soon the children were ready to proceed. Extending her open palms down toward the cavern floor again, the princess reestablished the gravitational field around their feet. As before, Jym held her close and did everything in his power to absorb her strain and pain.

An excited motion from the captain up ahead signaled something new. Squinting hard, Commander Kel attempted to focus on whatever Nado had indicated. Then she saw it. A light! Somewhere nearby, the tight crevice ended and there was a bluish illumination shining through. Gradually, one by one, they excised themselves from the claustrophobic passageway.

They found themselves inside another massive chamber, deep in the belly of the mountainside. Ancient runes lined the walls, giving off the blue hue. They seemed to be part of some kind of technological apparatus wherein tubing and wires ran from generators embedded in the rock. At the base of each generator was a man-made pool, where water that streamed down the craggy walls from the peak of the chamber gathered. Cabling from the generators ran across the ground, all connecting in the center of the space. There, at the hub of these landline spokes, rested a humongous, non-natural stalagmite. Its black housing was riddled with more of the glowing, cobalt writing and pulsing lines that indicated it was receiving power. Above, an obsidian-colored metallic stalactite mirrored it, both emitting an energy field that acted as the primary source of the lighting in this place.

The walls in this chamber glistened from the luminosity of these structures. Out of curiosity, Schiff, who had transformed back, lightly and nimbly ran a finger down the surface. Rubbing her fingers together as if feeling something gritty, she briefly tasted the substance. “Salt,” the lithe little woman mouthed, remembering to stay quiet.

That was all quite fascinating to the commander's engineering mind. As near as Kel could tell, the generators were recycling electricity from the salt deposits in the walls, as the water from the peak dissolved the mineral deposits and carried the salt to the pools. From there, as the pool water evaporated from the natural wind tunnels in the cave system, the salt crystals left behind could be harvested by the nanofluidic devices inside the generators. Genius, Kel mused. *Never let it be said again that the only technological breakthroughs of the Kritons are custom spacesuits and HVACs.*

Unfortunately, there was little time to dwell on these marvels, as ahead of them lay their ultimate goal. The data drive floated in an anti-gravitational field, probably maintained by the generators and the repelling forces of the black stalagmite and stalactite. Trepidation mounted within the crew as Captain Nado sidled forth, Princess Mara and Prince Jym softening his every step. Reaching toward the device with his upper right arm, the captain let out a long, steady breath and tried to sense if there was any danger. No heat exuded from the energy field, and no traps or alarms seemed to be attached to it. Nado stretched forth his hand inside the energy field, and tenderly took hold of the data drive, pinching it between two fingers. He started to smile until the huge housings burped an obnoxious pulse of energy, but nothing happened aside from a fluctuation in the power as the glow dimmed temporarily.

Proudly, Captain Nado withdrew the drive. As he did so, Schiff couldn't help whispering, "Well, that was super anti-climactic." That earned her a stern shushing from Kel and Rox. She shrugged and mouthed, "Sorry," back to them.

At that moment, the machinery hiccupped again and this time rings of super-heated, white lasers shot from the stalagmite up into the receivers in the stalactite! Had Captain Nado's hand been present still, it would have been sliced off by the weaponized beams. He gulped, and everyone stood motionless, waiting to hear if the thrumming and popping of the apparatus had alerted the sleeping girth worms close by. After several seconds, it appeared that the creatures remained in hibernation.

"Well, that was super lucky," Schiff whispered, forgetting herself yet again. Another hushing from the commander and doctor had her kowtowing once more, and mouthing, "Sorry," once more as well.

Speaking as quietly as possible, Nado murmured, "We've got it. Let's go."

Rox shook his head and pointed at the kids. "They need a rest. A long one. I have to check them out."

"Alright," the captain acquiesced. "Ten minutes."

"Then we need to get out of here," mumbled Kel, as the doctor crept to the young Vampyrials and began to examine their status.

"Why?"

"I suddenly have a weird feeling. Like the other boot is about to drop."

Nado looked at her quizzically. "Probably just the girth worms," he offered.

"It's not that," she replied, as soft and muted as she could manage. "Something else is wrong here."

"You sound like Mara," the captain jovially jested, still maintaining muffled tones. "Even the noise from these ancient machines didn't awaken the worms."

"Maybe." But the commander still wasn't ready to dismiss her feelings. It was as though someone else were watching them, lying in wait with a nasty trap. Try as she might, the cautious commander couldn't shake the sensation...

Hunting and searching, Klensh's band of murderous marauders trudged along the pathways, following the lead of their Kriton boss. The payday for this excursion was one that was long overdue, partially because they consistently underestimated the resolve of the Explorer 2000 crew, and partially because their boss' boss, Lord Hex, continuously held them at bay. His insistence that the kids and the captain remain unharmed was foolish and naïve, and today they were bound and determined to get their rewards.

Each one of their lives had been filled with one bad decision after another, none of them expressing remorse or regret over the things they had committed. It was all about money and power and getting it by any means necessary. Those who got in the way only received their just desserts according to this motley group of misfits.

Keeping their hefty arsenal of arms, traps, and snares at the ready, they were prepared for anything the Explorer crew could throw at them this time. Their prey was trapped in these tunnels, with only one way out. This time, they would hunt their quarry to extinction, and finally get paid the exorbitant sums that they had been promised. It felt so long ago that they had been initially released by the crooked warden who ran the Black Hole Penitentiary and hired by Klensh to complete this task.

First, they had been outsmarted on Vortex, then outmaneuvered on Hex II, followed by their defeat on Zen I, and the escape from the dreadnought during their last encounter at Khardan. The gang was beginning to doubt that Hex or Klensh could manage this upstart Explorer crew, but Klensh's cleverness back in the spaceport with Schlaar and Shtrepp had renewed some of their trust in him. Hex, on the other hand, could go eat space dust. The cat-and-mouse game he wanted to play had grown old for such scarred veterans of the criminal underworld, and they were all prepped and primed for vengeance. All those times they'd been unceremoniously humiliated by their targets would no longer go unanswered. A plasma bolt, bullet, arrow, spike trap, claw, or fang would at last find every single one of them, and the Explorer crew would be no more.

Marching along behind Klensh's bulky, swishing tail, they studied every dark nook and cranny they passed for a sign that someone had been there or was still there. So far, nothing. But that was about to change. Klensh had been so confident that they were on the right track, and his deception had worked flawlessly. They were here, but not for long.

An upheld claw from the albino Kriton leader halted them. He pointed into a shadowy chasm to their left. Inside, they could all barely perceive the colossal creatures that slept within. Coiled around each other were hordes of unimaginably large girth worms. Klensh glanced at the three-fingered emblem on the wall ahead, then back down at the worms. His cracked lips spread into a terrible, toothy grin...

Chapter 16

It was the dawn of a new cycle on Khardan, and even in the early morning hours the brutal desert heat bore down upon Captain O'Ryan, Warrant Officer Barsol, and the ever-enigmatic Mauve. While O'Ryan and Mauve appeared unfazed, their Zennian compatriot panted and sweated profusely, unused to the brutality of the Khardan sun. Though much taller than the other two, Barsol labored to keep up with their quickened gaits, being forced to extend the range of his own footsteps.

Noticing that his Warrant Officer was lagging behind, Captain O'Ryan admonished, "Come along, Barsol. This is not the kind of place you want to end up getting left in the dust."

The odd trio made their way to the spaceport town ahead, having disembarked from Mauve's sleek star cruiser. It was a third generation Seeker model, whose downward pointing prow and elongated, curved port and starboard fins gave it a distinct appearance like a bird of prey. This one was adorned with a specialty paint job that matched Mauve's armor and helmet. Armed with six rocket-propelled missiles and a fully rotational forward laser turret, the bounty hunter's

Seeker 3-86 was no laughing matter. Many of the thugs and grunts working the docks recognized the craft and gave a wide berth to those who egressed from within.

The Star Guard officers had long since doffed their uniforms and traded them for something far less conspicuous at Mauve's silent insistence. Without uttering a word, she had forced the pair to alter their attire so as to draw less attention on a hostile planet. Gone were their easily classifiable blue camouflage and badges, now replaced by rough brown leathers and hooded ponchos. The one distinguishable item that both of them kept on their persons were their Star Guard officer special-issued Fenton Commandments, a specially designed plasma pistol with a longer barrel and larger magazine than most others, outfitted with a scope and laser sights. These they hid under their ponchos and trappings, careful to keep the sidearms in their spring-loaded holsters for quick draw capabilities.

Despite their best efforts, neither man had the clout to convince the traffic controllers to divulge any info about incoming or outgoing spacecraft. Leaning back against a wall, Mauve gave the aura of someone who was mildly amused at their failure. Unwilling to break the laws of Taldish, loose as they may be, O'Ryan decided to look for clues in the little urbanite township instead.

In the middle of the town, O'Ryan spotted several Kritons milling about, bossing some Pyrian union workers around. Apparently, the laborers were moving the rather bulky shipment they had been charged with transporting a bit too slowly for the Kriton's liking. One of the scaly brutes picked up a Pyrian by the back of his collar and raised a fist. As the bossing threatened to devolve into bullying, Captain O'Ryan stepped into the situation.

"Pardon me, good citizen," he greeted lavishly. "It seems there is a disagreement here."

"Back off, Human," growled the Kriton woman. "Thish ish a private matter. Not that Humansss would know anything about that."

"Perhaps you'd rather speak to my associate then?" O'Ryan stuck a thumb over his shoulder, pointing at Mauve.

The Kriton started when she saw the infamous bounty hunter, merely grunting a single word. "Mauve…" She then calmly set the little Pyrian down. Brushing himself off, the green skinned fellow wiped his nasal cavities and set back to work. Meanwhile, Captain O'Ryan addressed the Kriton.

"My good woman," the ostentatious officer said, "we are in pursuit of dangerous fugitives who we believe have good reason to alight on your glorious globe. Have you seen an Explorer model ship recently?"

"Yesh," she blurted, still eyeing Mauve with uncertainty. "They were here for a short time, visssited the cantina, and left."

"Any idea where they went?"

"Ssscuttlebutt sssaysss they were headed for the Na'Kosh sssettlement in the Ghishnik mountainsss."

"Tell me, my dear," said O'Ryan, edging a little closer. "How do we get to the Na'Kosh settlement in the Ghishnik mountains?"

"I will make a map for you," the Kriton woman offered, never taking her gaze off of Mauve. All the while, the bounty hunter simply stood with her arms folded, tapping her right index finger on the pauldron covering her left bicep. "Jusht keep that hunter away from me."

"Do you have any outstanding bounties or warrants?" questioned the Star Guard captain.

"No..."

"Then you have nothing to fear." O'Ryan eased into a less intimidating position, almost taking an "at ease" military stance. "Now, is there any chance I could get that map?"

After requesting a scrap of paper and writing implement from the Pyrian union workers, the Kriton woman hastily scrawled a few images and words on the page. Handing it back to O'Ryan with a cowering, "Here you go," she backed away slowly, shifting her attention between a conveniently close alleyway and Mauve's steely presence. Having garnered what they required, the Star Guard captain was no longer interested in the woman and allowed her to flee.

After perusing the artless map and directions, O'Ryan handed it off. Barsol reached to retrieve it, thinking the document was meant for him. Instead, Mauve stepped forward and grabbed the scrap before the Warrant Officer could even get close to laying a single finger on it, leaving Barsol both looking and feeling rather silly.

"I believe we could make it by mid-afternoon if we left now," suggested Captain O'Ryan. Mauve's answer in return was once again a soft, steady nod of the head. O'Ryan continued. "Do you still have enough fuel reservoirs for a planet-side flight?"

Another nod.

"Good." Standing straight, O'Ryan shifted his belt and adjusted his accoutrements. "Warrant Officer Barsol?"

"Yes sir?" the faithful Zennian replied.

A wide, bright smile broke across Captain O'Ryan's face. "Prep the Seeker for launch. Today, we make history."

"Open fire!" Klensh roared at his gang.

The grisly goons eagerly commenced using the giant worms as target practice. Not that they were hard to hit. In fact, the real challenge would have been trying to miss one of the gargantuan creatures. Though nothing they utilized pierced the thick hides of the girth worms, it was enough to cause the great slumbering beasts to stir. However, it seemed that stirring was all they were going to do, as the massive worms gradually untangled themselves from their knotted sleeping arrangements.

"This is going to take too long," the Ranjeman huntress complained.

"Get the rail gun asssssembled," ordered Klensh with a scowl. "That'll get thoshe monsssstersss going." He chuckled grimly. "Then we fall back and let the Explorer 2000 crew flee right into ush."

Following orders, the two Fangorian crooks pulled a pile of gear from their packs and started snapping parts and pieces together. Within a few seconds, they had constructed a short tripod with a powerful laser emitter atop it. Against the girth worms it would probably only injure one of them, but Klensh relished the thought of maybe using this to turn Captain Nado and his dopey robot into ash heaps.

He powered up the device, and its heating core produced a red glare that shone in the Kriton's one good eye. Looking like a man possessed, Klensh wrapped his claws around the trigger mechanism. He lined up his shot and fired.

An enormous white beam blasted from the barrel of the rail gun, striking one of the worms and breaking through its leathery hide! With a screech that would have awakened the dead, it pulled free from the throng of its kind and fled, drilling into the rock walls with its unbreakable beak. As the thing tunneled away, the rest of the worms bellowed in chaos, all of them following suit and tunneling off in various directions, a veritable stampede.

"Now what?" asked the Pyrian thug.

"We ssset an ambush," answered Klensh.

Sunlight began to filter through the cracks and crevices far overhead in the data drive chamber. Observing this, Kel deduced that the crew of the Explorer 2000 must have spent all night in those caves. Everyone was utterly fatigued, especially Princess Mara and Prince Jym. There was still the return trip though, and despite their lucky break in finding the final Kathnarii data drive, the thought of hiking back to the surface was enough to depress every one of them. Except for Red of course, who was unable to feel such things. The dutiful robot had kept a lookout while the rest of them recuperated a bit.

No time to keep dallying, however, for there was still an arduous journey ahead of them. Staying as quiet as ever, Captain Nado roused the group after their respite and began the unwelcome task of rallying his team.

Rising and shaking off the fuzziness in her brain, Kel couldn't help but wonder, after they got out with this data drive, what next? The missing piece to the Kathnarii puzzle still rested in Graylon's clutches. How were they supposed to retrieve that one? They couldn't exactly barter with a madman bent on kidnapping the kids to use for whatever revolting experiments he had in store.

Amid these ruminations, Kel had another lingering thought that she hadn't wanted to entertain. What if the kids' mom and dad were gone? What if they had died years ago? What if all this, the danger, the injuries, the toll on the young ones' health, everything they were fighting to accomplish, was for naught?

Taking a page out of the captain's playbook, the commander chased those haunting scenarios from her mind with a surge of optimism. *No! We've got to keep going, to give those kids purpose and hope. They deserve that, and if any of us give in to despair then we've already lost this mission.* She vowed then and there to remove those what-ifs from her deliberations. They had a task at hand and needed to complete it first. If Kathnarii Base had no answers, then they'd figure things out from there.

Everyone was just getting ready to embark on the next stage in the expedition, to retrace their steps back to the cave entrance near the Na'Kosh village, when a rumbling caught their attention. It started low, reverberating the surfaces of the chamber, but began to build from a mild quivering into a steady quake. Kel shot a worried look to Nado, who clearly reciprocated her concern.

No pomp, no fanfare, no exciting introduction, the captain simply said, "Girth worm. Go."

"We were quiet!" fussed Schiff. "How did we wake them up?"

"Could have been these machines," Rox suggested.

"I don't think so," said Kel. "I think someone else is in here and woke them up."

"How do you know?"

"Just a feeling." The commander traded glances with the captain.

Jym lifted his weakened sister, placing her arm across his shoulders. "Shouldn't we stay quiet?"

"I think they already know we're here," Captain Nado replied. "Red, what do your scanners say?"

Studying a panel on its arm, Red reported, "Scanners indicate at least a dozen massive life forms in motion in the vicinity. One of them is coming this way."

"Time to go," Nado grunted, assisting Prince Jym by hefting the very weakened Mara onto his own shoulder. Her limp little body gave the appearance of a tiny ragdoll by comparison to the captain's own burly physique. He pocketed the data drive and slipped inside the crevice through which they had entered the chamber. Jym and Schiff were right behind him, with Rox and Kel following after that. Red took up a defensive position at the rear of the formation and they all squirmed along the scissure until they were back out on the other side.

With Nado pointing out where the three-fingered claw symbols were, they retraced their steps, all the while feeling the quakes and shocks underneath intensifying. This was nothing compared to what they'd dealt with in the village. Mukeh had been right. These girth worms were a force to be reckoned with, and they were on the move.

They bolted left, the captain indicating that he was still on the reverse trail of the claw emblems. Red tried to catch Captain Nado's attention. "Captain, this unit has detected additional life forms ahead. They are stationary."

"What?" queried the worthy Zennian, but he refused to halt his stride.

Breaking into another spacious chamber, they heard a gravelly voice call out, "There they are! Fire!"

"It's Klensh!" warned Kel, and the crew scattered for cover as lasers pelted the rock formations all around them. "Look out!"

Finding a suitable location to hide, Captain Nado laid Princess Mara, who was still trembling from exhaustion, on the floor of the cave where she remained stationary, but conscious. The captain drew his plasma guns and when there seemed to be a lull in the exchange, he popped out of hiding and returned with a volley of his own. It sent several of the brutes diving for cover themselves and gave Commander Kel the chance to advance. Klensh was clever though and had positioned his company in a higher crag where they enjoyed better cover and firing range. She got as close as she dared, popping off a couple of rounds from her pistol. The commander was now close enough to see the full arsenal of the nasty bunch and recoiled in surprise.

"Stay back, Captain!" she cautioned. "They have a rail gun!"

Remaining behind the decent cover that he had, Captain Nado rested his back against the rocky mound that currently protected them. "Jym, when I give the signal, I want you to run for it to the nearest exit from this cavern. Got it?" But the boy didn't answer. "Jym?" Nado whirled to see a terrified prince gripping his left arm as blood seeped through his fingers.

"I got hit," was all the lad could utter.

"You'll be alright," comforted Nado. "Time to get tough, okay? Get ready to run." He then twirled about as he stood, both plasma pistols firing rapidly. But his brave maneuver was short-lived as a white-hot beam of light struck the surface of the cave wall next to him, leaving a searing hole that was nearly a meter deep. "Never mind," the captain muttered to Jym. "We need a new plan of action."

Klensh's croaky laughter echoed throughout the chamber. "Thish time we got you, captain! Give up, and we'll make it a ssswift death!"

"Over my dead body!" Nado hollered back.

"That'sss kind of the idea," said a confused sounding Klensh. "You had your chance, now it'sss my turn. Eat grenade!"

With that, the Kriton warmonger hurled a gnarly looking spherical object through the air and it sailed down towards where the Explorer crew hid. It was as if time slowed for the commander, who watched in horror as the explosive hurtled along its trajectory. It would land smack in the center of the arena. She couldn't move fast enough to stop it, and even if she could, she'd be gunned down before taking her second step.

A flash of motion caught her eye. Maybe she wasn't fast enough, but someone else was. Kel looked up, seeing H-8-RED racing to intercept the grenade. Several shots and blasts plinked into its armor plating, but the robot stayed undeterred. It launched itself airborne, caught the explosive, and, taking careful aim, proceeded to drop the thing down a nearby shaft.

"Red!" fumed Kel. "Stupid stack of scrap! Why didn't you throw it back at them?!"

"You shall see shortly," the robot responded. No sooner had it vocalized that phrase, than the grenade exploded far beneath them, sending even more shockwaves pulsing across the caves. This was followed by a telltale screech and a violent rumbling.

"Curssse all of you!" snarled Klensh, snatching a smaller firearm from their pile of weapons. "Ssstart closhing in," he barked at his comrades. "They don't have enough firepower to hold ush off. We'll overwhelm them!"

"Almost out of time here," called Kel.

Red remained motionless. "Wait for it. Don't move."

Just as Klensh roared the command, "Charge!!" the ground beneath him and his gang opened and one of the great girth worms burst forth! Faces full of fear and dismay, every single one of the sour six was swallowed in the mammoth beast's maw. Klensh alone avoided this fate, able to balance atop the monster's beak as it continued its skyward arc.

"Aaugh!" the cruel Kriton screamed as the worm slammed into the ceiling of the chamber, drilling up into another tunnel.

There was little time to celebrate, however, as Red informed, "Captain, Commander, there are more girth worms converging on this location. Logic dictates that we leave. Now."

"Red, I'm sorry I doubted you," Kel puffed as they sprinted onward. "I take back all the awful things I said about you."

"One cannot withdraw words once they are spoken," the robot responded. "It is a physical impossibility. But this unit accepts your acknowledgement that the computerized mind out thinks your fleshy blob brain every time."

"And now I'm back to hating you..."

The crew continued to race along as the girth worms rumbled behind them, seeming to grow closer with every step. Turning her attention back to the head of their pack, Kel could see the consternation mounting on the captain's face. It was a mix of concern and frustration, his perturbed thoughts obviously starting to get the better of him.

"Captain?" she called out. "Everything okay?"

Without warning, he halted dead in his tracks. "We can't outpace the worms."

"What?"

"We can't outrun them!" he shouted. Addressing Red he said, "Take Mara and Jym. Get out of here, all of you. Enough is enough."

Commander Kel was thoroughly baffled. "What does that mean?"

Seeming to talk only to himself, the captain spoke on as he pushed past the rest of the crew to the rear of the group. "Enough is enough." He took up a wide stance on a raised section of stone, planting his right foot behind him. "First, my brother sent that assassin robot after us. Then he commissioned the Gnarfs to capture or kill us all. Then came Klensh and his goons. He lied to the Ranjemans and had them hunting us. Now, thanks to his involvement through Klensh, we have the girth worms to deal with. I'm done with Graylon's meddling. No one else is getting hurt because of my brother. Enough is enough!"

The shaking that heralded the arrival of the worms increased as Nado delivered his speech. Kel had never seen such anger in him, and it actually frightened her a bit. Everyone stood still and watched as the captain readied himself.

In a crashing wave of dirt, rock, and soil, the girth worm at the head of their pack bore through the wall next to Captain Nado. Standing his ground, the captain swung both of his left fists in an uppercut at the monster. Commander Kel had practically no time to think.

"Jym, give him some power!" she exclaimed, not really understanding what she was thinking herself.

Nevertheless, the young prince held out a hand toward the crazed captain as his meaty mitts connected with the girth worm's jaw. The thing was batted upward as if it were a punching bag, and Nado finished with a double haymaker with both right arms, sending the enormous creature reeling. It collapsed, apparently unconscious.

"Let's go." Trying to massage all four of his fists at once, Nado led his crew up the winding passages to the exit. Stunned silence fell upon all of them as they fled, and for now it appeared that the captain's stand had given the beasts second thoughts about their pursuit. Soon they had reached the end of the trail and darted for the cave entrance. Daylight had never looked so welcoming or felt so warm to any of them as they poured out of the mouth of the caves.

They all took some time for a respite, and the doctor had enough emergency supplies on hand to bind Jym's wound. Thankfully, it was nothing more than a surface injury. Unfortunately, as they trekked down the mountain trail, more devastation awaited them. They found Mukeh and Curik both in pretty bad shape. Dr. Rox and Kel immediately went to check on them, bandaging them as best they could, while the kids rested with Nado.

"Looks like it's not too grievous," Rox told the two Kriton men. "You should be okay to limp down the trail as long as you take your time."

"I'm fine," huffed Mukeh, picking up Curik in his strapping arms.

"Put me down," the elder Kriton protested, but Mukeh would hear no argument.

Together, they all gradually shuffled down the mountainside until at last they had reached the village around mid-cycle. They expected to see it as lively as it had been the night before, but all was eerily quiet. All of them were in too much of a weakened state for another battle.

"Hello?" Captain Nado yelled. "Is everyone okay?"

An all too familiar scratchy voice replied from the midst of the settlement. "Looksss like I sssurvived your little retaliation. Evidently, the higher powersss have a greater purpossse for me."

"Klensh?" Kel's mouth fell agape. "You've got to be kidding me!"

"I know," he called back. "I should be dead. But I wash ejected from that mountain cave and tumbled down the peak until I landed here again. Providential, ishn't it?"

Everyone moved into better spots to be able to spy their enemy. Peering around one of the yurts, Schiff got a good vantage. "He's got a kid and has his rifle trained on her," she told the rest of the party. "There's a few more Kritons lined up around the burn pit with their hands tied. He could kill them all quickly if he wanted to."

"We need a plan," whispered Nado, but nothing came to mind.

Meanwhile, their talkative antagonist proceeded to issue more threats. "Thish can be resssolved very quickly. If you will all drop your weaponsss, ssstep into the open, and let me blasht every sssingle one of you, I won't kill the little girl. Otherwissse, I ssstart checking to sssee what their insssidesss look like!"

Jym looked up to Nado. "Enough is enough, right?"

Before the captain could utter a response, Princess Mara chimed in, saying, "Right. I'm done with this guy."

Both Nado and Rox reached to stop the kids but weren't quick enough to grab either one. The siblings strode out of cover and revealed their positions to Klensh. The vicious criminal bared his fangs. "I guessss I can kill the two of you firsht." He trained his rifle on them.

Suddenly, to his shock and surprise, Klensh found he was no longer on the ground! Raising a hand, Mara bent the energies in the area to her will, lofting the albino Kriton high into the air. At the same time, Jym used his own abilities to pull the young Kriton girl out of Klensh's vile grip. The princess then slammed the brute into the ground, and before he could steady himself, Prince Jym charged forward and delivered a powered punch to the thug's jawline, knocking out at least a dozen teeth.

As Klensh toppled, so did the kids, both lapsing into unconsciousness. Rox raced to their aid, followed by Mukeh and Curik. The village leader gestured to his house. "Take them to my yurt to be healed. I will be there shortly."

Following Nado's indication, Red and Dr. Rox scooped up the unconscious Vampyrials and carried them to Curik's dwelling. Once they were safely ensconced within, the captain and commander untied the remaining Kritons and plopped onto the seating stones around the firepit. It had been a rough twelve hours, but they were finally through it.

Mukeh glanced down at the albino Kriton at his feet. "What do we do about thish one?"

"If that is the criminal Klensh," declared a garish and gaudy individual, "then we shall be taking him, along with the rest of the Explorer crew, into custody."

Three people stepped from behind another yurt. One of them was clad in rose-gold and onyx armor. The other two whipped back their brown hoods to reveal Warrant Officer Barsol and...

"Captain Bryant O'Ryan?" said Nado in disbelief.

"None other," proclaimed the Star Guard captain.

Kel held her head in her hands. "Oh, come on."

Chapter 17

Beaten, battered, bruised, and exhausted, Captain Nado, Commander Kel, and Schiff now faced down the hearty, healthy trio of Captain O'Ryan, Warrant Officer Barsol, and the third member of their little cadre, the woman in the distinctive armor. Like one of the characters in the serials Nado watched as a child, O'Ryan swept aside his poncho to reveal his Commandment sidearm. This act told Nado that this guy meant business.

"Come peaceably," O'Ryan instructed, "and we will not use force. There is no need for any conflict."

Nado started to rise to confront the opposing officer but was halted by a huge hand on his shoulder. "I know that gun," stated Mukeh. "You are Ssstar Guard. You have no jurisssdiction here, blue ssstar."

"You are correct, my good Kriton," admitted Captain O'Ryan. "She, on the other hand, does." Just as before, he stuck a thumb over his shoulder in Mauve's direction. As an aid to his intimidation, she powered up the plasma throwers that were built into her vambraces.

"Who is she?" queried Schiff.

"Mauve," replied Captain Nado. "She's a renowned bounty hunter." He nodded to O'Ryan. "Well played, Captain."

"Thank you, Captain." The voluble O'Ryan smiled proudly under his well-trimmed moustache. "Now, if you would be so kind as to turn yourselves in, we can avoid any...messy matters. Does that sound agreeable?"

"The officers of the Explorer 2000 will surrender," Nado answered.

"Nice try," O'Ryan chastised, wagging a finger in Nado's vicinity. "I've heard of your craftiness, Captain Burnay Nado. I am not here to apprehend only officers of your vessel. I want the entire crew, from yourself to Commander Kel, the petty criminal Schiff, Dr. Rox Garrison, your robot pilot, the two Vampyrial fugitives, and..." He glanced down. "I assume this is your quartermaster, Klensh, the intergalactic terrorist and warlord." O'Ryan grinned even wider at the stunned countenances before him. "Yes, I did my homework. Your merry little band of outlaws has reached the end of its short career. Where is the rest of your crew?"

Again, Nado started to stand up to his counterpart captain, and again Mukeh stopped him. "We will not tell you," sneered the big Kriton. "They have sssaved our village from certain dessstruction. They ressscued our leader, and me, from being food for the carrionsss. The Explorer 2000 ish welcome here anytime they like. You, however, are not. And I would sssuggessst you leave."

"I hardly think you alone have the capability to stop Mauve from claiming her bounty," O'Ryan jeered. But his chuckles turned to awkward grunts as a multitude of Kriton villagers began to surround the Explorer crew. Men, women, even children lined up, forming a barrier between the Star Guard captain and his quarry. Mauve aimed her plasma emitters at the crowd, but O'Ryan lowered her arms. "No. We will not harm innocent civilians. If you do, I will not pay you one single bit."

Though hesitantly, the famed bounty hunter backed down. Even still, more and more villagers joined the standoff, pitting themselves against the lawman and his squad. Barsol could only watch in awe as the Kriton people stepped in to protect these off-worlders from such a deadly threat as Mauve.

"Hm," hummed Captain O'Ryan. "Captain Nado, a moment ago you said 'well played' to me. It is now my turn to reciprocate. Well played, sir. Well played."

Too tired to answer, Nado only offered a tight expression of approval. Commander Kel, however, was not too tired to answer, so she did. "We're not playing a game here, Captain O'Ryan. We're trying to help people. And if you can't see that, then maybe you need to reevaluate your priorities."

"My priorities are perfectly aligned," snapped the Star Guard captain. "I follow our creed to the letter. 'To defend the poor and fatherless, to do justice to the afflicted and needy, and to deliver the innocent from the hand of the wicked.'"

"Take a look around you," retorted Kel. "What does it seem like we've been doing for these people?"

Captain O'Ryan placed both hands on his hips in indignation. "As far as I'm aware, the Explorer 2000 is harboring wanted fugitives and hiring criminals as crewmates. But you have made your point, and it is clear that you have at least done right by these villagers. For now, I have no other options but to release you, or risk maiming one of these civvies, which I assure you I will not do. Take the win, Commander."

Though she had plenty more to say, Kel decided it was better to stand down for today. She turned to Mukeh. "The Na'Kosh truly are the epitome of strength. What you have done for us today will not be forgotten."

"Nor will we forget you," he said. "Now go. Gather the resht of your teammatesss from Curik'sss hut and leave around the northern edge of the village. We will enshure that thessse outsssidersss do not follow."

"Thank you, Mukeh," Captain Nado saluted. "Thank you."

"It ish we who are to thank you," the warrior replied with a crooked grin. "Washte no more time. Leave, or I will tossss you off the mountain myssself."

In mere minutes, Nado and Kel, assisted by Schiff, had collected Rox, Red, and the kids and skirted the community using the northern trail as Mukeh had suggested. They could barely see amidst the yurts Captain O'Ryan and company being surrounded by the throng of Kritons. It had been a zany adventure on Khardan, one that none of them would ever forget.

It was nightfall again, the sun dipping behind the ridgeline, before they arrived at the Explorer. Everyone embarked and took up their various duties. Prince Jym and Princess Mara, now awake and recovering from their ordeal, got comfortable in a couple of the pods in med-bay while Dr. Rox performed an exam on each of them. With Red and Schiff on the bridge, Captain Nado left Commander Kel in command of the vessel while he retreated to his quarters to rest up.

As they lifted off to fly back to the Khardan spaceport, Schiff remarked, "That O'Ryan guy had some really piercing blue eyes. I liked that moustache too, very distinguished. He was kind of cute, don't you think?"

"Geez, Schiff," laughed Kel, as the Explorer 2000 sailed across the night sky.

Long after the Explorer crew had left, Mukeh and the villagers finally allowed Captain O'Ryan leeway to leave themselves. The grouping dispersed, going about their evening activities. Only Mukeh stayed nearby, watching the Star Guard captain closely.

Captain O'Ryan stared down at Klensh, who still hadn't found the ability to rise since his encounter with the kids. "Seems they forgot this crewmate."

"Nah," Mukeh grunted. "Klensh wash an enemy of theirsss, and oursss too. The Na'Kosh have no desssire for thish one to remain. If it ish a criminal you ssseek, take him."

"But he was on the manifest of crew members," stated Barsol. "There was a Kriton on that spacecraft when it docked."

"Not thish one," interjected Curik, walking into the conversation. "Rumorsss were that he hash been working for Lord Hex."

"The Warden of the Hexagon?" questioned O'Ryan. "Why him?"

"Asssk him yourssself if you ever meet," Mukeh growled, evidently finished with this conversation.

"I suppose the arrest of a very wanted intergalactic terrorist will do for today," the Star Guard officer conceded. "Very well, we shall remove him. Mauve, I hired you to claim a bounty, and here it is. We'll take Klensh back to GC space to stand trial. Is that agreeable?"

Mauve shrugged as if to say, "fair enough," leant to grab Klensh by his tail, and commenced dragging him away. Apparently, as far as she was concerned, a paycheck was a paycheck. After all, why not apprehend one criminal for the price of seven? Meanwhile, Barsol approached his superior officer.

"What of the Explorer, sir?" he asked. "Is it possible they aren't what we were led to believe?"

With a dour expression, Captain O'Ryan replied, "Possibly. Regardless, they have earned their freedom for today. I am honestly shocked that Klensh was seemingly not a member of the crew. But that is a mystery to be solved in another cycle. I am curious though, Curik, what was the Explorer 2000 doing here?"

"You ssseem honorable," replied the old Kriton, "ssso I will anssswer. They sssought the Kathnarii ssstar map. They believe it will reunite them with family, a noble goal to be ressspected. But that ish all I will tell you asside from thish warning: do not assssault them again. If you do, and we find out, resht ashurred the Na'Kosh will rissse to take up armsss once more."

"Accepted," said O'Ryan. "It appears your assessment of the Explorer 2000 crew is quite admirable."

"They are true and right," the sagacious elder declared. "And that ish all."

"Your finality on that subject is rather hard to debate."

"You would be wissse not to debate. I have decreed it. It ish ssso." Limping and leaning on his staff, the wizened old warrior left O'Ryan pondering these discussions.

"If the Explorer 2000 escaped, then why was I not informed?!" thundered Lord Hex into his radio transmitter. His vice-like grip threatened to crush the device into dust.

"Milord," crackled the receiver, "we did all that we could to apprehend them. If we had been given proper notice and intel, we might have caught them according to your wishes."

Calming himself, the masterful marquis spoke in his most charming tones. "Ascendant Ki'Vet, you were given all the necessary intel. Your job was to attempt to capture the occupants of that vessel and if unable to do so, you were to contact me...immediately!!" Roaring that last word vehemently, Lord Hex slammed his fist onto the console, something that would have rattled the ears of those listening on the other end.

"Milord," Ki'Vet angrily hissed, "are you insinuating that you never intended for us to actually catch these murderers? They killed one of the last descendants of the Dumrii. They must be made to face justice!"

"I am not insinuating anything other than the fact that your justiciars are completely inept at the simple task of communication," Hex growled back. "In regard to your demands for justice, do not forget to whom it is that you speak. I am the Marquis du Hex, Warden of the Hexagon system, and the only interplanetary ruler in this sector. Cross me, and I will turn my dreadnought against your planet next. Or has word of the fate of the Gnarfs not yet reached you?"

For the next several moments, there was silence on the other end of the line. Eventually, Ki'Vet responded, "I understand, milord. You have my apologies for the lack of communiques. It will not happen again."

"See to it." To seal the inevitability of his words, Lord Hex severed the radio connection, ensuring that a sudden static would be received by the Ranjeman warship. He then faced Cylor. "My son, we have been duped in some way. Set a new course to return to Khardan." As the boy led the command crew in preparing for their next warp, the lord of the vessel resumed his post on the overseer's deck above the bridge, all the while murmuring to himself.

Trying to help his frustrated father, Cylor offered, "Perhaps they went somewhere else first and you were too impatient – " A fiery scowl from Lord Hex stopped the young man in his tracks instantly. He tried to clarify. "I mean, perhaps we were too impatient – " Now he received a snarl from his lordship that gave the boy more reason to pause. With one final attempt, Cylor softly said, "Maybe 'impatient' is the wrong word. I was only trying to say that it is possible that the timing of everything simply didn't work out in our favor…" Cylor trailed off, feeling more insecure in his role than ever. This man was the only sliver of a family member he'd ever known, and now he felt as though Lord Hex disapproved of everything he had done since the trials in the temple. Still, his father hadn't put him out yet, and had remained as cordial as was manageable in such difficult situations. The stress of capturing the Vampyrial children was weighing heavily upon him. That had to be all that was wrong. Cylor had performed commendably for his father, so there was no reason to assume that anything was amiss between them. The young man returned to his operations, vowing he would work even harder for Hex's approval by doing anything he could to help. Soon the colossal craft was readjusted and primed, warping to Khardan in a flash.

A light knock sounded at the door to Captain Nado's quarters. Slowly, he answered the knock, pressing the button next to the entry that activated the magnetic controls. Swishing aside, the door opened to reveal Commander Kel standing just outside the frame. Beyond her, the captain also noticed Prince Jym and Princess Mara seated in the galley and enjoying a meal. From the aroma, he guessed it was oatmeal with cinnamon and brown sugar, and rehydrated chicken eggs. Those were hard to find anywhere outside the flotilla, but they'd earned even more delicacies than that after this most recent escapade.

"Captain, I wanted to check in on you," the commander stated. "You had a lot of built-up frustration in the caves. I'm glad you took it out on a girth worm and not...anywhere else."

Gritting his teeth, Nado admitted, "I've been letting Graylon get to me. He's given us a lot of trouble, and I don't want anyone else hurt by his treachery. I know I have to face him eventually, but I don't want to. He's my brother, what am I supposed to do?"

"Face him with backup." Kel put a comforting hand on her captain's lower left shoulder, as she was too short to reach his upper set. "I know I keep saying this, but you don't have to do it alone." The captain nodded, and she felt him relax. "Feels like you got a lot of that swirling mess of emotions out. Are you doing okay now?"

"Better," he replied.

"It's a good thing Jym was able to juice up your punches," the commander quipped. "Otherwise, you might not be standing here."

Apparently eavesdropping on their conversation, Jym chimed in from the galley, "Um...I didn't have time to do anything. I never boosted him at all."

"Me neither," Mara mumbled.

Hearing that surprising revelation, Kel turned to look at Captain Nado with a new perspective. "Huh, well, that's, um, something," she stuttered. "Remind me never to get on your bad side. Did you know you could hit that hard?"

"Not really," Nado shrugged. "In that moment, I sort of forgot everything else and just did what I thought I had to do."

"It was pretty impressive."

He shook his head. "Maybe. But I had to unleash all of my rage, anger, wrath, fury, every negative emotion I've been dealing with since I crossed paths with my brother again in order to output that level of strength." He paused for a moment. "And I didn't like it. I hope I never have to do anything like that ever again."

"Me too," Kel said soothingly. "Hopefully you won't."

"At first it felt good," the captain explained, "but afterward, the more I thought about it, the scarier it became." Nado then looked embarrassed. "Also, I think I may have sprained all four hands."

"Oh, no," chuckled Kel. "You should have Rox give you a checkup."

"I will." Now desirous to change the subject, Nado asked, "What about our course? Are we back at the spaceport yet?"

"It was a brief stopover," the commander answered. "Already spoke to the tower and got clearance for liftoff. For the time being, we're just in orbit around Khardan. I left a generic heading of Gentara Sector since we're fairly certain that's where the star base is located. That was enough to get takeoff permission."

"Good work, Commander," Captain Nado exhorted. "Let's get to the bridge. You and I can then plot out our next course of action. We still need the final drive from Graylon."

A quick jaunt through the galley and they were in the command center. Schiff greeted them both with a warm smile and a wave, while the robot only acknowledged their presence with a cold, clinical, "Captain. Commander." It then immediately resumed its work with the piloting controls. The sensation of new energy coursing in his veins flowed through Captain Nado as he stepped onto the bridge. As Kel assumed her own post, he started to regress to the med-bay but was halted by a daunting sight in the forward viewport. Outside, a mammoth spacecraft dropped out of warp just a few clicks from their location. It was Graylon's dreadnought.

"Hey, Captain?" called the commander. "Any chance you can punch a starship in half?"

"Milord," reported H-7-PRIME, in the typical monotone fashion, "there is another vessel in orbit. We have it on radar."

Lord Hex rushed to the front of his command deck to look out the forward viewport. He immediately recognized the spacecraft in question, and a wicked smile spread across his broad face. It was the Explorer 2000. They had come here after all.

"Patch me through to their frequency," he ordered.

"Captain, we are receiving a hail," Red informed.

"Figures," murmured Nado. "It's got to be Graylon. Let's hear him."

The robot flipped a few switches, and the radio speakers started to hum with the deep, resonating tonality of Lord Hex. "Explorer 2000. This is the Marquis du Hex, Warden of the Hexagon. With whom do I have the pleasure of speaking?"

Using his own transmitter, Captain Nado replied, "You know who we are, Graylon. I assume you're here to bargain?"

"I am," the elder brother proclaimed. "That is, if you're finally ready to offer something of substance in return. Trade is all I'm considering at this point. No firefights in space, you'll just slip away again anyway, and I'd prefer not to have to track you down. . .again."

"I don't understand you, Graylon," Burnay snipped. "You say you don't want to hurt us, but you just sent a bunch of murderers and killers with Klensh to hunt us and shoot us on Khardan. What do you really hope to accomplish here?"

"You've already been to the surface?" Graylon sounded genuinely shocked.

"And recovered the last Kathnarii data drive," the captain stated. "By the way, you can mark Klensh and his ilk as 'out of commission.' They won't be reporting back to you."

For the first time in a while, Graylon didn't sound overconfident. "Excuse me, brother. I'll be right back."

"Blast that useless Kriton!!" roared the marquis. "He was supposed to just inform me once they arrived. He wasn't supposed to take matters into his own hands! Blundering fool! How could he betray me like that?"

His stomping steps radiated like shockwaves throughout the bridge as he descended the stairs from the command deck. Several rolling carts piled with beverages received the brunt of his furious tirade. Many bottles and glasses were smashed and shattered before the marauding marquis was satisfied. Only the sound of his heavy breathing now resounded in the room.

Seeing that his father's wrath had mostly subsided, Cylor mentioned, "Father, I tried to warn you that Klensh was unreliable. I know you are fond of lessons. Perhaps we should take this as a lesson to search out better minions in the future."

Though the boy was truly only trying to help, his words were not received well. Long, swift strides carried Lord Hex to the console where the young man sat. Suddenly, and with frightening rapidity, the dark lord sped to Cylor and picked him up by the throat!

Throttling the helpless lad, Lord Hex seethed, "Mind your place, boy. You work for me, not I for you. Question me again, and I will put you back where I found you." With that, he dropped a simpering Cylor to the floor. Pulling the Ranjeman data drive from his belt, he addressed Zuugs. "Lock down every transceiver on the bridge. No communications are to leave this vessel without my authorization. It was intended that I should have both remaining data drives, but Klensh has made that impossible. I need a better bargaining chip." Waving the data drive in front of Zuugs' eyestalks, he instructed, "If my brother contacts us again, they don't get this information for anything less than both of those kids." In a whisper he added, "We have a tether to them via communications. Their robot may attempt to hack us. Put a trace on anything that might get out. I'll be right back."

Twirling with a flourish, Lord Hex left the bridge. Only then did Cylor feel confident that it was safe to rise from the floor. The boy was so shocked and scared, he couldn't stop the tears that streamed down his cheeks. As the young man stood, he saw that the data drive had been left behind on top of his console...

"Well, that was weird," commented Schiff. "Has Graylon ever done that before?"

"Not that I've witnessed," Captain Nado responded. "Something obviously didn't go according to plan."

"Captain," Red interrupted. "We are receiving another transmission."

"I guess he's ready to talk again," muttered the captain. "Patch him through."

"It is not a radio message," informed the robot. "It is being broadcast on our frequency, but it is an encrypted wireless transmission intended to be received by the onboard computers. Shall this unit access the computer system to retrieve said transmission?"

"NO!" Nado, Kel, and Schiff all yelled at the same time.

The captain explained. "As long as Cylor is still on the dreadnought, I don't want you anywhere near the Explorer's computer systems. We don't need another hacking attempt. Just make sure once we receive the message that we disconnect my terminal from the rest of the ship's network, and I'll try to decrypt it from there."

"Very well, Captain," Red acquiesced. "This unit will remain offline and will disconnect your terminal from the network at your command."

"Thank you," sighed Captain Nado. "Alright, go ahead." An audible ping notified them that the captain's computer terminal was offline. "Let's see what this message is...aha! It's from Cylor, he even signed it. Aren't you glad I wouldn't let you open it, Red?"

"This unit is incapable of gladness."

Everyone rolled their eyes. Nado continued reading the virtual documents. His demeanor quickly changed from suspicion to elation. "You're not going to believe this...it's the last piece of the star map."

"It has to be a trick," said Kel.

"There's some text here," the captain relayed. "It says, 'Please tell Jym I was wrong, and he was right. I need a friend.'"

"I knew Cylor wasn't all bad!" exclaimed the young prince from the bridge entryway. His sister stood beside him and smiled at him.

"This could still be a trap by Graylon," warned the commander.

"I'm not sure we can risk it," the doctor agreed.

Princess Mara spoke gently but firmly. "I trust my brother's judgment." She looked at Jym hearteningly. "I'm getting a good vibe from this."

Commander Kel sighed and nodded. "And we all trust you. Both of you."

"Good enough for me," declared Nado. "Let's all get strapped in and prepare for warp. Now that we have all the pieces, we should get to Kathnarii Base before Graylon realizes what happened."

"What about Cylor?" asked Prince Jym. "Won't he be in danger?"

Nado shared a concerned expression with the prince. "Maybe. But unfortunately, there's not much we can do about it right now. We can't assault the dreadnought. Rest assured though, we'll try to help him as soon as we can."

"Okay." Jym nodded grimly.

As everyone raced to take their places, Red issued another vocalization. "Captain, we are receiving another hail from the dreadnought."

"Patch it through," the captain replied.

Graylon's voiced oozed through the receivers. "Well, brother, have you come to a decision? Are we going to be able to make a trade? I might have a few other treasures I could add to sweeten the pot."

"I don't need your treasures," Burnay Nado stated plainly. "I have plenty already. Besides, you have nothing I need anymore. We have the whole map."

"What?! Impossible! How – "

"Goodbye Graylon." Nado turned off the transmitter.

Kel glanced over at him. "Was it really necessary to tell him we have the map?"

"No," he confessed, "but it felt really good to gloat. Commander Kel, have you assembled the map data?"

"Aye, Captain," she responded.

"Set our course for Kathnarii Base!"

Just like that, they were gone.

Yet again, below them in the engine room, the warp drive spluttered and popped, sending sparks across the floor. It still functioned, but this time the noises and reactions were worse than ever before. The Casimir drive was dying.

Chapter 18

Things were in a frenzy in Ranjeman space as the Drakewing ended its warp travel to the planet. Through his viewport, the mysterious man observed the fleet of warships in a constant state of flux. It was as if there had been orders for changing the guard, but no one knew which guard was supposed to be at which station, and none of them had been briefed on patrol routes.

Closing his eyes, the man tried to sense the energy trails he had been following. He was definitely on the right track. Immediately, he picked up on a faint trace of the Hex-man's power. Whoever this new ruler of the Hexagon was, he certainly left an easy trail to detect in his wake. There were others here as well, though. Those of the traitor lineage were instantly recognizable, but now a fourth energy was introduced. It was strong and controlled, but still raw and juvenile. There was something familiar about this one as well. It reminded the man of his own aura of power. *Strange...that will have to be a secret to unravel another time.* For now, he had other matters that needed to be addressed.

He tried a radio hail. "This is Drakewing V, calling the Ranjeman forces. Requesting an audience with a vessel officer. Please come in. Over."

The man didn't want to wait too long for a response, and thankfully he didn't have to. Someone answered his hail within seconds. "Drakewing V, this is Arch-Venerate Pra'Tor of the Stalker 920. We have received your hail. What is your business on Ranjeman?"

"I am seeking someone who may have passed by here recently," answered the stranger. "He is known as 'Lord Hex' in this sector."

"I know of whom you speak," the Arch-Venerate said, with a distinct note of disgust in his tone. "It is he who has our justiciars wound up and resituating the entire fleet as a sign of genuflection. They are readying their forces in case either he or the Explorer 2000 ever return."

"The Explorer 2000 was here as well?"

"Yes. You also seek them, I presume?"

Weighing whether to share more information about his mission or less, the man decided that the risk was worth the reward. "I do. I also have it on good authority that Lord Hex is pursuing the Explorer. I assume he was here to continue his chase, but do you have any knowledge as to why the Explorer 2000 was here?"

"You would have to ask someone other than myself," replied Pra'Tor. "I am a retired hunter, too old to continue with the hunt. I have been 'elevated' to the status of a ruler among our people. More like relegated, if you ask me. Your best bet would be to contact Ascendant Ki'Vet of the justiciars. She was the leading huntress for the stalking and apprehension of the Explorer crew."

"The justiciars wished to arrest them? What were their crimes?"

"Again, I am but a timeworn relic among our kind. However, I can patch your radio frequency through to Ki'Vet's vessel. If she is available to converse, she can provide you with the knowledge you seek. Just do me one favor, and do not tell her that I was the one who referred you to her."

"Thank you, Arch-Venerate, you remain one with the shadows," the man flattered. Static and interference buzzed through the receiver for several minutes, until finally a woman's voice rang out.

"This is Ascendant Ki'Vet," said the justiciar, rather snippily. "I do not really have the time to partake in petty questionings, but as it may pertain to the objects of our current reformation, I am willing to indulge you. You may ask away but do so quickly."

"You have my gratitude, Ascendant." The enigmatic individual poured on the charm. He needed to milk these people for all the information he could glean. Tactics such as intimidation and violence may work on crime lords and brainless brutes, but Ranjemans were neither of these. Unlike the Gnarfs or the Trells, Ranjemans could not be bullied into submission. They were a proud race, capable of building the grand culture that existed today.

From the lowly scavengers to the lodges of hunters, each with their own hierarchical system, to the governors like Arch-Venerate Pra'Tor, the Ranjemans kept a tight hold on their society. They had even formed their own police force, the justiciars, who had their own hierarchy and internal governance as well. It would be hard to bend a people group like that to his will through a mere show of strength. More likely than not, they would have their own show of strength in return.

He was powerful, but not that powerful. Only his master had ever held such potency in his grip.

Continuing with the matter at hand, the man asked, "Can you confirm if a vessel bearing the name 'Explorer 2000,' and a person called 'Lord Hex,' were on or near your planet recently?"

"They were here," muttered the justiciar. "They caused quite a stir."

"That seems to be their mode of operation," quipped the stranger. "I take it they are no longer here then."

"You would be correct."

"Do you know where they went?"

"I do not."

That was unfortunate. Nevertheless, there may still have been more to learn from the Ranjemans. "What transpired with the Explorer and Lord Hex? Why were they here?"

"My understanding is that they visited the Great Temple to compete in the challenges of the Dumrii," answered Ki'Vet.

"The Dumrii?" queried the man. "I thought they had been absorbed into the Kathnarii. I didn't realize that legendary order still persisted."

"Only their descendants," the Ranjeman woman corrected. "They are the guardians of the temple and the moderators of the games. Our involvement came after, when we were alerted by Lord Hex that one of the Explorer crew had murdered a guardian."

"What do you know of the murder?"

"How many more interrogatories do you intend to ask?" Ki'Vet sounded impatient. "I remind you, I have very little time for this."

"Please, only a bit more," he pleaded.

"Fine," she huffed. "It was a woman named Li'Nora. Her skull was crushed against a wall. My understanding is that she was attempting to prevent them from stealing an artifact from the relic room."

With his curiosity now piqued, the man had to know more. It may shed light on the situation between the two opposing groups. "What was stolen?"

"That is classified," the justiciar curtly answered. "Why are you asking? Are you a bounty hunter?"

"Not quite." Searching for just the right words, he reached deep into his artificial memories for the charismatic nature of his master. "I am a warrior, a seeker of truth and justice, a proponent for the perpetuation of peace in this galaxy. If I am not mistaken, that is what you fight for as well, is it not?"

For a while, the man received no reply. When Ki'Vet at last spoke, she sounded approving. "I like your moxie," she purred. "If you can promise me that you will do all in your power to escort the killers back to Ranjeman to be hunted and punished, I will tell you what I can."

"Consider it done."

"The stolen artifact is a data drive," Ki'Vet responded. "It contained secret information about Kathnarii Base. There is only one reason to take it."

"To attempt an expedition to find the base itself," the stranger concluded. "Thank you, Ascendant Ki'Vet. You have been most helpful. I will leave you to your work now."

Apparently too busy for a final salutation, Ascendant Ki'Vet simply severed their connection. That didn't bother the mysterious man, though. He had other, bigger thoughts swirling in his mind. There were many clandestine documents and items secured in that place. It would be troublesome if the children found them first. He had to get to Kathnarii Base ahead of them. His master's memories should contain something about its pathing and current location. Taking advantage of the sheer silence inside the Drakewing, the man consulted his master's vast array of remembrances. A mental library of forbidden information, these recollections were sure to grant him some insight into the next stage of his quest.

Yes, he remembered. The pathing of the station was already implemented when his master spent time there. Now, it was only a matter of construing the timeline with the ambit of the station's automated routine. It would take time to calculate the necessary trajectory for warp travel to Gentara Sector. Hopefully, he would not be too late...

Many hours had passed since the showdown in the Ghishnik village, and Captain O'Ryan had been unable to shake the words spoken to him by Curik. Was it possible that the renegades he had been sent to catch weren't as dangerous as he'd been led to believe?

He'd read their files. When it came to Captain Burnay Nado, the only blemish on his record was taking in the Vampyrial escapees. As for Commander Kel, how could he question the integrity of one who had been cleared as a top officer for the Star Guard? Then there was Dr. Rox Garrison. That man was about as squeaky clean as one could get.

The matter of Klensh had been resolved, whether the Kriton warlord had been part of the Explorer crew or not. If so, they had obviously willingly handed the criminal over to him. If not, as Curik and Mukeh indicated, then the Explorer crew had been instrumental in affecting Klensh's capture. What about Schiff the shapeshifter? She had a record, to be sure, but she was nowhere near the status of intergalactic terrorist. So she'd sown a few wild oats, who cared? Besides, that mop of purple hair and infectious smile were not the mark of a hardened criminal, and her file made it seem that she'd left that life behind, turning over a new leaf.

There was not enough information concerning their robot to suggest whether it was a threat, but if it was only a pilot then it couldn't be that much of an issue. Robotic pilots were not unheard of and were simply the next technological leap succeeding automated piloting systems. The only passengers he knew absolutely nothing about were the two Vampyrials, whose identity had thus far evaded him. Even Councilman Legis had not offered any intel on that subject. Perhaps it was time to reconnect with the SGS Victorious, try to make contact with the councilman, and lay these doubts to rest once and for all.

All these musings and more pervaded the Star Guard officer's thoughts during the return flight to the spaceport, and the subsequent warp travel to Star Base 143. His mind in a haze, Captain O'Ryan walked through the motions of dismissing Warrant Officer Barsol, paying Mauve for her ultimately unneeded services, and relieving his secondary executive officer of command as he boarded the SGS Victorious once again.

Salutes abounded as his faithful crew greeted him back. By rote, the captain saluted in response, still lost in his contemplations. Questions galore were murmured under every breath, the scuttlebutt amongst the crew members being that their commanding officer had been away on some top-secret mission. They all had various speculations as to what that mission may have been, but everyone agreed that a covert operation was undoubtedly in the works.

Tired and worn, Captain O'Ryan retreated to his quarters for a much needed sleep cycle. Along the way he gave orders to the command staff to set a course for Octagon V. Once they had arrived, he would be able to connect to the planetary network and attempt a video conference with Legis. It had been several cycles since the captain had been given this assignment, and since then too many unknowns had entered the equation. Who were these Vampyrials? How did they survive all this time? How and why were they under house arrest? He himself had been too enraptured by the concept of being the first Star Guard captain in this generation to tussle with Vampyrials again to ask any further into the matter. Add to that the fact that Legis had been all too eager to send him on his way without offering additional details. Something was amiss.

Continuing to ruminate all through his sleep cycle, the usually outgoing officer kept his communicator deactivated. He was eventually awakened when his intercom beeped. Captain O'Ryan activated the device. "This is the captain. Go ahead."

"Sir, we have made all necessary preparations and are ready for warp travel." It was the ensign helmsman.

"Very good, Ensign. I will be up to the bridge momentarily." O'Ryan ended the exchange and turned off the intercom. After getting freshened up and redressed in his military garb, Captain O'Ryan paraded to the command center of the grand cruiser in his typical fashion. Though he was developing grave doubts now about their current task, this was no reason to alarm the crew of the Victorious and have them thinking that their leader was questioning the governing powers.

Entering the bridge with significantly less bravado than he typically employed, the captain still maintained an air of authority. Exuding an aura of command and quiet strength, Captain O'Ryan took his seat in the central chair. His bridge crew seemed surprised at their superior officer's newfound meekness, but he put any rumors to rest when he resumed command of the vessel.

"Deputy Lieutenant, is our course set?" the captain loudly queried.

"Yes, sir," answered the junior officer.

"Deputy Commander, are all crew members at their postings? All supplies accounted for and secured for warp?"

Another crewmate replied, "Yes, sir."

"Then let's get the Victorious on the move!" bellowed O'Ryan. "Prepare for warp travel. Ensign, activate the warp drive!"

Being in full command of the SGS Victorious again was already beginning to alter Captain O'Ryan's deportment. As the dark energy bubble enwrapped his spacecraft, his old confidence started to re-envelope him. There were still many details that he wanted to know and inquiries that he wanted to make, but at least he wouldn't look, or sound, deflated in his encounter with Councilman Legis.

In an instant, the forward viewport was filled with the spectacular sight of the Octagon, an enormous gas giant of a planet sporting a luminescent cerulean coloration with streaks of pure white stretching like ribbons across the surface. In orbit around this gorgeous celestial body were seven moons, each the size of a planet themselves. Octo I was the gas giant itself, while Octo II was the original homeworld of the Aronites. Octo III and IV belonged to the Gonians and Baldins respectively, while V had become the seat of government for the Galactic Community. Octo VI had been granted to the Star Guard for training and recruitment bases, and Octo VII was primarily utilized as an agricultural world to support the massive cities of Octo V. Finally, Octo VIII was rich in natural mineral and ore resources, thus had been transformed into a world of mines and refineries. Seeing all of these moons in quiet rotation filled Captain O'Ryan with a sense of awe. Though born on the flotilla, he considered the Octagon his home, and every time he returned it was a beautiful thing to him.

With the planet now in range, O'Ryan gave a new command. "Deputy Lieutenant, open a line with the Octagon V planetary network. I need a secure connection to Councilman Legis' offices."

"Yes, sir," came the reply.

"Set up a video call in my private conference chamber," the captain instructed. "Let me know once the councilman responds."

"Sir, we're patched in," reported the Deputy Lieutenant. "Shouldn't take more than a couple of hours to get a – " She stopped as her console pinged. "Wow. That was fast. They must have been expecting us. Your call is waiting in your private chamber, sir."

"Thank you, Deputy Lieutenant," O'Ryan commended. "Everyone, remain at stations. I'll return shortly."

Rising dramatically from his command seat, Captain O'Ryan marched to a side room of the bridge. Inside was a small room with a large array of monitors, featuring one that was massive and had been mounted in the middle of the rest of the much smaller screens. A comfy, high backed swivel chair allowed for easy viewing of all the displays, while a plethora of tiny bulbs dotting the walls provided just the right amount of lighting.

After sitting down, O'Ryan activated the video call by typing in a series of passwords for the security firewalls. Despite his recent misgivings, this was still a classified project, and he intended to follow procedure where all of that was concerned. Soon thereafter, the councilman's ascetic countenance filled the main screen.

"Captain Bryant O'Ryan," he calmly greeted. "I hope you have good news for me."

"Not yet," the captain responded. "I have made contact with the Explorer 2000, but so far they have been able to elude capture."

Legis was unimpressed. "Then why are we having this conversation?"

"Councilman, the last time we met regarding this assignment, I believe there was much left unsaid in reference to the escaped POIs," O'Ryan posited. "In order to be as effective as possible, I need answers to these questions."

"Proceed," sighed Legis.

"Do you know the identity of the Vampyrials?"

"I do not. I only know that they were in custody and subsequently escaped." The Aronite leaned toward his camera. "That is why I contacted you to apprehend them."

"I see," Captain O'Ryan said. "Then can you give me a rundown on their history at least? Where did they come from? How were they detained? That may give us some clues as to how we can better incarcerate them once we recapture them."

"I know little," answered Legis, "but I will divulge what I can. To the best of my knowledge, these two Vampyrials were discovered by salvagers aboard a derelict craft. They were brought to the council, who voted on whether to save the abominations or allow them to be executed. It was ultimately elected that they would be kept alive in stasis aboard the Human flotilla."

"Why the flotilla? Why not a GC facility?"

"The flotilla has the best stasis bays in the galaxy. Unfortunately, there was an accident. An explosion in that stasis chamber meant that the Vampyrials had to be moved. They were temporarily awakened while awaiting transfer to a new location. That is when they escaped."

"How did they escape?" queried O'Ryan.

"They were helped." Legis now looked decidedly disgusted. "The anonymity of their benefactors is a problem that is being investigated separately. Any other pesky questions, or are we done here?"

"Almost," assured the captain. "There was also the matter of your previous agent assigned to this task. You referred to them as a colleague before. Who was this person?"

The cranky councilman rubbed his forehead. "If you must know, I had commissioned the Marquis du Hex to track the movements of the Explorer 2000 while they dithered about in Taldish Sector as he does represent the Galactic Community in that region. Like I stated prior, he was unsuccessful in his attempts."

"You had Lord Hex trying to catch these Vampyrials?"

"Yes!" groused Legis. "Must you force me to relive that most regrettable decision?"

Time to drop the bombshell and see what came of the fallout. "Were you aware, Councilman Legis, that Lord Hex had employed the intergalactic terrorist and warlord Klensh for his services?"

But the stoicism of the Aronite councilman remained unfazed. "Where did you receive that information?"

"There were several witnesses who all claimed this to be the case," replied Captain O'Ryan.

"What witnesses?"

Legis wasn't going to let this go. Perhaps O'Ryan's bombshell had been ill timed. He admitted, "It was Kriton villagers. They claimed to have knowledge on the subject and were well acquainted with the criminal in question."

"Ha!" scoffed Legis. "I would not believe everything you hear from primitive tribesmen, Captain O'Ryan. Any other news you wish to share?"

"I only had one more inquiry for you, Councilman," murmured a humbled O'Ryan. "The Vampyrials, exactly how dangerous are they?"

Without batting an eye, without losing a beat, with utmost confidence, Legis gave only one word as a reply. "Very." Pulling away from the camera and making himself appear taller and even more imposing, the pretentious politician threatened, "Do your job,

Captain O'Ryan, and bring these fugitives to justice. If you are unable to do so, I can always find more suitable candidates for the captain's chair of the Victorious."

"Councilman, I have reason to believe that the Explorer is searching for Kathnarii Base, and may go into Gentara Sector," O'Ryan mentioned. "How are we to apprehend them if that is the case?"

"Do whatever you must, Captain," Legis said darkly. "If they are in Gentara Sector, then go to Gentara Sector. You have my express permission. Any means necessary, Captain. Bring them in alive or dead." And the call ended.

The captain had been a law officer for too long not to suspect that Legis was still hiding something. There was more to this tale than he was receiving, but now was not the time. No matter what, if there was danger in the galaxy, he would rise up to face it. Hearing the creed of the Star Guard buzzing in his mind, the captain gave renewed purpose to his mission. If these Vampyrials were as deadly as Legis claimed them to be, then he would do his duty and arrest them. Yes, Captain Bryant O'Ryan of the SGS Victorious was back on the case!

As the Explorer shifted out of warp, the forward viewport displayed an eerie but awe inducing sight. Floating before them, almost invisible in the near black expanse, was a massive and ancient-looking structure. A humongous bronze colored ring dominated the architecture of the derelict space station, with a series of spires like the towers of a citadel jutting from its center. They were all varying heights but had been constructed so that the shortest spires were closer to the outer edges of the ring, the tallest spires rising from the center.

Inversely, from the bottom of the great ring protruded a long, tapered housing that was twice as altitudinous as the most colossal of the towers. It was accompanied by additional antennae, solar panels, and thruster rods all extending in the same direction, their points aligned with the tip of the large housing. They seemed to hang from the ring like technological stalactites, and also ranged from shortest to longest in the same manner as the spires. No lights shone from within any of the portholes. In fact, the whole place offered a dark and spooky visage.

"This must be it," Kel murmured. "Kathnarii Base."

Chapter 19

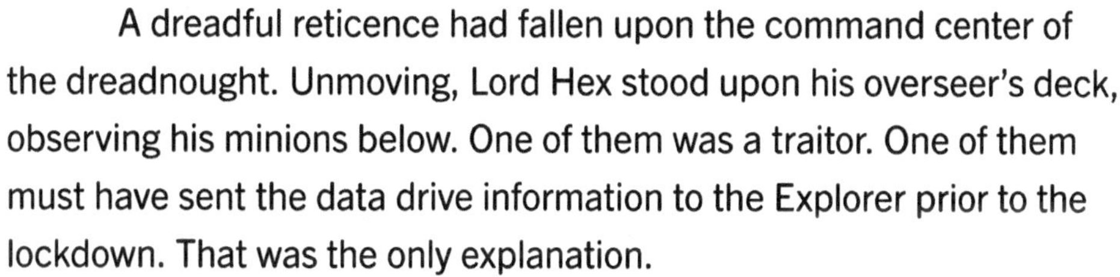

A dreadful reticence had fallen upon the command center of the dreadnought. Unmoving, Lord Hex stood upon his overseer's deck, observing his minions below. One of them was a traitor. One of them must have sent the data drive information to the Explorer prior to the lockdown. That was the only explanation.

The silence was shattered with one thunderous bellow, "Zuugs!!"

Scampering to Hex's side, the Sorogan foreman swiftly responded, "Yes, milord?"

"I thought I had given you orders to lock every transceiver on this vessel," rumbled the malicious marquis. "If you followed those orders, as you should have, then how did my brother receive the data from my drive?"

"Milord, every single console was made secure through the puppet master server," explained Zuugs. "The task was performed immediately following your orders. But all we can do through that measure is prevent the users from logging in to their profiles. There are ways to circumvent that – "

Zuugs was abruptly interrupted, finding himself unexpectedly in Lord Hex's powerful grip once again. Pulling the little fellow close, Hex intimidated, "If you wish to avoid being blasted out an airlock, I'd suggest you figure out how to fix this, and fast!"

"Milord," squeaked the foreman, "it would not be difficult to identify which console sent the message. We can dig through the logs on the master server."

"Do it." Not wanting to miss any clues, Lord Hex carried Zuugs to the master server, a terminal that could only be accessed by the foreman and himself. "Show me."

As the marquis held him in position, the small Sorogan typed away on the keyboard, sweat beads pouring from his face. "There," he indicated. "That series of letters and numbers is the node key of the console in question. It was sent from there."

They followed the evidence to the suspect computer. The operator thereof was another Sorogan worker, who shook and shivered with fright as the Marquis du Hex's shadow fell across him. Sensing the horrifying glower that must be underneath that hood, the worker almost fainted.

"Why did you disobey my orders?" Hex demanded to know.

"I swear to you, milord," the worker answered, "I followed lockdown procedure. I swear it!"

"Swear all you like," fumed Lord Hex, "from a cell in the brig! I shall deal with your failure later. Guards! Escort this miserable excuse for a laborer to the cells." Responding to their master's beckon, H-7-

PRIME ordered several other units armed with electric prods to usher the operator from the bridge, him still maintaining his innocence all the while. Having now dealt with that issue, Hex turned his attention back to Zuugs. "Now then, let us get to work. Did you trace all outgoing data as I requested?"

"Yes, milord."

"Can we track them even post warp travel?"

"Now that we have identified the culprit's console, we should be able to follow the signal of the tether, milord."

It was as if a hellish fire glowed through Lord Hex's eyes from the shadows of his cowl. "Excellent work Zuugs. I think we're finally developing a good professional relationship, you and I."

"Yes, milord." The Sorogan foreman gulped for air. "Could you please put me down now?"

Allowing Zuugs to plop to the floor, Lord Hex resumed his post at the command deck. Meanwhile, Cylor, who had remained completely silent through the whole affair, internally kicked himself for not suspecting the traceability of his transmission. He winced when his father barked the next directive.

"Cylor, set our course for the coordinates provided by Zuugs! All hands, prepare for warp travel!" He grinned, quietly murmuring to himself. "I'm coming for you, Burnay. You won't get away again."

Finding a place to dock and connect an airlock tether to Kathnarii Base proved more difficult than Captain Nado and Commander Kel had expected. It took several passes around the structure before they were able to locate a suitable berth. With as much disrepair as the station had suffered over the decades, it was remarkable that there were any docking fetters still in operation. Carefully, Red expertly piloted the spacecraft into position, connecting to the station's automated airlock subroutines.

"This unit detects that life support systems are still online," the robot reported. "The atmosphere within is breathable and will sustain flesh blobs without the need for spacesuits."

"Call me a flesh blob one more time," threatened Kel.

"Very well. You are a flesh blob."

"Blast you!" the commander fussed. "Hapless hunk of hardware. I ought to turn you into spare parts."

"Have we completed the docking procedure?" asked Captain Nado.

"Indeed," answered Red. "Access through our cargo bay bulkhead is now possible."

"Let's head out then," the captain said. "Red, stay here and keep a watch on the radar. Alert us if anyone else shows up. Dr. Rox?"

Replying from med-bay via his own communicator, Rox responded, "I'll also stay on board the Explorer. Red and I will keep the engines primed in case we need to make a quick getaway."

"Anyone else want to remain behind?" Nado inquired. "There's no telling how dangerous it could be in there."

"We're going," Mara insisted. She was showing a lot of mettle despite still being in a very weakened state from their affairs on Khardan. "If there are any clues about Mom and Dad here, we want to see it."

"I've got your back, Captain," the commander chimed in.

"Oh, you couldn't beat me away with a Hydran water whip!" Schiff excitedly exclaimed. After receiving odd looks from the rest of the crew, she explained, "Hydrans have some weird religious rituals. . ."

"Okay," stated the captain. "Move out."

Shortly thereafter, the group had assembled at the airlock bulkhead and lowered the bay ramp. It opened into darkness, so Nado and Kel were forced to use their flashlights to illuminate the path. At the end of the corridor, they reached the internal airlock. Beyond lay the remainder of Kathnarii Base, and whatever secrets it may hold.

On approach, a camera affixed to a mechanical arm extended from the wall. This was followed by a monotone, robotic message that played, warbling and staticky. "Present your Kathnarii identification. Present your Kathnarii identification."

"We don't have Kathnarii identification, do we?" worried Schiff.

"Try the ring," whispered Prince Jym.

Withdrawing the miniscule item from her necklace, Princess Mara held the ring up to the camera's eye. The repetitive message ended, replaced by a new phrase. "Welcome, Senior Member. May you ever follow the ways of honor, strength, and cunning."

As the camera retreated into its orifice, a hiss exuded from the airlock, and the triple layered bulkhead split open. Auxiliary lights embedded behind railing along the walls flickered on, shining their dim amber glow upward to the high ceilings. Directly ahead of them was a rounded reception desk with a trio of matching computer terminals spaced evenly across the surface. All of them were dead, their blackened screens reflecting only the lighting from the walls.

Mounted above the desk was a humongous sangria crest in the shape of an inverted triangle with an indigo circle at each corner. Within the circles were intricate symbols, each depicting a different aspect of the Kathnarii Order. One held a shield, denoting honor, another held crossed swords, denoting strength, and the final one held an eye, denoting cunning. Gold filigree encircled the whole crest, connecting each of the three smaller circles together. The center of the triangle boasted more gold filigree, shaped into the words "Honor, Strength, Cunning," the creed of the Kathnarii, and the entire heraldry was bordered on either side by long, intricate drapes.

In front of the curved desk was a large plaque with a silvery frame. Upon closer inspection, it turned out to be a directory and map of the facility. Captain Nado went to check, but when he realized that the tablet was adhered to the desk itself, he tore it loose.

"Captain!" Kel reproved. "I don't think we ought to go around breaking things in here."

"Why not?" he defended. "It's not like the Kathnarii are going to pitch a fit. Besides, we need the map on this thing so we can find our way around."

"Fair point," the commander conceded. "Let's just try and keep it to a minimum, shall we?"

"Understood," Nado complied. "According to this, we're on the outer ring. We need to get to Bastion Seven to find the bunkhouses. Mantis' room here is where we'll find all of his belongings."

"Good idea, Cap," chirped Schiff. "We'll follow your lead."

They all kept a wary watch for traps or defenses, but it seemed that practically nothing here was active anymore at all. Just the basic life support functions, some auxiliary utilities, the artificial gravity, and the automated piloting. It raised quite a few questions in Commander Kel's critical mind. "I wonder how they set it up to keep the star base in motion all this time. The power would be easy, I'm sure this place is rigged with enough UPS batteries and luxonite panels for low level power output. But you would think it'd run out of air reserves for the thruster jets at some point, not to mention oxygen output for life support. I'd be curious to check their navigation logs, see where and how often it stops to resupply.

"It's probably outfitted with moisture inductors in order to harvest water from the clouds of the planets that it passes by, then the onboard filters in the recyclers transform it into breathable air. That would explain it." At that point she noticed the kids staring at her. "What? I like to know these things. I'm an engineer."

"No judgment," said Jym, putting both hands up in mock surrender.

"Well, a little," Mara added. "But I promise it's silent judgment. I won't say it out loud."

Smiling warmly, Kel grabbed them both and gruffly pulled them into a friendly squeeze. "Alright, you punks. We'll see how you like it if I give you the patented, old, Kel family headlock hug!"

Squirming and even giggling a bit, the kids fought back. They wriggled free and the good-natured wrestling match was over. An awed muteness overcame them as they delved deeper inside the labyrinthian space station. The further they went, the more deterioration and decay they found. Tapestries of varying make and design that had once hung proudly now littered the walkway, having fallen from their mounts long ago. One of them featured a now faded portrayal of a Zennian Kathnarii knight that stood out to the captain. Piles of cargo and supplies meant to be ported to other areas of the station lay abandoned and discarded. A few robotic sentries stood in a corner, but they were in rough condition. Kel doubted they could even be repaired at this point.

Passing through a massive double door, they found themselves inside a colossal chamber with even higher ceilings that arched to a sharp apex. Elongated pews sat in neat rows on either side of a single aisle which was decorated with a once brilliant runner, now faded and scuffed from time. A raised platform with a podium rested at the fore of this room, surrounded by ornate columns and unique carvings. On the far wall, above the podium, the Kathnarii crest adorned the surface, framed in the same velvety curtains as before.

"What is this place?" inquired Schiff. "I thought this was a military installation. This looks more like a religious cathedral."

"There's a lot about the Kathnarii Order that we still don't know," replied Nado. "Who knows what they taught here? Could be a chapel for one of the many religions of one of the many races that formed the order. Or it could be a place of worship for the three aspects of the Kathnarii. Could be anything, really. Unfortunately, we don't have time to investigate everything on the base. Though I'm sure it would be enlightening." A touch of nostalgia swept across the captain's expression. Kel could sense it. That old explorer's spirit was welling up inside him. He shrugged it off and sighed, "Let's keep moving."

"Fine by me," Schiff uttered. "This place gives me the creeps."

They rounded a few more corners and eventually arrived at a hallway that featured a series of monorail shuttles. One of them was marked with the numeral for seven. "I think we need to go through here," said the captain.

"Do you suppose these things are still operational?" asked Kel.

"Only one way to find out." Nado pressed the button beside the number seven. A chime rang out. "I guess it is." Magnetic doors sealing away the shuttle swished aside. "I'll go first. I'm the heaviest, so if it'll hold me, it'll most likely hold the rest of you."

"Most likely?" the commander questioned.

Ignoring her caution, Captain Nado stepped aboard. Though creaking and groaning with age, the monorail shuttle remained intact. One by one, they all clambered inside until the car was full. With a push of the activation button, they were whisked away. It was about a two-minute ride to their destination. Exiting the monorail, they were now in a new corridor, but with much of the same deterioration as before.

They were definitely inside one of the spires, as everything here was round and spiraled. Still, the remnants of the former glory of the Kathnarii told the tale of a once thriving and wealthy faction. Carpets softened their treading here, and the structure of the bunking quarters resembled that of a hotel, with private rooms tucked behind soundproof doors.

"This is a barracks?" Schiff quipped. "It has all the appearance and trappings of a daytime spa."

"Ooh, a spa," mumbled Kel. "I could go for a spa cycle."

"Me too..."

"Ladies," Nado interrupted. "Can we stay focused?"

Schiff and Kel spoke simultaneously. "Sorry."

"We're looking for Bunk Room 297," informed the captain, staring up the spiral staircase in the center of the tower. "I think we have quite the climb ahead of us."

Up the staircase they trotted, Nado checking his directory all the way. They wound around in the helix, ever onward and upward, until Commander Kel thought they'd all get sick. It was many minutes into the ascent before they reached their final stop.

"This is it," Nado happily told them. "Bunk Room 297 is on this story." He explored the landing that acted as the floor for this level. "Here!"

Everyone joined him at the hefty door frame. Prince Jym looked for a way to open the portal. "There's no activation switches or buttons. Just that little indentation."

Without a word Princess Mara stepped forward, looking as though she'd been hypnotized. She stretched forth her hand, placing the Kathnarii ring on her finger. The tiny bauble fit perfectly into the notch, which caused another panel to open just above it. Everyone instantly recognized the handprint reader that lit up with a blondish hue. With a simple touch of Mara's palm, the heavy door opened.

What they saw inside actually surprised Kel. She wasn't sure what she expected to see, but the simply furnished bedchamber and humble private bathroom weren't what jumped to mind when thinking about the infamous Prime Executor. Aside from a bed and side tables, the only other articles of note in the room were a writing desk and chair.

Wasting no time, the kids rushed inside and dug through the drawers of the little desk. It was empty, barring one single item. Therein lay a thick, leather-bound tome. It had been preserved well. There wasn't even any dust in the pages when Mara flipped it open.

"Whoa," she phonated. "It's Mantis' notes. His notes on everything. Look! There are techniques for learning the mastery of dark energy manipulation, sections on experimentation for DNA alteration, a whole segment devoted to cloning and...Schiff, you should see this."

The shapeshifter left Nado and Kel in the doorway and walked over to the princess to see what she was talking about. Her eyes danced with light as she read. "Oh my gosh! It's all about the shapeshifters! Why would he have notes on the shapeshifters? Maybe Mantis found our homeworld or something..." Schiff trailed off, her countenance drooping as she read further. "Oh. That's, well, depressing actually."

"What is it?" Nado wanted to know.

No one had ever seen Schiff as defeated as she looked now. "According to this, we weren't born this way. Mantis changed my people, turned us into what we are. We were meant to be part of his army. We were made to be monsters."

"Hold on," Mara stopped her, placing a gentle hand on the young woman's shoulder. "Schiff, you can't let someone else's actions dictate who you are. You are a part of our family, not a monster. And look here. It says that he used Vampyrial DNA in the alteration process. That means we're related. You're like, my half-sister!"

Tears formed in Schiff's limpid eyes as she wrapped Mara in a tight embrace. "I can't think of anything I'd rather be."

"And there's more," Princess Mara pointed out. "Your shapeshifting powers do somewhat morph your body, but it's your people's connection to photonic energy that allows you to complete the illusion. You're bending the light the same way we bend dark energy."

"Wow," stated Schiff. "I didn't even know completely how my abilities work. That's pretty neat."

"There's so much more here," the princess commented. "Maybe there's a clue to where our parents are. Maybe there's a secret hideout or something he knew about. What's this? 'Project: Mysterious Vampyrial.' I wonder what that's all about."

"Hey," Prince Jym interjected. "Check this out." Hanging above the bed where the boy was pointing was a long, dark blade with a thick hilt.

"That must be Mantis' Kathnarii blade," Captain Nado remarked. "Those are highly dangerous weapons. The hilt contains liquified plasma that is controlled by an electro-magnetic field much like our starship's shield. It also houses a powerful heating core that weaponizes the plasma, turning this simple sword into a fiery foil. Looks like it's crafted out of morbidium. That would explain why the energy field works so easily. Morbidium is a natural conductor for electro-magnetism."

"Ooh." Jym grabbed for the weapon. "Fire sword. That beats chainsaw sword every time." He pulled it from the wall, and nearly fell over from the weight. "Whoa! That's heavy. I don't think I could actually wield it unless I was infusing it with all my power."

"We'll have to look into that another time," the commander said. "I say we get that book back to the Explorer and dive into it there. If there's a clue about your parents, we'll find it."

"Huh?" Mara glanced up. She was still pouring over the pages looking at every item intensely. "Right, we can go."

It was then that the captain's communicator came to life with Red's suave but clinical tones. "Captain, Commander, there is another vessel that has entered radar range. It is too large to be anything other than the dreadnought."

"How did he track us here?" Commander Kel groused. "I knew that message from Cylor was a trick!"

"It couldn't be," Jym protested. "It just couldn't be."

Closing the tome, Princess Mara came to his side. "It wasn't. Lord Hex must have tracked us another way."

"Regardless, we need to get out of here before we get trapped," Captain Nado warned. "Back to the monorail, hurry!"

Taking in the sights of the ancient star base would have been an ecstatic experience for Graylon were he not in the throes of trying to trap and capture two pureblooded Vampyrial children that could unlock the entire galaxy to his machinations. There was so much to do, and so little time to do it. The longer the Aronites and Humans remained in power, the harder it would be to overthrow their prejudiced regime and build a new, freer, more inclusive Galactic Community. For now, the tourism would have to be placed on hold.

After selecting Cylor and a contingent of three H-7 units to accompany him, Lord Hex boarded his shuttle craft and piloted his extraction team to the pinnacle of the tallest spire. Using internal airlocks and the robots, he had them blast an opening and craft his own tether, connecting them straight into the topmost section of the main tower. He was sure that the primary control center and security offices would be there.

Finesse would be required to excise his prey from this locale. An attack from the dreadnought could cause irreparable damage to Kathnarii Base, or to the children inside. He needed them alive for his experiments. His brother was another matter. The elder Nado wanted no harm to befall his younger sibling.

Once the tether was in place, he and Cylor crossed into the dark, murky desolation of the base. All the H-7s were equipped with flashlights, which they utilized until they came to an area where auxiliary lighting had been activated. Nearby was the entrance to the command center and security station, just as the marquis had suspected. It required some kind of passcode or key for entry.

"Cylor," Hex ordered, "open the door, son."

Obeying quickly, the boy bent the energies around them into a strong grasp that pried the magnetically sealed door panels apart. Just beyond, they discovered the security room, a round chamber with monitors all along the walls. Rolling chairs dotted the floor all around, unused for a century. Spying a switch on one wall, Lord Hex flipped it, bringing the dead displays to life.

Images of the derelict station sprung up on each screen. Observing closely, Cylor noticed that a couple of them had activity. Apparently, some of the cameras were operational even when the receiving monitors were not. What he saw enraptured the young boy. There was Prince Jym, and presumably his sister, walking with another woman who lovingly wrestled them into a hug, playing on a broken loop. On another display, he saw the frozen picture of the little girl hugging another woman tightly as they cried together.

Something welled up inside him, causing him to shed his apprehension to ask, "Father? Do you love me?"

"What?" grunted the marquis.

"Do you love me?"

"What do you mean? Where is this coming from?"

Cylor referenced his augments. "I am in constant pain. Can we fix it?"

"Son, I have told you, those are necessary for you to be an asset," dismissed Lord Hex.

"But, they hurt," said the boy. "Friends and family do not purposely harm each other. That is why I ask. Do you love me?"

"Our relationship is...complicated," Hex answered, clearly perturbed and wishing to end this conversation.

"It does not seem complicated for them." Cylor pointed to the screens that portrayed the Explorer crew. "These are shows of affection. You have never treated me in such a way, yet it seems to be quite natural to them. I would like that, wouldn't you?"

"Cylor, I have told you – " the Marquis du Hex started to say, then he caught himself. Something dawned on him. He slowly turned to face the lad. "You bounced the transmission off the secondary console, didn't you? You sent them the Kathnarii map data. It was you! Treacherous, traitorous whelp! After I saved you, raised you, how could you betray me like this?"

Now stammering and shaking with fright, Cylor began to back away. "Father, I – "

"Do not call me that!! You are a wretch, and no son of mine!" Snapping his right arm forward, Lord Hex caught the boy with a surge of dark energy. One after the other he launched each arm out to strengthen his hold, his fury blinding him to the blood snaking down from his nostrils. "I will bind you and imprison you and take you back to your pod on Hex II. I will – "

This time it was Hex who was cut off, as Cylor used all of his own power to break the wicked warden's grip! The young man dashed into the next room, which happened to be the command center, and sealed the door behind him. That reinforced hermetic seal was tough enough that even he would have trouble opening it with his abilities. As Lord Hex slammed on the door, Cylor spotted an emergency distress signal. It had an intercom linked to it. He pressed the button.

Chapter 20

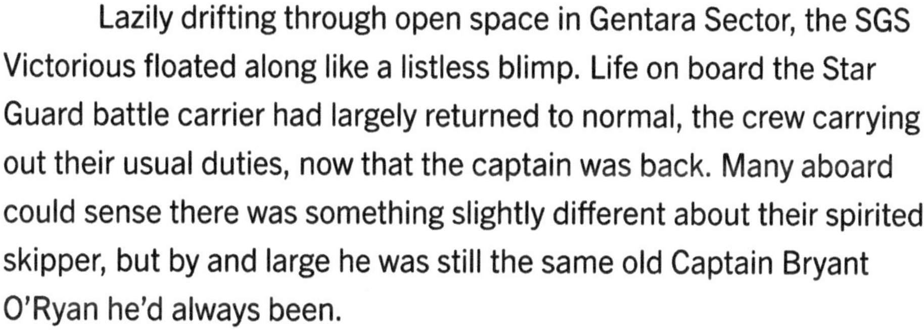

Lazily drifting through open space in Gentara Sector, the SGS Victorious floated along like a listless blimp. Life on board the Star Guard battle carrier had largely returned to normal, the crew carrying out their usual duties, now that the captain was back. Many aboard could sense there was something slightly different about their spirited skipper, but by and large he was still the same old Captain Bryant O'Ryan he'd always been.

He now occupied his command chair in the center of the Victorious' bridge, watching over his subordinates with his characteristic force of personality. Whether for good or ill, they had been granted permission to be in Gentara, well outside the Star Guard's jurisdiction, but the captain appeared unfazed. His excitement over the mission had returned tenfold. Not only was he on the prowl for his missing escapees, but there was also something else that had him twisting things over in his mind. His crew knew him too well to let it go unnoticed. After the capture of these fugitives, there would be another phase to the operation for sure.

Nevertheless, many were getting antsy being so far away from their home turf. Dorthal Sector, Murrigan Sector, and parts of Amaransk were their domain. Out here in Gentara, they could be easy prey for a claim of warmongering against them.

An alarm sounded from the communications officer's console. The Deputy Lieutenant checked the broadcast. "Sir," she reported, "we have an emergency distress signal coming across the generic Gentara satellite system. It's an older code."

"What code, Deputy Lieutenant?" queried Captain O'Ryan.

"It's not possible, sir," said the young woman. "It's reading as the old Kathnarii code."

O'Ryan practically leapt from his seat. "Haha! Are they transmitting coordinates?"

"Yes, sir."

"Lock in on those coordinates, Deputy Lieutenant! Don't lose that signal!" Emphasizing his words with a wagging finger, the garrulous captain turned to the helmsman. "Ensign, send an alert. All hands prepare for warp. It's Kathnarii Base. It's them!"

Alarms blared throughout the station, making Commander Kel's ears ring. She wasn't the only one covering her head from the noise. Nado, Schiff, and the kids also cupped their hands around their ears in a desperate attempt to block out the cacophony.

When it quieted, they heard a demure, almost flat, child's voice come through the base's emergency broadcast speakers. "Explorer crew, this is Cylor. I don't have much time. Lord Hex will probably cut me off. He wants to hurt me more. I'm sorry for what I've done to you. I hope I have been able to make it up to you with the star map data from the Ranjeman drive. Please help me. I'm trapped in the control room. Prince Jym, you were right. I want a friend...a family. Please – " The message ended abruptly.

"I guess Graylon did cut him off," the prince muttered.

"Unless this is all part of another trap," cautioned Kel. "Come on, how did Graylon track us here in the first place?"

"I have a feeling about him," replied Jym. "He's just a scared kid, lost and lonely, like we were before we met you. It's not his fault Lord Hex got to him first. I'm going to the control tower to rescue him. Who's with me?"

"I am," Mara bravely stated.

Nado and Schiff looked at Commander Kel, both seemingly begging with all their feelings for a positive answer. She studied both of the young Vampyrials standing in front of her. After a deep breath, she said, "We're going to need a plan."

Banging on the reinforced door was doing no good, and Lord Hex didn't have the ability to pry it asunder with dark energy. He was wasting time on this petty child. He needed the purebloods. Even now, they could be getting away. Angrily, he spun toward the monitors where their images had remained stuck on screen. Where was that located? Running through the index, he discovered that for which he was searching. It was the bunkrooms in Bastion Seven. But were they still there?

His communicator crackled with static. "We need. . .the other bastions. . .to take. . .back to the main ring. . ." That was Burnay's voice! They had somehow crossed their communications frequency with his own. Tuning the device, he listened further.

"I'll explain again. I want you all to avoid the other bastions and just head straight back to the Explorer once we're done here," Burnay was saying.

A young girl's voice chimed in. "There's still so much to uncover, though. Let me finish sifting through this tome. Maybe I'll find something we can use."

"I don't like it." That was Commander Kel. "Neither you nor Jym have recovered from the ordeal on Khardan. You're in a weakened state."

"Please," the girl pleaded. "We may not get a chance like this again. What if this is the only way to find our parents?"

"Alright, fine," responded Graylon's brother. "The commander and I will escort Jym to the exit. Schiff and Mara, you two stay here and finish up, then meet us back in the chapel. Follow the directory and don't forget where you're starting from. Bunk Room 297, got it?"

More static garbled the rest of the conversation. That was enough, though. Burnay was in for a big surprise. "H-7s, come with me. We're headed for Bunk Room 297. Move out!"

Leaving the security room, Lord Hex led his robotic lackeys around the corridor to an elevator lift. It was operational, so they rode it down to a monorail station. From there it was a short ride to Bastion Seven, where his prey awaited. This time, he'd have the drop on them and would be able to easily overpower the whole lot. He didn't need Cylor, or Klensh, or anyone else for that matter. He was the Marquis du Hex, Warden of the Hexagon, master of dark energy and soon-to-be overcomer of the Galactic Community. He'd made it this far on his own, he could make it the rest of the way by himself as well.

Shushing his sentries, Lord Hex crept up the spiral staircase of Bastion Seven. They hadn't passed Burnay or Kel, which means he wouldn't catch the Vampyrial boy. However, he would get the girl and the shapeshifter, and that was fine. Using their safety as a bargaining chip, he could easily sway Burnay into handing over the boy too. As quietly as ever, he slipped up the steps until they at last reached the landing that housed bunkroom 297. Peering just past the ledge, he could see the two young women still inside, looking at some kind of book resting on the unassuming desktop.

With swift hand motions, he directed his H-7s into position. Neither girl saw them as they snuck onto the landing and took up posts on either side of the doorway. Readying his dark powers, Lord Hex gave the signal and rushed into the room with his deadly robotic force, screaming a blood curdling battle cry.

A flash of light blinded him temporarily, and when it had diminished, the two young women were gone! "Where did they go?!" he belligerently bellowed. "Where are they?!"

"Right behind you, your lordship," quipped the shapeshifter. "Fooled you!" Into a communicator she held in her hand, she then reported, "We got him, Cap!"

Bewildered and furious, Hex whirled to see the pair standing in the doorframe. The little Vampyrial girl waved mockingly at him and placed her palm on a panel next to the entrance. It began automatically closing, and though he raced to stop it, Lord Hex was not fast enough. The door clicked into place with irrevocability.

"NO!" he thundered, slamming his huge fists against the door. A panel inside the entry with a handprint opened, glowing in a faint yellowish shade. After several attempts, it was clear he could not activate it. "How? How did this happen?"

His communicator spluttered again. Burnay's voice rang through. "We have your H-8-RED, Graylon. It still knows your frequencies and everything. It was a cinch to hack into them."

"It's not like you to gloat, Burnay," the elder Nado sibling seethed.

"I'm not gloating," explained the younger brother. "It doesn't have to be this way, Graylon."

"For now, it appears it does." With those final words, Lord Hex destroyed his communicator with one hand, crushing it in his grip. He addressed his H-7s. "Blow this door down. We are getting out of this room."

A knock resounded at the control room entryway. Afraid to answer, Cylor called out, "Who's there?"

There was a familiar sound on the other side. “It’s me, Cylor! It’s Prince Jym. We’re here to rescue you!”

The little cyborg boy opened the door to see Jym, Captain Nado, and Commander Kel on the other side. “I am so relieved to see you all,” he gushed.

“No time to chit chat,” Nado said quickly. “We need to meet Schiff and Mara at the airlock and get out of here.”

Grabbing Cylor’s upper left hand, Prince Jym led him out of the command center, through the security room, and around the corridor to the lift. Guns drawn, Nado and Kel took defensive positions beside the boys, the captain out in front and the commander at the rear guard. Now to meet Schiff and Mara at the airlock and escape.

With three plasma rifles pounding away at the soundproof door, coupled with a powerful energy surge from Lord Hex, it eventually caved in, breaking from the frame and collapsing on the landing floor with a crash. Smoke and dust filled the area but was no deterrence to the villainous quartet. Exploding from within, Hex and his robots tore down the staircase in hot pursuit of his quarry!

As soon as Nado and company had exited the lift and taken the monorail car back to the outer ring, they raced along the rounded halls searching for Schiff and Princess Mara. Reaching the airlock, they made a horrid discovery. The two young ladies weren't there.

Raising his lapel to speak into his communicator, the captain very nearly hollered, "Schiff, where are you and the princess?"

"I tried to blink us along to move faster, but we ended up getting lost!" was her crackling reply. "I'm sorry, I thought I had a handle on it."

"Don't fret," calmed Nado. "Tell me what you see."

"Um...a bunch of fallen tapestries."

"Does one of them have a Zennian knight on it?"

"Yeah!" Schiff excitedly exclaimed. "It's just ahead of us!"

"Do you see a set of big double doors?" asked the captain.

"I do."

"That's the chapel. Run in the opposite direction. We're coming, we'll meet you halfway." Releasing the PTT activator on his communication device, Captain Nado sped past the airlock and sprinted further along the grand halls, with Commander Kel, Prince Jym, and Cylor right on his heels. Within a couple of minutes, they had reconnected with Schiff and the princess, who carted the tremendous tome under her arm.

They were all just beginning to greet and welcome each other, when they received quite the shock. Another entryway from the inner section of the facility burst open, as Lord Hex and his trio of computerized cohorts erupted from within! Exercising his dark energy mastery, Hex held out one set of hands to grip the two Vampyrial siblings, using the other two to send Schiff and Kel sprawling across the floor. Plasma bolts whizzed through the air from the robots' rifles, but Nado expertly rolled aside and fired off three shots of his own, temporarily disabling the automatons. He then turned to train a pistol on his elder brother, but Cylor had beaten him to the punch. The young cyborg boy utilized his own abilities to disrupt Graylon's hold on Mara and Jym. Once they were free, all three of them locked into a struggle with Hex, power for power, slowly pushing him back.

Captain Nado could see the blood trails coming from each of their noses, even from Cylor, and kept his firearm aimed. He dared not fire though, for fear that it could cause some kind of energy backlash. Instead, he waited and watched.

Tears from Cylor's eyes mingled with the blood from his nostrils as he softly spoke to Graylon. "I hope one day, we can learn to love each other…Father."

Then Burnay Nado saw something in Graylon that he hadn't seen or felt in a long time. No one else would have caught it, but he knew his brother. Somewhere deep inside his older sibling's soul, something emotional broke, and for a brief moment there was profound vulnerability. It was enough to catch him off his guard and allow Cylor to launch Graylon backward, removing him from the fray for now. Having expended so much power, the boy crumpled, unconscious. Also weakened, Mara and Jym staggered but remained awake. Seeing the commander and Schiff rising to their feet, Nado scooped up all three kids.

"To the airlock, let's move!" he ordered.

Dashing back the way they had come, the party quickly reached their berth. A swift activation of the airlock tether and they were aboard the Explorer once more. While securing the kids in the galley and Cylor in a med-bay pod, Kel mentioned to Nado, "Hey, we live to fight another cycle, right? Don't worry, we'll defeat Graylon someday."

"I don't want to defeat him," Captain Nado resolvedly replied. "I want to save him."

Pulling himself from the rubble in which he'd landed, Lord Hex rose from the debris. He was alone, abandoned by Cylor and robbed of his H-7 units. With no communicator, he had to get back to the dreadnought, lest the Explorer evade him yet again. With incredible speed, he darted to the monorails and took the one that brought him to the command center elevator. One excruciatingly slow lift ride later, he found himself in the security room again. The control room had a communications array, maybe he could contact the dreadnought from here...

True to his word, Dr. Rox had kept the engines primed for a rapid regression. As Captain Nado and the crew took their positions, he gave the command, "Red, untether from the docking hatch. Let's get to a safe warp distance and beat it!"

"Acknowledged, Captain," the robot responded. In seconds they were jetting away from Kathnarii Base. "Captain, radar readouts suggest that the dreadnought is heading our way."

"Are we at safe warp distance?"

It took a couple of seconds to reply. "Affirmative."

"Kel, set our coordinates for Zen I," the captain requested. "Graylon won't try anything there, and it'll be nice to see Mom again."

Kel nodded back. "Done."

Looking to Red, Captain Nado barked, "Punch it Red! Activate the warp drive!"

A noise like that of a droning insectoid spiraling out of control resounded throughout the little starship. Nothing else happened. Checking the multiple consoles surrounding the pilot's controls, Red informed, "It appears that the Casimir warp drive is unresponsive, Captain. It may be damaged. If this unit had been allowed to connect to the ship's onboard computers, this unit would have discovered any flaws – "

"Oh, give it a rest, you bag of bolts!" the commander hushed the machine. "What do we do, Captain?"

"You and Red stay on the controls," instructed the captain. "I'll head down to the engine room and see what's going on. Perhaps I can figure it out and do a quick repair."

"Shouldn't I do that?" questioned Kel.

"No. I need you on navigation so we can zip out of here fast. Red, get the shields up. If they fail, take evasive maneuvers." Having given those last commands, he leapt from his seat and made a beeline for the engine room.

"Can I help?" Schiff queried.

"Help Rox watch the kids," answered Nado. "He's got his hands full trying to stabilize Cylor." With that, he dropped through the hatch.

Following his orders, the nimble shapeshifter also skipped out of her seat and scuttled to the galley. Meanwhile, Commander Kel and Red got the vessel's shields up only moments before they started hearing the thudding of laser fire blasting into them. Apparently, the dreadnought had gotten into firing range.

"Commander, radar indicates another spacecraft has entered the area," Red coldly informed.

"I thought this base was supposed to be hard to find!" fumed the commander. "Who's coming here now?"

"It seems that the emergency distress signal that was sounded was more far-reaching than assumed," explained the robot. "That vessel must have followed the beacon. Also, they are hailing us."

"Patch it through..."

The radio blared with an obnoxious and boisterous tone. "Greetings, crew of the Explorer 2000. This is Captain Bryant O'Ryan of the SGS Victorious. We are here to apprehend your craft. Please turn yourselves over to the Star Guard, and I will personally guarantee your safety as we escort you back to GC space."

"Oh, good grief," groaned Kel.

Aboard the bridge of the SGS Victorious, the atmosphere buzzed with excitement. O'Ryan himself was feeding the anticipation with his own energetic activity. Even seated in his command chair, the dynamism he exuded was infectious as he eagerly awaited the Explorer's reply.

The speakers crackled, "Captain O'Ryan, this is Commander Kel. Can't you see we're under attack from this dreadnought?"

"We have that under observation," assured the Star Guard captain. "I have the Warden of the Hexagon on another frequency. We can patch the calls together on one. Standby." O'Ryan turned to his communications officer. "Deputy Lieutenant, can you connect both radio hails?"

"Aye, sir," she answered. "You should be able to reach the Warden now."

"Warden Hex," greeted the captain. "Can you hear me?"

"I can," grumbled a disgruntled Lord Hex.

"Commander Kel, can you still hear me?"

"Loud and clear," stated the commander. "We're still getting pelted here!"

"Warden Hex, the SGS Victorious requests that you cease fire immediately!" Captain O'Ryan demanded.

"I'm going to capture that Explorer and take them into my custody," spat Hex. "You have no jurisdiction here, O'Ryan."

"Neither do you, Warden," the captain of the Victorious retorted. "We are here to apprehend the Explorer and escort them back to GC space. Now cease fire!"

"I will stop my onslaught, but only if you will allow me to detain the Explorer," Hex bartered.

"You are currently suspected of working with intergalactic terrorists," snipped O'Ryan. "I hardly think that qualifies you to act in a humane manner when it comes to escorting prisoners."

Suddenly, a third dark voice joined the conversation. "It seems I am late to the party. Nevertheless, commanders of the Explorer 2000 I demand that you surrender to me and turn over any documents uncovered on Kathnarii Base."

Staring out the forward viewport, Captain O'Ryan and his command crew watched another vessel slip in out of warp travel. It was shadowy and sleek, sporting a laser turret at its forward tip, with stylishly curved wings and top fin. Everyone gawked at the unusual sight with trepidation.

"Captain," the helmsman inquired, "what is that?"

Leaning forward dramatically, O'Ryan replied, "That, my dear Ensign, is a Drakewing."

"What's a Drakewing?"

"A specially designed battle schooner of the Vampyrials." The Star Guard officer was grim. "Nobody's seen one in over a hundred years."

That gloomy, husky voice spoke again. "Will you surrender, Explorer 2000?"

Next came Commander Kel's response. "We're not surrendering to anyone today!"

"Then I shall force you to submit." Now the Drakewing opened laser fire on the small spacecraft!

"That's my quarry!" fumed Lord Hex. The call ended.

Watching in frustration, O'Ryan could only observe as the Drakewing swept around the Explorer. Whoever was operating it was an expert combat pilot. Next, the dreadnought's weaponry resumed its assault. The much smaller vessel was struggling to avoid attacks from both assailants. They certainly wouldn't hold out very long. He didn't want to lose the Explorer, but what could he do?

Now being beset on two sides, Commander Kel used the intercom to try and reach Captain Nado, as Schiff still held her communicator. "Nado, any updates with the repairs?"

"I'm struggling here!" he yelled. "Ow! I need to pry open the housing, but I can't. My hands are still injured."

"You were supposed to get those checked!"

"We've been a little busy..."

In a last-ditch effort, Kel hailed the Victorious. "Captain O'Ryan, any assistance you can offer would be greatly appreciated!"

"We have no authorization to engage!" he shouted in response. "Agree to allow us to tow you aboard and I can help you. Turn over your dangerous Vampyrial fugitives, and we can keep you safe!"

"Dangerous Vampyrial fugitives?!" the commander blustered. Calling down through the hatch, she hollered, "Schiff, use that communicator with the kids. Have them introduce themselves." Acting quickly, Kel patched her own communicator transmitter into the starship's radio console. "Go ahead!"

"O'Ryan, give a listen to this!" the commander's tonality warbled through the receivers of the Victorious' bridge.

Listening intently, Captain O'Ryan heard two small voices in succession say, "This is Prince Jym."

"And I'm Princess Mara."

The cadence of their speech patterns was unmistakable. Kel confirmed what O'Ryan was already thinking. "They're kids, O'Ryan! A couple of orphans looking for their mom and dad. Just two lost, scared little kids! That's who you're chasing. Now do the right thing or leave! I don't have time for this...Red, maintain evasive action!" After that, the line went dead.

"What are our orders, sir?" asked the Ensign.

Slumped in his chair, O'Ryan mumbled, "To defend the poor and fatherless..."

"Sir, what was that? Do you have orders?"

The captain murmured on. "To do justice to the afflicted and needy..."

"Sir, we can't hear you."

"To deliver the innocent..."

With the bridge crew growing more concerned with each passing second, the Ensign almost shouted, "Orders, sir?"

Slowly rising from his defeated posture, Captain Bryant O'Ryan squared his shoulders, standing strong and resolute, loudly proclaiming, "'To defend the poor and fatherless, to do justice to the afflicted and needy, and to deliver the innocent from the hand of the wicked.'" Pointing his authoritative index finger as he bellowed, O'Ryan ordered, "Commander, scramble the twelfth squadron and have them intercept that Drakewing! Lieutenant, target all laser turrets on the dreadnought! Ensign, bring us about! We're going to help the Explorer 2000 escape."

Seeing the chaos from his post in the Kathnarii command center, Lord Hex growled, "O'Ryan, you boastful buffoon. I'll see you burn for this!"

Meanwhile, the mysterious stranger was suddenly assailed by an entire wing of Star Guard fighters and was forced to take evasive maneuvers himself. Cursed fools. He tried to fight back, but several laser blasts caused a minor explosion in his engine chamber...

From the galley, Schiff and the kids heard Commander Kel celebrating, "Captain, we've got some breathing room! How's that warp drive?"

"I can't fix it!" the annoyed Zennian responded.

"O'Ryan can't keep them occupied forever. We need to warp out of this!"

"Wait!" shouted Princess Mara. "Look here, in the book." She showed the entry to Jym and Schiff. "There's a page here labeled 'Operation: Backdoor.' It's a portal opened via a blending of photonic manipulation and dark energy manipulation. If the three of us work together, we can escape through the portal."

"But where does it lead?" queried her brother.

"It doesn't say," the princess admitted, "but with a name like 'Backdoor' maybe it's a secret hideout. Maybe it'll take us to our parents."

"Worth a try," boomed the captain, who had scooted up the cargo bay ladder. "I say give it a go."

"But I've never blinked anything as big as a starship," protested Schiff. "Besides that, I can hardly ever get the blink thing to work consistently anyway."

"We'll be here backing you up, sis." Mara smiled at her.

"You can do it," encouraged Jym.

Captain Nado took the little shapeshifter by the shoulders. "We need you, Schiff. Remember, you're not a monster. None of you are. Today, you're my heroes."

"Okay," said Schiff. "Show me the book."

Following the directions listed, the trio held forth their hands. Schiff reached out with both, flanked on either side by the kids. Mara held out her left hand, her right supporting her newfound sister. On the other side, Jym mirrored the princess' actions. Outside the forward viewport, a wormhole of light and shadow swirled in front of the Explorer.

Through the still active radio transceiver, Kel overheard the effects of the battle. Graylon was first to speak, blasting, "What's that energy field? H-7-PRIME, fire all available turrets at the Explorer! Stop them!!"

This was followed by O'Ryan's gallant cry, "All starboard cannons, prepare to fire on the dreadnought...Fire!"

Below in the galley, Schiff's tiny voice repeated, "I can do this, I can do this, I can do this...

As combat raged between the Victorious, the dreadnought, the twelfth squadron fighters, and the Drakewing, the Explorer was swallowed by the churning maelstrom in front of it. In a brilliant flare, the wormhole disappeared. A calm settled over the battle arena. The Drakewing was disabled, the dreadnought damaged, with the Victorious and her fighters having won the conflict. There were no other spacecraft present, however. The Explorer 2000 had vanished.

...to be continued

Epilogue

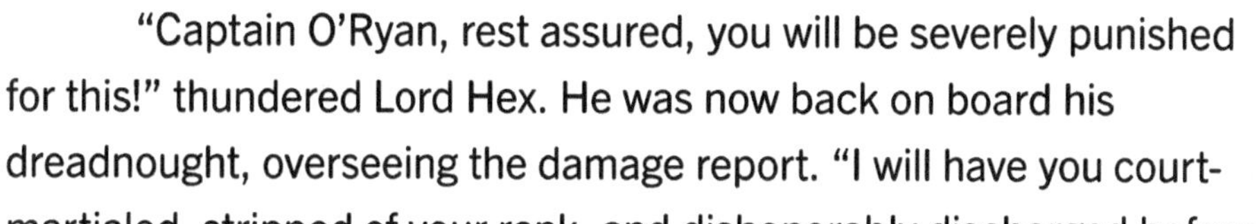

"Captain O'Ryan, rest assured, you will be severely punished for this!" thundered Lord Hex. He was now back on board his dreadnought, overseeing the damage report. "I will have you court-martialed, stripped of your rank, and dishonorably discharged before I'm through with you!"

"We shall deal with that when the time comes," O'Ryan unflappably answered, severing their connection.

Addressing H-7-PRIME and Zuugs, Hex rumbled, "What is our status post battle?"

"Well, milord," gulped Zuugs, "the shield systems are unresponsive, the laser turrets are once again inactive, and all starboard generators of our primary weapon have been destroyed."

"BLAST!!" the manic marquis roared. "I thought this was supposed to be an engineering marvel. I thought we were supposed to be a flying fortress!"

"The dreadnought is all of those things, milord," the Sorogan explained. "But we are not invulnerable."

"What would it take to be invulnerable?"

"A lot more resources, time, and hard labor."

Lord Hex loomed over the diminutive foreman. "Then I guess we'll be extending your contract yet again, won't we Zuugs?"

Lowering his face, eyestalks drooping, the small Sorogan dejectedly replied, "Yes, milord."

Aboard the Victorious, Captain O'Ryan had just cut off his call with Lord Hex. All was quiet. The Ensign helmsman, true to fashion, was first to speak. "Any further orders, sir?"

"Yes," declared the exuberant O'Ryan. "Have the twelfth squadron tow that Drakewing into our carrier bay. I want to know who, or what, is on board. If the occupants are injured, I want them confined to med-bay pods. If not, escort them to the brig. Deputy Commander, ready a security team. And bring me my Commandment. It's time we start getting some answers."

Did the Explorer survive their escape attempt? If so, where did they go? Find out next time in:

EXPLORER 2000

Book Three

Melgite Invasion!

www.ingramcontent.com/pod-product-compliance
Lightning Source LLC
LaVergne TN
LVHW010601100826
845148LV00014B/2805